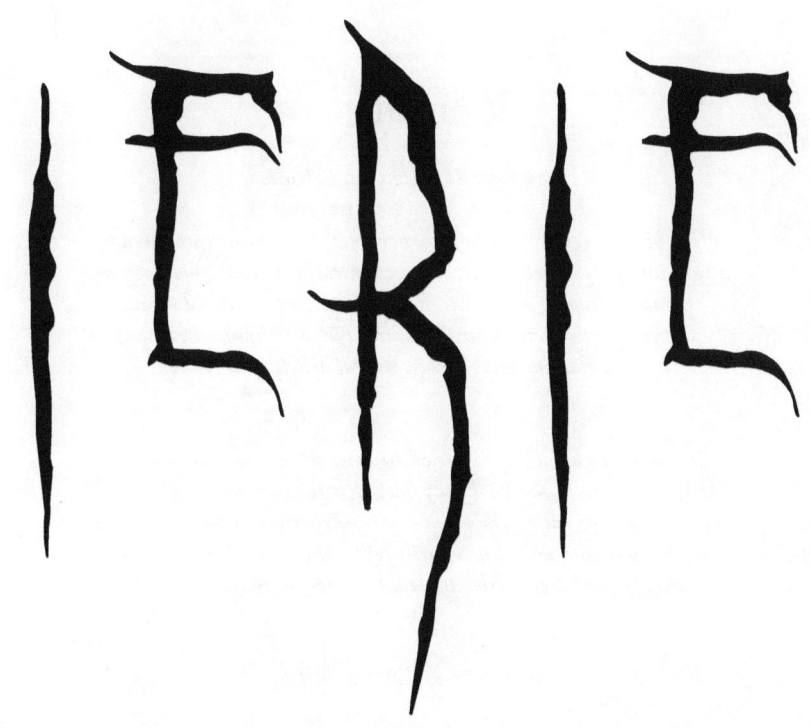

C. J. SAHADEO

IERIE

Copyright © 2022 C. J. Sahadeo.

All rights reserved. No part of this book may be used or reproduced by any means, graphic, electronic, or mechanical, including photocopying, recording, taping or by any information storage retrieval system without the written permission of the author except in the case of brief quotations embodied in critical articles and reviews.

Because of the dynamic nature of the Internet, any web addresses or links contained in this book may have changed since publication and may no longer be valid. The views expressed in this work are solely those of the author and do not necessarily reflect the views of the publisher, and the publisher hereby disclaims any responsibility for them.

ISBN: 978-976-8290-28-1 (sc)

Print information available on the last page.

ACKNOWLEDGEMENTS

The writing of this book would not have been possible without the help of God who has carried me though many long years. I would also like to thank my family who has supported me and my writing, in various ways, and have really been the driving force behind getting this book published. I couldn't do it without you guys.

CHAPTER 1

Sadika ran into the room upon hearing her young niece cry out. Reshma was sitting upright on her bed, with the covers pulled up to her eyes.

"What is it?" asked Sadika.

"Jumbie!" said Reshma, shrinking beneath the covers even more.

"Oh," said Sadika, relief flooding her chest. She sat on the edge of the bed and smoothed back Reshma's hair. "Did a Moko Jumbie look in your window?"

Reshma nodded vigorously in agreement.

"Don't worry," Sadika said, "He won't hurt you. Jumbies only scare those children who are up too late."

"Not my fault!" said Reshma, indignantly "We had a party."

"I know it's not your fault," Sadika assured her, "He didn't know this time. Don't worry; he won't bother you again. Okay?"

Reshma nodded and Sadika leaned forward and kissed her on her forehead. She helped the little girl get settled back down and waited for her to fall asleep before leaving the room.

She closed the door softly and then, frowning, went through the house until she found a window facing the same direction as Reshma's. Sadika pushed it open and looked out.

After a moment, a tall, thin figure stepped out from behind a coconut tree in the distance. The tall figure gave Sadika a grudging nod and disappeared behind the tree. A few moments later, she caught sight of its slim figure threading its way through the estate, a slip of a shadow hiding within larger ones.

She sighed and pulled the window firmly closed.

A leisurely wind wound its way through the rooftops, ruffling the top of the trees and rustling the small unsecured hairs on Amrika head. She shivered a little, the ocean's cold bite still present on the breeze, as she shifted position on the rooftop carefully.

Thin metal sheets and thatched roofs didn't give the most secure footing but she'd learned over time where the support beams were. Keeping her presence silent, however, was something she still had to work on despite her skill gaining steadily over the years.

Mosquitoes, the ever-present bane of her existence buzzed around her head, several resting on the bare skin of her neck and hands, others seeking to push their hungry proboscis through her clothes.

Amrika waved irritably at them, while trying not to be seen.

She was on the edge of a roof on the border between the saikan town and boerin village. It was a place where less savory businesses flourished and where saikan with money came to sate their various vices.

It was a perfect hunting ground for a part-time thief and Amrika had made off with many a spoil over the years.

A saikan man walking down the road caught her eye. This member of the highest class of society was wavering as he moved. The hood he'd had up to hide his fair hair had slipped down revealing what he was. Not that it had mattered anyway. No boerin or jotlin person had clothes that fine, even if they were plain.

The man stopped, belched loudly and then continued down the road, humming off-key to himself. Amrika crept to the edge of her roof, catlike and silent, preparing to stand up and leap; taking him down in smooth movement, when a soft hiss came from the alleyway the saikan was approaching.

The man stopped and watched the alleyway suspiciously. Another hiss came, alluring in its deepness. Sweet, honeyed words poured out of the lips that spoke to him. A hint of a beckoning hand peeked out of the alleyway, then a long slender leg, moonlight somehow casting the limb in perfect artistic relief.

The saikan man grinned and went purposefully towards the woman in the shadows. She leaned out the alleyway, continuing to beckon coyly to the man, tilting low to show her over-endowed bosom to advantage. Amrika wondered if it was his drunkenness that kept him from noticing that the bosom was a little too over-endowed to be natural or if it were the Dame Lorraine's abilities that kept his mind in a fog.

At any rate her target was gone. Amrika sat back down on the roof and sighed. The Dame Lorraine, one of Ierie's dark things, the children of its heart, had struck again. She wondered if the saikan would be alive tomorrow to discover he'd been robbed or if he'd simply disappear without a trace.

She was still on the roof, marking targets, belt a little heavier with coin, when the clock struck twelve, huge heavy chimes ringing over the town. A pervasive blackness settled over the area, people in the street glancing up worriedly before retreating indoors. A shrill whistle broke the night air, raising the hair on her arms.

Below, those who hadn't gone inside rushed for shelter despite having no notion of why. Amrika however, crouched in the shadows of her roof, knew the reason, and hoped that she wouldn't be seen up here.

She wasn't so lucky.

A soft voice addressed her.

"And who dares to walk in the Robber's domain and tries to dip into his spoils?"

"Spoils are for those who can grab them," Amrika responded, whirling to her feet to face the man on the roof and trying not to let him know how much he'd unsettled her by his silent arrival.

He tilted his head and paced closer. "And if I consider you a spoil?"

"You'll lose yuh hand!" Amrika snapped back.

A deep laugh, rippling with malice and something darker, broke the night. "Run along child. Yuh brave but yuh is no match for de Robber. We are blackness and yuh is ah stained white cloth. Run now 'fore I clap you into ah coffin before yuh time, eh?"

Amrika stood her ground angrily for a second before spinning and making her way off the roof.

Another shrill whistle broke the night's air when she touched the ground and then the Midnight Robber was gone, carrying with him his miasma of darkness.

She stood in the street until he was gone, glaring at the sky and wondering if she could get back to her work. At last, however, she blew out a breath and gave up the endeavor. It was not worth it. All of the boerin, the true peoples of Ierie, knew about the dark things that stalked the night. They were the children of Ierie's heart, the island's adopted ones, granted their own kind of power much like the kalinag. And they were born out of them.

But the dark things did not care for them. The Midnight Robber was as likely to steal from them as a saikan. It was their nature to be dangerous, to see all that were not them as prey.

Dark things haunt all men's dreams.

But the people that lay beneath the skin of the dark things, they cared. The Dame Lorraine might not care for the poor girl being assaulted in the alleyway, but the woman who had been in the same position years ago just might. The Dame Lorraine might not care enough to do anything but the woman just might slip a Dame Lorraine's knife across his throat.

Dark things were scary because they were also people underneath.

When Kirish came home it was to find Amrika waiting up for him, arms crossed, mouth pouting. He glared at her, angry too.

"Surish tell me that he find yuh on the roof after de whistle blow!" he snapped at her.

"Wha wrong wit that?!" she yelled back.

"You mad gurl? Wha wrong wit you? Yuh tryin to dead?"

"Ah not!" she snapped, "You know dat! Is not fair you is a Robber and I cah be!" Because the stinging wild call always haunted her, like it had haunted her brother before his abilities had appeared. And yet, yet she remained unchanged.

"You cah be a Robber!" Kirish said, taking her by the shoulders and shaking her.

"Why, cause I is a gyal?"

"No, cause you doh have the temperament to be ah Robber!"

"I have de blood!" she shouted at him, tempted to raise her wrist as if showing him her veins would enable him to see the black blood in them.

"Blood doh give temperament!" he yelled back at her. He ran his hands through his hair and then sighed and said, "'Rika, you doh want this. Don't you know wha de Robber is?"

"I know," she said, voice trembling, "I grow up in de same house you did, yuh know. I hear de same stories and de the same warnings." She had heard too many stories, had too many of them settle into her bones with their whispers of blessings and curses.

"Den you know is not nuttin to want," he said, and his gaze was earnest and real, but she knew he loved it too. "If you want dis, yuh mad."

"We whole family is," she said, bitterly looking away.

"The Robber is born from de blackest blood," he said, "You and me, we didn't have full black blood. I choose dis but you Amrika, yuh could do something different. Be something better. Be better. The Robber blood is nuh good."

"But it runs in your veins," she said, eyes fluttering shut for a moment, "Yuh feel alive, when you walk as the Robber. I hear yuh joy, when you blow the whistle, yuh laughter when yuh drink fear, yuh exhilaration when you move across the night. Yuh really think the blood in meh veins longs for anyting else?"

Kirish's shoulders slumped. "Please, Amrika. Yuh is mih sister. I know what this really is like. I doh want yuh to be in dis. Please don't. Black blood has its nice side and it have it price to pay even Robbers doh get way from the Bookman," he added darkly.

"I cah help it," Amrika admitted. "De night calls me de same way it calls you."

"But yuh cah be ah Robber," Kirish said shaking his head, "Yuh really doh have de temperament. Maybe de night really calls to you buh is not to be ah Robber. Ah could tell yuh dat!"

"Den what?" she demanded.

"I doh know," Kirish shrugged. "But next time Miss Lady, yuh hear de whistle, you get yuh tail inside, eh!"

Despite all his arguments earlier, there was one thing that Kirish never discouraged her from. After she had changed out of her street clothes, Amrika sat at their small wooden table, sorting through the spoils that her brother had brought in a few nights before. Some of it went to join the meager funds their combined jobs provided. Amrika made sure there was enough for the budget required for her and Kirish to live on for the next fortnight and then turned her attention to other concerns.

She pulled out her own small sack of spoils that she had gained on her nightly raids and weighed the bag in her hand. For a moment memory assaulted her, and she was five and weighing the sack of coins her father had brought back from his time out as the Robber. Her father had peered down at her from under the wide brim of his hat and cupped his hands under her small ones.

"Feel that?" he had whispered. "Dais the feeling of ah full belly."

She exhaled a sigh and let the memory go. She and Kirish did not need the extra money to gain full bellies anymore, though it wouldn't be comfortable. But Amrika, shorn of both her parents too early, clung to this little thing she had left of her father, this little thing of her heritage, though she did not have it all the way Kirish did. Black blood yes, but real blood drove her out into town night after night to ply her clever fingers against saikan targets.

With another breath, she tore herself from the sentimental air that had descended and emptied the bag of coins next to Kirish's haul. With quick motions she began to separate the coins into piles that would go to others. Two piles to extended family whose jobs did not pay as well as the ones she and her brother held. Another pile to go to the family at the end of the street, a unit of four children and one father. The mother and the babe she had carried, buried only in the last month. Three more piles were to go to the elders in the village, too old to do much work and too proud, too caring, to ask for help that would be difficult for others to give, they were always the greatest challenge, she and Kirish having to sneak in, place the money where the grandmother or grandfather of the village hid their own small savings, and get out before they awoke. But it was worth it; the Midnight Robber stole, but Kirish and Amrika gave.

Sadika checked in on her niece in the morning, cracking the door open gently and peeking through at the lump under the pile of covers. She was pleased to see the child sleeping well.

"Morning," said her father from behind her. Sadika gently closed Reshma's door and said

"Morning daddy!"

"Everything good?" asked her father.

"Yeah," said Sadika, "A Moko Jumbie peered in last night and scared her."

"A jumbie in the estate?" her father said, eyebrows rising. "Is a long time since one of dem was here."

"Not too long," said Sadika, shrugging. "They canvas parts of the island, remember? They're almost right on schedule."

Her father made a harrumphing noise. Sadika shrugged and offered him her arm to help him down the stairs. Her father gave her an amused look and said, "I'm not that old."

"Of course not," she said cheerfully, "I just thought you'd like to escort me down."

Her father gave her a look that said he clearly saw through her but took her arm. She moved slowly so as not to cause his arthritic ankles pain.

They made their way down the staircase in relatively good time today, Sadika noted. When they almost came to the end of the staircase, her father paused. Sadika frowned, wondering what had stopped him and then saw the large, furry spider on the bannister.

Her father reached out a hand and coaxed the spider onto the back of his palm. He held it toward Sadika, who held out her own hand and allowed the spider to scramble onto her palm. She let go of her father's arm and went down towards one of the windows. She opened the window with her free hand and put the spider on the sill. The spider rewarded her by biting her twice. Sadika hissed at the pain, huffed at the spider and then moved back to her father. She hooked her arm through his and helped him into the dining room.

"You should run some water over that," her father observed of the two growing red splotches on her palm.

"Yes," she agreed and left to do just that.

CHAPTER 2

The governor of Ierie, stood with his hands clasped behind his back and stared out at the scene from the window of his office. Below him, Port-of-Gold was spread out, stretching from the water and crawling further inland as more and more buildings were built. From where he stood, the buildings were larger, the pattern of them more orderly, a thriving city that was a proud addition to the Motherland's colonies. But as one moved out from the city's center and thus towards where the saikans did not inhabit, the city presented a less than desirable sight.

The borein village was a poor collection of buildings; structures with enough shape to stop them from being shacks. The distance it had from the city was not enough to stop the governor's mouth from curling in distaste.

Still, these people, secondary though they were, were under the Motherland's protection. A generosity the Motherland had decided to grant its ex-slaves and their progeny. And the governor did not argue with this generosity, he did not even begrudge it, for it made much easier in his life.

But there were those who were not under the Motherland's protection, not considered its own. There were those who had rejected such overtures of generosity and had had the gall to reject the Motherland's claim of the island. The kalinag, the native peoples who had lived on the island before it had been discovered by the civilized world and though there were little of them left, disease having its way with them, they persisted, setting up their villages and refusing entry to anyone they wished as if they had ownership of the land they stood on. It soured something in the Governor's stomach, that they should so blatantly deny the Motherland what was its own.

At last, the governor turned around and addressed the group of men sitting at the table, waiting patiently for him to speak.

"The lushest part of the island is taken up by those uncultured natives," said the governor of Port of Gold. "If we truly want to build a community fitting those of our rank we must do so in appropriate grounds."

The other saikan businessmen nodded.

"The kalinag have long been a blemish on our land," one added, wrinkling his nose in distaste.

"Yes," agreed the governor. "The Motherland gave us this colony to rule. How can we do so in good faith if we allow these... things to run unchecked over our land? How can we do so in good faith if we do not develop this colony and bring it to the greatest height that it can aspire to?"

"Quite true, Governor," the other man agreed.

"So, you are on board with my proposal?" the Governor asked.

"You have our support."

CHAPTER 3

Disgust, anger, ambition, the proud arrogance of ownership, caught on the wind. Vile intent was tossed on the ocean breeze, through the wavering branches of the coconut trees, filtering words from the saikans who walked here as if they were the rulers of the earth they moved over with each careless step. The words trembled through the trees, words rattling down the hollows in the trunks, seeping into the earth below. The echoes of the words hummed through the crystalline edge of the water that saturated the earth, tangling with more roots, being absorbed into rocks, all the way to the core of Ierie, spreading across the length and breadth of it, all screaming the same message. Danger. Danger to its children. Danger to those it had chosen to share with itself, those it had chosen as its own.

Rage and righteous indignation rose in swiftly in answer, rolling out over the island. There would be a reckoning for this threat. There would be repercussions to these petty would-be usurpers who dared threaten those that belonged to Ierie. The island hummed and then sent out a message of its own. It was time for its dark things to end their play and get to work.

Come! Come children of my heart. Come children of the night. Come children of Ierie! Come or your feet will dance on your own graves. Come!

Protect the children of my womb. Protect the children sculpted out of my dirt and bark and salt and waters. Protect the first born. Protect the children of my womb!

The message passed as a whisper along the. The land had called out the dark things. Ierie itself had called to the dark things and told them to protect the kalinag. They were bound because the shadows belonged to Ierie. Their power was bound to the land in a way the boerin could not truly understand and yet could not escape understanding. They too could feel the beats coiling down their bones on the days they were allowed to dance. Dark things were born out of them, after all.

Sadika mended one of her dresses while listening to Reshma trying to spell the list of words she was given to learn as an assignment.

Her fingers froze as the breeze blew through the open window bringing with it the humming words of Ierie.

Protect the first born!

"Sadika?" She flinched at the voice of her niece.

"Yes sweetheart?" she said.

"You okay? You're... far away today."

"I'm fine," Sadika smiled. "I'm just thinking about something, is all."

"What?" asked the child.

"Grown up ting," said Sadika, smiling. "Don't hurt yuh head, I'm fine."

The child huffed but returned to spelling her words. Sadika smiled at her and returned to her sewing, hiding a shiver as the breeze brought Ierie's words to her again.

Jamal raked the yard of the saikan man who employed him, using the motion to hide his agitation. He needed to move, run, kill, destroy. His hands ached to do more and the bottom of his feet itched terribly. It felt like the bones were pushing against the soles of his feet needing to get out, the itching increasing as the bones stretched. The claustrophobic feeling was even worse, growing steadily each minute until he was sure it would strangle him. Jamal tightened his grip and raked viciously.

When night finally fell, Jamal breathed a sigh of relief and carefully moved from his hiding place in the grounds of his employer. He was supposed to have left several hours ago but he still had business here. His employer was an important saikan and he had little doubt that the man would not know of the governor's plans.

He moved over to where he had hidden his stilts early that morning and pulled them out of the brush. He sat on the ground and put his feet into the stilts, strapping them on.

After a moment, the straps melted into his skin and his bones pierced the soles of his feet. They merged into the wood and the wood itself warped and twisted into solid flesh.

Jamal sighed in relief and rose into the air, body slimming into the thin figure of the Moko Jumbie. At last he was free of the claustrophobia. He was free, towering above the world, a sentinel in the darkness, a terror that did not miss your misdeeds.

He breathed in deeply of the night air that brought him whispers of words and the scent of wrongness. The saikan's house stank of evil.

Protect the first born!!

Ierie's words rang in his ears. And so he would.

CHAPTER 1

When Amrika was younger, a child barely in her teens, she'd asked a question with the toes of one foot dragging in the dirt as she swayed in a hammock in the kalinag village, sipping sweet water from a coconut.

"Why? Why had the Kalinag not killed all the intruders from the motherland, the saikan?"

Sure she knew the stories; that at first the saikan had pretended to be friends before their true nature's as conquerors and enslavers had spilled out.

But after, when they knew, when kalinag blood had been spilled, when they were dying by bullet and sword and disease, why had they not killed them?

The children of Ierie's womb were not without power. They were entwined with the land, its very essence run through them to make them Ierie's and not merely travelers from across the sea in canoes.

Amrika knew that the power of the kalinag was great and terrible, the pull of the tide and the strength of the mountains and the burn of the lava their world drifted on. She had heard the stories all her life, knew too well the power of Ierie's adopted children, the children of its heart to not believe that the power of the children of its womb was real.

So she'd asked why.

Wizened, amused eyes had glittered at her, folds and folds of brown skin creased around the corners, thin, sly yet kind lips curving up into a smile.

And then the old kalinag woman had told her,

"Some things are meant to be."

For an inquisitive teen, for anyone really, it was not enough of an answer so, she pushed and asked and tried her best to understand because she couldn't believe that sometimes bad things had to happen before you could get to the good, that sometimes the best things only came from the worst.

It did not bear thinking of.

But the kalinag had tried to explain because she was a child and she was their little sister and because it was her right to try and understand.

They tried to tell her how the world had a shape and sometimes terrible things had to happen for it to become its best state. But in the end, it all boiled down to this: some things are meant to be.

They said it in a hushed tone, almost reverent, with a gravitas she could and could not understand.

The kalinag's power could have put an end to the saikan long before Amrika's people had ever been brought to Ierie but they had not.

Because... Some things were meant to be. She could almost see the threads tying them to the world when they said the words. Some things were meant to be, in the way the waves were meant to wash up to the shore and wind was meant to rifle through the leaves and the rich dark soil was meant to grow food and the way the sun was meant to shine down on them all.

Amrika still did not understand it. Could not she thought, because she was only human and not one blessed with this knowledge. But she could accept it.

Some things were meant to be. This was her world as it was meant to be and it was still growing and changing and she was nothing but a part of that.

Her hair heats up under the sun's bright rays as she walks home from the shop she works at in the town. The dry season sun is both a beauty and a bane to its inhabitants. Good weather for planting, for building. Entirely too hot to be truly enjoyed without the oceans' waves nearby or under the cool trees by the river, toes dipping in lapping water, wriggling in blue mud.

The evenings are usually used by the boerin to do their own chores when they are finished for the day, but the carnival days are approaching so the barest minimum of chores are being done and rest of the time devoted to preparing for the festival.

Carnival.

Their tribute to freedom. Their wild mockery of those who had enslaved them. The days when they could dance. The days of secret tribute to the dark things who had stolen food from the masters when the slaves were hungry, who had distracted the masters so slaves could be freed, who had fought the masters to protect their own. The saikan thought the costumes of midnight robber and Dame Lorraine, Moko Jumbie and Fancy Sailors, Jab Jabs and the feared Bookman were merely characters borne out of the figment of their imagination, that the Stickfighters were merely some form of barbaric entertainment. The saikan knew nothing.

People were outside carefully sewing their costumes in the evening light, piecing together old clothes and whatever little scraps of cloth they'd found that the saikan didn't care for anymore. More cloth was being dyed in barrels and buckets set out, men and women's hand being stained and they dipped and re-dipped the cloth.

Amrika could see old man Seiko and his sons Arjun and Timal splitting bamboo and sanding it down in preparation for building a frame. Bente, their neighbour was sitting next to them, frowning hard at something he was drawing in the dirt. He must be trying to figure out the design for the cloth to drape over the frame. Bente was playing the dragon mas this year. The biggest and fiercest of all their carnival characters. It was sure to be something spectacular and Amrika couldn't wait to see it in its finished glory.

Echoing from outside the village were the sounds of tamboo bamboo bands warming up. Tamboo bamboo bands were the backbone of carnival, providing the music, the beat itself, for the parade. The bands practiced for long hours, until carnival itself, learning to thump their various lengths of bamboo in time to come up with the most pleasing rhythms. The competition between the various bands were fierce but friendly and the playoffs were a delight for anyone listening.

Amrika looked forward to spending the night before Carnival eating hot pholourie, with sweet sauce dripping down her fingers and then gorging on too sweet barfi, sitting on a roof to get the best view of the bands with Kirish beside her, still sweaty from participating in the stickfighting competitions, knuckles red and weeping from where they'd been rapped at. They'd be joined by their peers while the older and less nimble family members stayed on the streets clapping and shouting.

Later in the night, she and Kirish would slip down to one of the stalls and slurp oysters from their shells, enriched with pepper sauce, bandanya and salt. The tasty treat would burn going all the way down, spreading a tingling to her lips and making her breathe harshly and the only way to stop it would to be to slurp down more and more for the brief reprieve of tasty before burning came back to full force.

She never quite remembers making it back to their house on those nights, too tired and too alive, head swimming with music and the smoke from the flambeaus and the alcohol on people's breath.

Amrika has both her and her brother's costumes to make this year. So she finishes the bare minimum of her chores and joins her neighbors outside while she waits for Kirish to return from his job in the town. She is soon caught up in her work; needle in hand as she fits the pieces of the black cloth together to form the costume of a Bat, and so doesn't see her brother until he nudges her gently. She still jumps and nearly says a word that would have all the tantes around her washing her mouth out with sand and water. She restrains herself in time but glares at Kirish who laughs at her.

"Come gyal," he says kindly, eyes still twinkling, "De sun almost gone, leh we go home." Grumbling Amrika stows her needle and gathers up her work, says goodbye to the rest of their neighbors who are still stubbornly working in the last orange rays of the sun, and follows him back to their house. He magnanimously takes the bundle of cloth she shoves at him.

"There are a lot of interesting meetings going on," Amrika reported to Kirish the moment they are safe within the walls of their own home.

Her brother groaned, throwing his head back so far, his back bowed. "Ah thought ah tell yuh stay inside?"

"Yuh did," she said cheerfully. "Relax, ah went inside when de Robber pass."

He sighed and acquiesced to her prodding for information. "Yes, dere was some interesting meetings going on."

"You get close enough to find out wha they was saying?"

"Lil bit," he admitted, "Nuh for all ah dem." The tick in his jaw gave away his annoyance at that fact.

Amrika shivered. "We go hear the rest. Ah saw a Jab Jab last night by one of de windows." She shuddered again at the memory of the sleek, blue-skinned person with the wide, almost friendly grin. It would have been more convincing if the teeth weren't sharply pointed and the Jab Jab hadn't been holding his long black whip that twisted and turned of its own accord. Jab Jabs were beautiful, with angled faces and graceful, well-toned bodies that moved as smoothly as an undulating river. Amrika had never been more afraid of anything before.

"Are you alright?" Kirish asked with concern. Even Midnight Robbers were wary of tangling with Jab Jabs.

"Yes," she said, "He didn't do anything."

"Dais why I does tell you stay inside!"

"I good," she said, irritated now. "He eh do meh nothing and ah was far away."

"One day you won't be far away enough," her brother predicted darkly.

"Dika!" Reshma's small voice pierced through the house.

Sadika ran up the stairs. "Wha is it chile?"

The little girl stood naked outside the bathroom and pointed. "Spider."

"Oh," said Sadika and laughed. "Okay, wait a moment." She stepped into the shower and found the spider on the pump handle. She held out her hand to the funnel-web spider and allowed the creature to scramble onto it.

"Easy, sir," she murmured to the spider as she turned and carried it over to the window under Reshma's watchful gaze. She set the spider free on the side of the house and shivered as the spider's beady eyes bore into hers. It wove a quick web which hummed

"Protect the children of my womb!"

And the spider was gone.

"It's gone," she said to the child.

"Thanks," said Reshma as she retreated into the shower.

"Welcome," Sadika said cheerfully and left the room.

When Reshma finished dressing after her bath, she went over to the window and looked out. Sure enough, there was the large furry spider from the bathroom. She hesitated and then reached out with a finger and stroked its large back. Its hairs were stiff but pleasing all the same.

"Hello Mr. Spider," she said. The spider moved its mouthlike appendages at her and she took it as a greeting. She smiled back at it.

She continued to stroke the spider until suddenly, she felt a sharp sting in her hand. She cried out and jerked back her hand, gripping it tightly. She stared at the spider with betrayed eyes until the spreading pain made her burst into tears.

Sadika rushed upstairs at the sound of her niece wailing.

"Reshma! Wha happen!"

She was hit by a wailing bundle of child as she entered the door. It took her a few moments but finally Reshma was able to show her her hand

and the point of pain. Sadika stared at the red splotch and felt the blood drain from her head.

"Which spider!" She said frantically, "Reshma, which spider?"

"Bathroom!"

"The one from the bathroom this morning?" she asked, heart sinking.

Reshma nodded though her tears.

At this point Sadika's father had made it to them.

"She was bitten by a funnel-web spider," Sadika said faintly. "Oh, I'm so stupid!"

"There's nothing we can do now," replied her father gravely, "Either she makes it or she doesn't."

Reshma wailed even louder.

"It's okay chile, yuh going an be okay." Sadika assured her, rubbing the back of the child's head in a futile attempt to comfort her. "Come, leh we put some water and ice on that, okay?"

Reshma nodded and Sadika lifted the child into her arms and carried her into the bathroom.

The sun was brushing the top of the cane fields when the stickfighters assembled in the dirt yard on the edge of the boerin village. The yard was edged with a tall fence, made of thick board slats and was familiar to them all. Many of them had learned here. The house, also within the fence, belonged to the family of Markus; another stickfighter.

The inhabitants of the house had watched many a stickfighter be trained and even now, Markus' grandmother was sitting on the porch, rocking back and forth in her rocking chair, peering at them with sharp, black eyes, set in her wrinkled face. Khion remembered a time when she used to have a stick leaning against the wall next to her chair and her wiry curls were still shot through with black.

"Alright," Markus began as the unofficial leader here. "We hah all three ah de kalinag villages to protect. We go have to do them in shifts. Everybody go take a night. I want two people on each village. One with de village itself and ah next one ah allyuh on de roads leading to de village. Right?"

"Rite," they agreed.

The meeting quickly descended into the intricacies of logistics, and Khion found himself being assigned to alternate between Chagna and Tarigua. He took note of the others he would be working with, catching their eyes in acknowledgement before turning his attention back to the schedule being laid out.

It would be long and tiring, he mused, to stand guard all night, but it was not a duty he would shirk. The kalinag were friends, they were brothers and sisters in spirit and they had welcomed them; they had made Ierie a home instead of a jail the saikan had dragged some to and tricked others into entering.

Protect the first born!

"Of course," Khion murmured.

Two nights later, Khion was moving through the dirt road, leading to Chagna in languid patrol. The bare earth under his equally bare feet pulsed with a rhythm that vibrated through his bones as if they were hollow and exacerbated the sound. He swayed as he moved, twirling the stick in his hand and waiting for the moment when the land's rhythm roared in response to the intrusion of the saikan. While the other things of the night sought to unravel the saikan's plots, he was here, hovering on the perimeter of the kalinag village, a silent shield for the firstborn of Ierie

CHAPTER 5

It took two days for Reshma's fever to break. Sadika had spent much of that time with the little girl, pressing wet cloths to her forehead and talking soothing nonsense as the fatal venom raged through her small body.

It took another day before she woke up properly and was coherent. She spent a great deal of that day fussing and crying, but Sadika had never been so relieved to hear cranky cries. Her father visited the child and was much comforted when he came out of the room.

"She will live," he declared wearily.

"Will it happen again?" asked Sadika anxiously.

Her father shook his head. "It has never happened for any of us, so I doubt it will do so for her." "She'll be fine."

She watched as he rubbed his wrist where she knew he'd gotten his first fatal spider bite. He'd told her the story frequently when she was younger and prone to sitting at his feet, begging for his attention even though he'd been beyond tired from working in the estate fields. She'd been horrified to hear of the pain from the spider bite but fascinated how it sparked their abilities as dark things.

"A meeting," her father had said of the incident, "Like the meeting between Anansi and Ierie."

Still, despite knowing their family history, Sadika sighed in relief at her father's reply and slumped, dropping her face into her hands.

"Good. I can't go through a next few days like that again."

She breathed shakily into her hands, swallowing hard. It was times like this that made her miss her older sister acutely. Prisha had always been better at handling crises. She'd helped their father take care of Sadika after their mother had died from some disease that had flooded the area when Sadika had been very small, despite the fact that Prisha had only been a few years older than her little sister.

She'd thought then, when she was young and naïve, that Prisha would be there forever. It had never crossed her childish mind that her happy, daredevil, ridiculously kind and acutely skilled sister would die before she reached twenty-five. So when Prisha and her husband had never returned from their humanitarian mission of freeing slaves from a ship, still transporting them after the ban on slavery had passed, Sadika's world had almost crumbled. She and her father had clung together to survive their grief and Sadika had done everything in her power to care for her sister's eleven-month-old baby.

If Reshma hadn't made it, she wasn't sure she'd have been able to endure that kind of grief again. There were too many gaping holes ripped in her heart already.

"So, what now?"

Jamal looks at Jessica. The ex-jotlin class girl was of saikan decent but now lived with his boerin class family because her own were dead and none of the other jotlin or saikan families would take her in. The jotlin class was the middle class in more than one way, being made up of saikans who were too poor to gain status in the saikan class despite their heritage and boerins who had managed to catapult themselves into moderate wealth. As such the jotlin class was always careful about who they associated with. The right connections could catapult a saikan-born jotlin higher while the wrong connections would send a boerin-born jotlin back down. The daughter of a saikan-born jotlin with no remaining wealth was not a connection to have, so Jessica had come to them. She was not what Jamal would have wanted in a sister, but she had adapted rather well to life in the boerin class.

As a jotlin, she had heard tales of the dark things but had never expected the stories she'd heard whispered by the bored youth at fancy parties to be real. Needless to say, the truth of Jamal and his family had been a shock, but she had adjusted well to the surprising news often asking him for an explanation of the things she didn't understand.

Currently, she was curious as to what they were going to do with the information he had gleaned from the saikan's house the night he'd spied on them.

He shrugs, "Doh know, we'll see after it's passed round to everybody. All de dark things are gathering info, so we need to get everything first."

"I don't understand though," Jessica says, "Why didn't Ierie grant her firstborn abilities too?"

"She did," Jamal tells her patiently.

"Then why don't they protect themselves?"

"Because," he says, "we don't want them to awaken their power. It's a last resort. It's not something anyone would want awake yes? So, de dark things, we will fight them so worse don't come, rite? Trust me Jess, nobody wah the kalinag power raising."

"Is it dark?" she asks.

"Dark?" he says, "No. It is the force of a land, the rush of the sea, intent on drowning everything in its path, it is the strength of a people who have managed to survive in a land when it was untamed and intent on their death. Ierie only let those who live, who prove themselves yes? And the Kalinag survived, proved that Ierie didn't make a mistake taking them as its own. Their power is like the slow-moving fire of the earth, the drowning rain and howling wind of a hurricane. It is everything of the island along with the determination of men who have not been defeated. It is and always will be, a last resort because such power should never be raised lightly."

"It sounds scary," she says honestly.

Jamal lets out a little laugh and slings an arm around her shoulders. "I know. De rel scary thing though? It doesn't seem scary at all."

"So, what is it that our interlopers have planned for de first born?"

It is a Dame Lorraine who speaks, her inhuman beauty is not hidden by the night. Despite the darkness, there is something that lures men to her. Her voice is warm and deep and perfect for starting the meeting because everyone is paying attention.

"From what we have seen," a Moko Jumbie answers her, "is that they want the kalinag land for dey own, cause it lush, and also cause dere might be gold dere."

"They not mining gold already in the mountains?" another Dame Lorraine asks.

"Yes," says a Stickfighter. "Buh that may run out, and they greedy so eh? Dem saikan eye too big."

"Which land they want?" a Midnight Robber asks next.

"All of it." The voice that answers is the smooth vocals of a Jab Jab.

"So, what do we do?" Another Stickfighter breaks the silence.

"Protect the first born," says an aged voice, the speaker hidden in the shadows.

"Shall we kill them?" The Jab Jab is bored.

"Killing saikan do not stop their plans," a Moko Jumbie observes. "They are quick to revenge death and brutal when they do, they must be disillusioned from their plans."

"In what way?" a Robber asks.

"In the ways we do best," the aged voice answers. "Dame Lorraine and Midnight Robbers, steal their coin, Moko Jumbies scare their meetings, destroy the places they meet, Stickfighters, protect the village and my kin shall make it very difficult for the villages to be found."

"And us?" asks the Jab Jab.

"As you please," the aged voice says. And the Jab Jab laughs.

"As for the others who are not here, pass the word, don't let their shipments make it to them, do not let their goods travel unharassed."

"And if dat doh work?" a Robber asks.

"We are de dark things," says the aged voice. "We'll remind them why we are called so."

"As you say," says the Midnight Robber, amused. "The saikan live here on Ierie's sufferance. They really doh want to know what it like when the land does not permit them to live here anymore."

The dark things all laugh in agreement.

"Sadika whey you going?"

Sadika paused as Reshma's tiny voice pierced the air.

"What you doing waking?" asked Sadika.

"I heard you going back downstairs you doh do that."

"Go back to sleep," Sadika told her, "Granpa and I have some wok to do."

"Wha wok?"

"I tell you ask that?" asked Sadika, lifting an eyebrow, dangerously.

The little girl shrank back and shook her head.

"Good, go back an sleep, we won't be too long."

She went over to the child and ruffled her hair and gave her a little hug to let her know that she wasn't angry. The child clung to her and then scampered off to bed. Sadika closed the little girl's door and went downstairs to where her father waited.

"Are we going together?" she asked.

Her father shook his head, "Is too many, I'd rather have as much covered as fast as possible."

"Okay," Sadika nodded. She hugged her father and he hugged her back tightly.

"Be careful," she said.

"I know," her father said brushing back her hair. He knew how long it had taken for her to resume usage of her abilities as a dark thing after her sister's death. He knew that she'd had blamed their abilities for Prisha's death, before her father had pointed out that dark thing of Ierie or not, Prisha would have still gone to help because that's just who she was. He knew and she didn't need to say, that she couldn't lose him too.

"You be careful yuhself eh, young lady?"

She laughed. "Of course!"

Her father laughed and went off to the carriage and Sadika herself mounted a horse. She took a deep breath, eyes fluttering shut as she attempted to center herself. It'd been years since she'd refused to use her abilities; too stung by Priya's death and blaming anything she could. But even though she'd made her peace, she still didn't often use her abilities. This would be the first time in a long time that she would ply the trickster's thread so wide and long, cast her web with intent to catch prey and laugh at their futile struggles. She let out the breath and gave a slow and sly smile. She would be okay.

She adjusted the wide brim hat on her head and pulled the veil down from it. She didn't need to be recognized by any saikan that might catch a glimpse of her tonight.

She took the roads to the north whilst her father took the roads to the south. As she neared the rest of the boerin houses, she caught a glimpse of a dark figure in a long cape, sliding along the roofs. A shrill whistle met her ears a moment later and a miasma of darkness flooded over the area.

The Midnight Robber kept pace with her until she was past the boerin village. Then she was thundering down a dirt road to the nearest kalinag village. Before she intersected the village, a figure placed itself in her path.

She shouldn't have been able to see the figure. It was pitch black and the figure was not dressed brightly. But it stood there, staff in the road, giving note of its presence by its aura alone.

Guardian. Warrior. Stickfighter.

If necessary, the Stickfighter would throw both her and her horse in another direction.

Sadika pulled back on the reins and her horse slowed to a trot. She halted a few feet away from the figure.

"Who comes?" asked the Stickfighter softly.

"A friend of the kalinag," Sadika replied gently. "I come to make your job easier, guardian."

"How so?" asked the figure.

Sadika smiled. "I'm going to make the road disappear. The saikan will have a difficult time finding what's not there. And if they do breach the roads well, you are there."

There was a pause and then the Stickfighter nodded slowly. "Work, dark neighbor."

Sadika tipped her hat to him and slid off her horse. She felt in her saddlebags and pulled out a spool of sticky, grey material.

"Where's best for me to start working?" she asked the guardian of the road.

"Here good," he said.

"Alright," she said and started working.

CHAPTER 6

Amrika said nothing as her brother walked over to the window and stood poised on the sill there. He tilted his head a little to let her know he knew she was there, and as always, a shiver went down her spine. Kirish was her brother and he loved her, but he was the Midnight Robber tonight and it was the Robber who was acknowledging her presence and choosing not to harm her.

Then he leaned out the window, twisted and lifted himself up to the roof. Amrika exhaled slowly and waited for the footsteps of the Robber, her brother, to fade away. A few moments later she heard the shrill cry of the whistle and knew the Robber was hunting his next victim.

Protect the first born!

Ierie's words still rang out, still shivered on the air, still thrummed beneath her skin. Black blood. No matter how much Kirish might wish that she did not have it, she did. Black blood drummed through her veins, tugging at her, telling her to dance, telling her to destroy, telling her to walk the night like it was her own, to walk Ierie and not fear. She was one of the dark things and she was adopted by Ierie.

Only she wasn't. Black blood ran in her veins but she wasn't a dark thing, not yet.

Protect the first born!!

Amrika paced inside the house, tugging against the call.

Protect the children of my heart!

Amrika paced some more.

Protect the first born!

She gave an angry sigh and crawled up onto the roof to sit in a corner, hoping that just being outside would ease the call of the land.

Protect the first born!

It did not. The land's whispers were much fiercer now, blowing on the cool night breeze. Ierie was insistent and though the dark things were answering, it was determined not to let them forget or slack off.

After a frustrated hour, Amrika gave up and simply prowled the roofs, searching for some saikan targets to release her annoyance upon. She found some, but the areas were too well lit, and others carried bodyguards. She might have black blood but she wasn't a dark thing yet. Bodyguards were beyond her.

She spied another saikan man and was just about to strike when two other men appeared and moved to join him, guards for his person. Amrika sighed, frustrated, but then let out a startled noise when, just before the bodyguards met the saikan, a tiny child brushed past the man and snatched his wallet.

The saikan man let out a shout and his bodyguards immediately set off after the child. Amrika stared for a frozen moment and then set off over the roofs after them. Saikan merchants had no fondness for pickpockets and the fact that this one was a child would not lessen the severity of the punishment meted out. The bodyguards would most likely beat the child to death.

Amrika ran as fast as she could and by some clever maneuvering managed to get in between the child and the men, as she dropped into the dark alley.

"Hey!" she snapped at the child, "Dais a dead end!"

The child paused, looked at her and then nodded and followed down the path Amrika indicated. Amrika ran behind her, nudging her into various paths and corners as she sought to lose the men behind them. When she thought that there was enough distance, she stopped the child and they took a few moments to rest.

After she caught her breath, she took a good look at the child and seeing the almond eyes and sharp cheekbones, realized that the little girl was a kalinag child. She was very grateful then that she'd helped the child. Who knew what Ierie would do if a saikan killed a kalinag right now?

"Wha village yuh come from?" asked Amrika, stooping down to the child's level.

"Chagna," said the little girl. "I wit meh cousins rite now."

"Whey yuh cousins?" asked Amrika.

"Dong de road dere," said the child, "After de parlour."

"Alright," said Amrika, "Leh we get you dere and doh thief nobody money again eh! Cause if they ketch yuh they go kill yuh."

The little girl nodded solemnly and took the hand that Amrika held out. They were almost to the parlour when the two bodyguards reappeared behind them.

Both of the hulking men held long pieces of wood and were brandishing them menacingly. Amrika shoved the child behind her and backed slowly down the road.

"When I say run, you run," Amrika told the girl.

"Buh!" the child protested.

"No buts!" she snapped, "Just do it!"

There was silence but Amrika took it as a positive.

"Leave she 'lone," Amrika told the men. "Is a chile!"

"She took our master's money," said one, "She must pay."

Amrika held her hand out behind her and after a moment the child placed the wallet in it. Amrika tossed the wallet at the bodyguards and one caught it but they still advanced.

"Like we said," said the second one, "She took our master's money. It doesn't matter if we get it back. She must be punished for even daring!" The men smiled identical wicked smiles and then surged forward.

"Run!" Amrika shouted. Tiny feet pounded behind her and Amrika managed to catch the first of the descending pieces of wood before it smacked her in the head. She pushed it away and threw the man off balance, managing to twist in time to trip the other man who'd gone after the child. He sprawled on the ground but scrambled to his feet quickly.

The first one had recovered and smacked Amrika on the back. The blow stung and she couldn't breathe. The force of it knocked her off her feet and she sprawled face down in the dirt.

The second man, in revenge for being tripped, stomped on her before turning away to go after the child.

Amrika heard him running after the girl before her mind could process what it meant. She tried to struggle to her feet, but the first man didn't let her make it up. Another bone crushing blow landed on her back and then on her head and shoulders and continued cracking against her until all she could hear was the dull thumps as the wood impacted on her body.

Thump! Thump! Thump! Th-thump! Thump! Thump! Th-Thump!

It sounded like a beat, she thought abstractly, as pain seared through her and the sound of bones breaking crackled through her, a fast, heavy bass beat. Kinda nice actually, it could make a good rhythm.

She coughed out blood as the wood hit her back again. It looked almost black in the pale moonlight. The wood descended again and again.

Thump! Thump! Cough! Thump! Thump! Cough!

More blood. Seeping into her eyes now, leaking out her nose.

And then a beat. At first, she thought it was the wood, but it sounded all wrong. *Idiot*, she thought dazedly, *it's my heart beating*. And it was, only her heartbeat was matching something else, matching the thrum of the land, the rhythm of Ierie.

Then, there was a scream in the night, a child's scream, a girl's scream.

There was silence then it was broken by the first bodyguard laughing.

"He's got her now, little boerin!" he sneered to Amrika then he swung down to deliver the final crushing blow to her skull.

However, it did not connect. Amrika rolled away just in time and the wood smacked into the ground. She rolled again and slid gracefully to her feet.

"And you lil saikan," she said, "now yuh dead!"

The man swung his makeshift weapon at her, but she slipped out of the way, whirling and snatching the piece of wood from his grip as she did so and then smacked him across the face.

The man staggered back and then rushed at her, but the beat of the land was thrumming through her bones now, and he was no match for her. She sidestepped him, smacking the wood into the back of his neck and then his back, driving him to the ground.

She whirled the wood over her head and delivered a final, crushing blow to the bodyguard's head. He was knocked unconscious for what would probably be a very long time. Amrika then spun and fled down the street.

The second bodyguard had apparently managed to lose his hold on the child in the interim and was cornering her again. Several residents had also apparently tried to stop him, but their unconscious or softly moaning bodies littering the ground spoke of their failure. Only the young and women were left. Even as Amrika advanced, a middle-aged boerin woman stepped out against the man waving a kitchen knife, but he simply swung the wood, snapping her wrist when it impacted with her hand. The woman cried out, dropping the knife and grabbing her hand.

The man would have swung at the woman again but Amrika said, "Swing an you'll lose your han'!"

The man turned to see who had spoken and she could feel his surprise at seeing her there and the state she was in.

After a moment though, he smirked, "And what can you do to me?" he asked, clearly amused.

"The same I did to your partner," she said coolly.

The man snorted and then twisted and swung at the child. Amrika's piece of wood impacted into his shoulder a second later, knocking him off balance and causing him to miss his target. Amrika slammed into him a moment later. He threw her off, but she had retrieved her weapon. He then swung at her and she parried and then lashed out at him. Her blow struck and enraged him; he lashed out again.

She danced away, struck again. The man roared in frustration and swung wildly at her. She nimbly stepped out of the way and laughed, loud and scornful.

She paused, swaying to the beat and then raised her piece of wood over her head, pointing one end at him.

"Come nah!"

But the saikan man paused. It was finally starting to dawn on him that Amrika should not be able to even be walking, let alone fighting. Blood streaked down her face giving her a frightening visage, and the blood smeared smile did not help to soften it.

"Yuh fraid?" she drawled out. She danced lightly towards him, bouncing on the balls of her feet and the man shuffled away.

"What are you?" he said.

"I? I is a woman. You fraid a woman? You should."

"You are no woman," the bodyguard said, staring at her, staring at the way she moved, so very at odds with the broken bones still sticking out of her.

"I am," she said cheerfully.

She swayed to the beats that coiled down her bones and then suddenly the night was disturbed by a clap and then another, and another. Amrika shifted to see that the woman and children in the houses surrounding them were clapping, but they weren't applauding; they were setting up a beat. They were grim-faced but their eyes twinkled as they rapped a rhythm between their palms. It wasn't drums, Amrika acknowledged, but it was good enough.

She turned back to the bodyguard who looked both furious and afraid.

"Leh we dance nah?" she said and twirled her stick above her head.

The man yelled and struck at her. She parried and struck out, gashing him on the cheek. The man staggered, and she did not let him recover. Her piece of wood was no longer a blocky, discarded beam, but a smooth, sleek stick, thick and flexible.

It swooped through the air and cracked against the man's arms, side, shoulders and ankles. He fought to block her but he wasn't fast enough. The stick crackled over him and shattered bone; first one arm and then another hung useless and then the stick whirled down and gave him the buss head of a century and he fell unconscious.

Amrika was standing and breathing hard in the middle of the street. After a moment, the clapping wound down and the beat vibrating along her bones slowly flowed out. Her grip loosened, and the blocky piece of wood hit the street. Amrika's knees hit the ground a moment later as she lost consciousness.

CHAPTER 7

When she was a child and free of the responsibilities of someone older, she'd spent a lot of time in the kalinag villages, running barefoot with their children, eating food in their homes, getting her hair braided by the aunties and being taught to fish by the uncles.

She'd spent a lot of time learning to bask in the scent of brine, in the shade of mangrove trees, feet buried in the mud, salt and green on her tongue, oysters on the tree roots not too far from her, soaking in the peace of the island.

She has too many memories buried in the warmth and contentment of the kalinag villages, too much and not enough. She misses it sometimes, fiercely, when the bustle of the saikan town is too much, when even her own little boerin village is too busy, people hustling about as they try to get their work at home done as well as do all the extra work their saikan employers would demand of them whenever some big to-do would happen.

She is not the only one, she knows.

Many of the boerin; the people who once were slaves and now are free, had spent time in the kalinag villages. Many of those who were Ierie's dark things, or who held a history of such in their blood, had spent a lot of their formative years flitting in and around the kalinag village, soaking up the wisdom of the elders and making friends.

It feels like home, the best parts, concentrated and living in her chest.

For a long time, it felt like she was cradled in that warmth, until the sharpness of reality poked its way through and she blearily opened her eyes.

"Chile, if you know how much I want to cut yuh tail eh?"

Kirish's voice came as Amrika blinked slowly.

"Eh?" she said, voice rough and hoarse.

A sigh, and then her brother loomed over her, shaking his head. Despite his earlier words, worry had lines etched into his forehead.

"Yuh alrite?"

Amrika attempted to sit up and groaned.

"Doh move," said her brother exasperatedly. "Yuh does heal buh it does still hurt chile."

"Heal?" Her voice was confused. She swallowed hard; her throat dry.

"Doh tell meh you ent remember inno," said Kirish.

Amrika frowned and then the memories came back, the saikan, the child, the fight.

"De gurl!"

"She alrite," said Kirish. "Better dan you!"

Amrika attempted to sit up again but her brother pushed her back. Still, she lifted her head and peered at herself.

"Kirish," she said hoarsely, "I shouldn't be healing, I should be dead."

Kirish snorted. "I realized," he said dryly.

"How?"

"I thought you remembered," he said.

"I... Maybe?"

Kirish sighed and shook his head. "I don't know if to be happy or if to kill you." The darkness of the Robber was in his voice but he was also strangely affectionate.

"Why meh ribs not break?"

"They were, yuh healed."

"Buh..." Amrika trailed off as her mind caught up with what memory she had. The beat, the clapping, the stick swinging in her hands.

"The stick," she said hoarsely, "The beat."

"Yeah de stick." He shook his head again, "Black blood. Cah get way from it! At least, at least yuh is not a Robber."

"Stickfighter," she said. "Kirish how?"

He shrugged. "Doh know, but Ierie is a mix up country, I eh going an be surprised if we had Stickfighter blood somewhere. But I eh going an be surprised if you is a first line either. I tell you you ent have the temperament to be a Robber."

She laughed. "Yuh did."

Kirish smiled at her. "Doh do dat again eh? Yuh may be Stickfighter and ting now but if I have to come and see yuh lying in a pool ah yuh blood again I going an kill you mehself."

"You found me?"

Kirish laughed. "The boerin clapping? Ierie thrumming under our feet? We knew something was happening, so we came."

"We?"

"We in Ierie," said Kirish, "Everybody fas so."

Amrika laughed. "What now?"

"Now you going an sleep," said Kirish, "then you going and go home, and after that, then yuh go pick up ah stick again."

"What, precisely, do you mean by 'you lost them'?" His master's voice was smooth and cool and utterly furious.

Jamal raked the yard and continued to eavesdrop.

"The men stated that they were ambushed by a group of the boerin," the guard master said carefully.

"Ambushed," repeated the saikan man carefully. "Your trained men were ambushed by things, who scarcely have half a mind enough to survive? Your trained men lost my money!" Jamal's saikan employer slammed a hand down on the table.

The guard master did not jump. Jamal smiled and then tried to hide it, raking industriously.

"It will be rectified," the guard master said.

"If it is not," the saikan said silkily, "You will find your life very unpleasant."

The guard master didn't reply and the saikan eventually waved a hand to dismiss him.

"Dem does rel lie eh?" said a smooth, rich voice.

Jamal spun to see a young man, leaning against the side of the house, eyeing him lazily.

"Wha you doing?" Jamal hissed at him.

"Listning," the young man said unconcernedly.

"I go do dat here," Jamal said angrily. "Now geh out before I get meh head buss, de bossman ain't too happy with boerin today."

"Yuh bossman nuh going an be happy with any boerin fuh a while," the young man said. "He guard man done gone an say is plenty ah we who hit he guards instead of ah gyul. Now they going an fight up all ah we."

"We go deal," said Jamal.

"Will yuh?"

"Shoo Jab Jab," said Jamal. "This saikan go get what coming to he tail jus now. I's a protector, you is jus a nightmare."

The Jab Jab laughed. "Alright, buh that guard master is mine."

"Tear him apart," Jamal said carelessly, negligently. "I will continue to mek sure that de saikan here never go be happy 'gain."

The Jab Jab laughed again and sketched a bow before striding off. Jamal snorted and set back to work.

The Governor, Sir Archibald, was visited by a certain man employed by him.

"Yes, Mr. Kit, how are things progressing?"

Mr. Kit took a seat and said, "Rather unusually." He took the drink that the mayor poured for him.

"How so?" said the mayor.

"Well I sent men to survey the villages so that I could get an idea of how many men were required. I don't believe in wasting resources you see. But the men I sent, very competent men I might add, could not find the villages."

There was a pause.

"I don't understand, Mr. Kit." "Do you mean to tell me the villages have moved?"

"I mean to say, the roads leading to the villages, don't appear to lead to them anymore," Mr. Kit stated neutrally.

"What?" said Governor Archibald, sitting up.

"The roads curved away from where they used to," said Mr. Kit. "The men I sent attempted to follow the road and seemingly knocked into things that they could not see. After several tries, they retreated to report to me."

The governor blinked. "How are the roads changed?"

"If I knew that," said Mr. Kit, "I would not be here mi' lord. We are attempting another breach tonight."

"You may try from another direction," the governor suggested.

"Be assured we will," said Mr. Kit. "Good day mi 'lord."

Protect the first born!

"Alright, alright!" murmured Sadika as she moved around the house, going about her chores. She blinked and rubbed her eyes with the back of her hand. She was tired from her late-night escapades. Unlike the rest of the dark things, she wasn't in the habit of trundling around the country late at night.

"Dika!" called Reshma.

"What is it chile?" she called back, muffling a yawn.

"Ah throw down the flour."

"What?!" she exclaimed exasperatedly. "Reshma, why?"

"I doh know," said the little girl sulkily.

Sadika rubbed her forehead with a hand. Ever since she had been bitten, Reshma had been like this. She would throw down things or tear them up just for wickedness sake. Not that she meant it to be wicked, she just thought it was funny at the time. Sadika knew it would pass, eventually. Anasi's trickster tendencies eventually went down to a simmer. She too had gone through the same thing, but it was frustrating when you were in the position of parent and not child.

"Well next time chile, don't do it, even if yuh think it is funny. Now get the broom and sweep it up. I not going to do it fuh you."

There was a clatter of movement as Reshma went to get the broom and scoop.

"She'll get over it soon," said Sadika's father.

"I know," huffed Sadika.

Her father laughed at her expression. "You wasn't easy either chile. You did shave off meh beard a day."

Sadika laughed. "I don't remember that."

"It still did happen," said her father. "Doh worry. And doh get annoyed at de chile. It does take some time for yuh to get a handle on it. We lineage ain't easy."

"I know," said Sadika, sighing. "I think it's cause I blaming meself. If I didn't pick up de spider where she could see, she wouldn't ah get bitten."

"It woulda happen sometime," Sadika's father advised her. "It always does. Best she get it over with."

"I know. I know," said Sadika. "But with Ierie calling de dark things... I just wish it wasn't now."

"It may help, or it may hurt," her father shrugged. "Reshma will deal fine. We family never gained we lineage by runnin or standing down."

Sadika sketched a shallow, mocking bow to her father. "No, we didn't," she said and moved to the next room.

She crossed the room to the basket of clothes on the bed and began sorting and folding them.

Protect the children of my womb!

The words hummed from the spider's web in the corner. Sadika went over to it and carefully spooled the threads in her hands.

"Working on it," she replied.

CHAPTER 8

A day after she had awakened, Amrika found herself outside in her backyard. She took her time, stretching leisurely and moving carefully on the hard-packed earth. Once she was satisfied that everything was healed and nothing was likely to rip, something she still had trouble believing, she moved faster, breaking into a little run. After a few laps around the tiny backyard, she stopped and stretched again.

This time she put a little more effort into the stretching. This wasn't to ascertain if she was well. This was to pull at her muscles, yank them until they uncoiled and lay loose and heavy with untapped power. This was so that she could move, really move. This was so that she could tap into the black blood that ran through her veins.

Once she was loose and limber, limbs warming with a pleasant burn she started to move, gentle quick steps, then a sharp twist to the body, a turn and a few gliding steps. It was half-dancing, half her carving her way through the world. She turned and swayed again, trying to find the beat that had echoed through her bones on that night.

She lost track of how long she had been moving, but suddenly there it was, a whisper of an answer, the rhythm of the land, Ierie's song playing like the drumming of a thousand feet. Her heart stuttered in her chest and then picked up the rhythm, and for the first time, since she'd begun, Amrika felt like she was finally, really moving.

Something flew through the air and Amrika heard the song vibrating along its shaft. She reached out and snatched the stick from the air, twirling it through her hands before she turned and faced her brother.

"I hear stickfighting does work better with ah stick," he said, grinning at her.

She grinned back and twirled the stick in her hand again before raising it above her head, sinking down into the Stickfighter's stance.

Her brother drummed on the bench he was sitting on and Amrika whirled into motion, trying to get a feel of how she was now. She was faster, she knew. She had realized that already but she didn't really feel the strength until she had a stick in her hands. But now that she was gripping the smooth wood, she was aware of just how much power really laid in her limbs. Here encased in her skin was the ability to toss men through stone. It was certainly going to take some getting used to. Aches and pains also faded faster than she expected and she wasn't as tired as she should be.

Her practice with the stick was suddenly cut short as the stick clanged against a knife. She looked up to find her brother holding a knife against her staff. She frowned at him and he smiled. It was the Robber's smile. Amrika suddenly realized that night had fallen whilst she had practiced.

"Yuh should move," Kirish told her, almost gently. The hair on the back of her neck prickled and Amrika hastily heeded his advice. She knocked back his knife and danced back. He recovered in the next moment and dashed at her. Amrika parried one blow and almost got sliced open by the other. Her breath hissed as she exhaled in some mix of exhilaration and fear. She blocked the next one and got a knife to her throat in the next second.

"Yuh cah be a Stickfighter without fighting," her brother told her.

"So, ah hadda fight you?" she asked breathlessly. Adrenaline and Ierie's song mixed into an intoxicating drug that had her body shaking with anticipation, Amrika was not entirely sure her body could handle the strain. "Yuh rather fight another Robber?" Kirish asked. "It have other Stickfighters and yuh go hadda learn from dem," he said. "Buh until yuh ask dem, is me you hadda work with."

"Is meh first day!" she told him, irritated.

"And you does never not stick yuh nose in someting too big fuh yuh," Kirish told her. "So yuh should be just fine fighting on yuh first day!"

Amrika snorted. "You just real want to cut meh tail ent?"

Kirish laughed. "Come 'Rika. Ierie calling so leh we get you ready. Yuh doh know wha going an happen. You done nearly dead fuh all dis. And if yuh didn't have black blood in yuh then yuh woulda really been dead."

Amrika studied her brother and saw that even though there was the Robber's darkness swirling around him, his eyes were that of her brother and they were worried.

"Alright," she said and raised her stick over her head.

"Whey yuh going?" Reshma's voice was timid as she surveyed Sadika. Sadika sighed.

"Ent you supposed to be asleep?"

"I can't," said the little girl. "What you doing? You does never go out like this unless is a party and it don't have any party and you not dressed fuh one either."

"Is not any of your business," Sadika told her flatly, but the little girl stared at her stubbornly.

"It is! Both you and granpa going out late and allyuh not coming back home till late late!"

"We have things to do," Sadika told her. "And you have to go to sleep."

"But I can't!" said Reshma frustrated, eyes welling up with angry tears. "I can't. I can't. I want to, but I can't!"

Sadika sighed in sudden sympathy and her anger drained out. "Come here," she said, stooping down. Reshma ran into her arms and Sadika held her tight.

"Yuh going to be alright, I'm sorry you feeling like that, it's like that for me too. But I can't bring you along. If you want though, you run around a bit downstairs, it helps to tired out yuhself."

There was a pause and then the little girl nodded, head still buried in Sadika's shoulder.

"Okay," she said in a little voice. "Yuh coming back rite?"

"Of course, I'm coming back," said Sadika smiling at the little girl. "Doh worry. Now go and sleep... or run." With that she stood up and headed down the stairs.

Her father had already left, and so, Sadika swung up on her horse, affixed her hat on her head, shrouded her face with her veil and headed off into the night.

CHAPTER 9

Khion felt the humming of Ierie in response to the approaching rider far before he felt the pounding of the hooves travelling through the earth. Like before, the rider stopped before she came to him.

"Stickfighter." Her voice was measured and calm.

"Neighbour," he replied.

"Good night," she said, clear voice not muffled by the veil she wore over her face.

"Good night," he said.

"Did they come close to breaching any of the illusions?" she asked.

"Nuh yet," he replied. "I think dey will try tonight though."

"Den leh me get to wok," she said, sliding off her horse. Like before, she pulled out a thick roll of sticky, off-white stuff. This time she backed further away from the village and began stringing the sticky stuff across the road, pulling it between trees and holding it down with rocks. She worked fast for all that it was an unwieldy task and although all Khion could see from his side was the gray and off-white threads crisscrossing the area in particularly ugly fashion, he knew that for anyone approaching, the road would appear to have come to a dead end. He stopped and considered, no, not a dead end, a corner. She twisted the road and then continued into the trees and brush, stringing her web as she went, creating a road that wasn't there and littered with obstacles hidden behind her illusions.

When she had finished making her false road meet up with another fake one she had made the night before, she carefully stepped through the threads until she was behind Khion and began stringing up a second illusion.

This one, Khion could not see what exactly it was she building. Unlike the previous times, the illusion did not shimmer into being as soon as she pulled the string across an area. The young woman worked with skilled hands, plying the sticky thread between trees, zigzagging them across the road and then weaving them into each other in an intricate pattern. As she worked ,Ierie's beat hummed louder and stronger, in approval.

Finally, the young woman's spool of thread ran out and she tied the end off to a branch. Khion looked with interest to see what it was exactly she had crafted. He did not expect her to drag her hand over the threads causing more of them to suddenly spill out, dropping from the existing ones like curtains falling, vast, billowy, white sheets, waving eerily in the light breeze.

The young woman stood back and surveyed the result with satisfaction and then, with a wicked grin he could somehow see through the heavy veil, she let her illusion flow.

It started with a spark of light, then another, and another and suddenly there were torches, apparently flickering in the distance. Houses came next, some shadowed in the night, others half lit by torchlight. Hammocks hung from poles and people sat around a central fire. No. not just people, kalinags sat around a fire and children darted here and there, little figures barely discernible from a distance.

Khion blinked in astonishment as he surveyed the illusionary village that the young woman had crafted. He gave a shallow bow of respect to the dark thing.

She laughed. "Ah not done yet." She moved forward and touched the illusion and after a moment her body tensed with pain. She gave a little gasp after several minutes of struggle and a sort of blurred quality rolled over the whole illusion for a moment before settling back into its normal state.

The woman's skin was pale when she finished and Khion noted the drops of liquid at her fingertips.

"Doh touch de web," she cautioned him.

"Alright," he said. He turned to watch the illusion again and Ierie's words hummed, vibrating along the threads.

Protect the first born! Protect those sculpted out of my dirt and bark and salt and waters!

Khion laughed and thumped his stick in the earth in answer.

I here!

I here and none goin an pass me!

Beside him, his dark neighbour reached out and twanged one of her threads. The husky hiss of the threads sliding over one another was reply enough.

They were the dark things and the saikan would soon be reminded of that.

His name was Mr. Denning and he was the guard master of a particular saikan by the name of Lord Ainsley. At the moment, he and several of the men under his command were converging on the boerin section of town where two saikan guardsmen had been beaten into unconsciousness and his master's money stolen. The Jab Jab studied the group of men who were charging towards the boerin, intent on performing violence on them. He did not care for the boerin, but boerin had been harmed in protecting one of the kalinag and had offered aid to a Stickfighter. And also, the guard master had lied, had downplayed the strength of the Stickfighter who had taken down two of his men, had implied that they, the dark things, were weak. The Jab Jab intended to fix that lie with a little truth.

He waited until the men passed a narrow space between two houses and then his whip flicked out from the darkness of that space. It wrapped around the neck of one the men in the back of the group. The Jab Jab leisurely yanked the whip back, causing the man to knock into the house and fall unconscious. He did the same to another man and by that time, the group of saikan bodyguards was spinning to find out who was attacking them.

The Jab Jab waited until they rushed the narrow alley and then cracked his whip against the ground. It sparked on impact with the floor and the Jab Jab inhaled, taking in all the evil and malice of the men rushing him. A quick flick of his wrist brought the tip of his whip in front of his face, still sparking, and then he blew.

Flame sprouted as he burned their evil.

The men attacking him, reared back, but it was too late to save them. Their clothes ignited and with a cry they fled; they didn't get far. The Jab Jab plied his whip to devastating effect, bearing all of them to the ground.

The whip flicked over them again and again, shredding their skin but putting out the flames. When the men were suitably chastised, the Jab Jab laughed and melted back into the shadows.

CHAPTER 10

The men came sometime after midnight. Sadika went to her feet the moment the Stickfighter stiffened. He glanced at her and then put a warning finger to his lips. Sadika nodded back solemnly and touched the cutlass hanging at her waist to reassure herself. She was no Stickfighter but at least it should give her a chance to get away. No dark thing ever stayed helpless for long after their inception.

The men moved down the road in a clatter of horses' hooves and paused at the start of her illusions. They attempted, cautiously, to follow the false road, but when it became clear that doing so would only lead to injury, they withdrew.

After a moment of conferring, one of the men let out a loud whistle. The Stickfighter cocked his head, eyeing off to the side.

"Dey coming from the side now," he said. His body swayed slightly to a beat Sadika couldn't hear. Then he turned and strode off into the trees. Sadika paused, unsure of whether or not to follow him or guard against the men standing at the road. Eventually, she followed the Stickfighter. Any men who came through her illusions would eventually run into the illusion she had made of the village.

Following the Stickfighter was not easy. He slipped through the forest without a sound, a dark shadow blending into the night. Sadika had to move much slower to keep from making a sound.

She eventually caught up with him when he paused to look at the group of men creeping through the forest, their pistols at the ready. Surveying the large group, Sadika was glad she had chosen to come even though butterflies were fluttering in her stomach.

After a moment of calculation, the Stickfighter made as if to attack, but Sadika laid a hand on his arm.

"Nuh yet," she said. "Save yuh strength."

"Wha you could do?" he hissed back. "You cah get close to spin any illusions."

Sadika gave him a trickster's smile. "It ha plenty spiders in the forest yuh know. And dey does all spin web."

It took a second for what she was saying to penetrate and then his eyes widened. Sadika stretched out a hand and concentrated. It wasn't a trick she used much but it wasn't something she'd ever forget how to do either.

The men, creeping forward, began to see things moving out of the corners of their eyes. It wasn't much, just shadows, twitching away whenever you happened to glance at them. But then those little incidents increased. The forest came alive in the dead of night, the tall trees becoming sinister, the leaves hiding stalking predators and preying eyes.

When the first flash of light flickered across a web, men jumped with angry, fearful shouts. Their leader snapped at them and although they settled down, their minds certainly weren't at ease. Sadika had heard tell of the Motherland's folktales. These men might not be afraid of Ierie, but they had had the fears of their own land ingrained since childhood. One of those things she had heard that they feared was the illusive willow o' the wisp. Little lights that lead men astray in dark forests, until they never wandered out again.

Sadika waited for a moment and then the Stickfighter said softly, "Now, neighbour."

Pretty blue lights erupted in the forest, shining out of strategically chosen spiderwebs. The men cried out and recoiled. Their leader snapped at them, but men were already covering their eyes, fearing for their lives. The distraction was all that the Stickfighter needed.

He burst from his spot beside Sadika with frightening speed, appearing in the middle of the men before anyone quite knew what was happening. Ierie thrummed with barely concealed rage but the Stickfighter was smiling. His stick whirled, and men lost hold of their pistols, bones shattering as the stick made its rounds. A couple of men recovered in time to launch a few shots, but they were already confused and most of them went wide. Two hit the Stickfighter but they were merely scrapes, and they didn't slow him for an instant.

Sadika cut the lights, plunging them back into the darkness of the forest, creating more chaos. It didn't take long for the Stickfighter to incapacitate them all. When he was done, the Stickfighter said, "It ha more, on de next side." Then he was off and running at a speed Sadika could not hope to match, but she tried anyway.

Soft delighted laughter rang out into the night as the young couple traversed the promenade. The young man's hair was fair, blue eyes sparkling in the light. The young lady's hair was dark brown and so were her eyes. Unlike her companion, her clothes weren't of the finest make, even though they were quite lovely.

She was a boerin class girl embarking on an exciting, forbidden romance. He was a bored, saikan class noble who was rebelling against his parents and having some fun along the way, though he doubted, his lovely, delicate companion knew anything of the sort. Still she was exciting enough, certainly a beauty and her boerin class accent could be called charming when paired with fluttering lashes and hips that swayed unconsciously in the most alluring fashion.

The young couple chatted away, flirting with each other, him boldly and her shyly. In between, the young lady asked him questions about his life as a saikan noble. *What was it like to ride in a carriage? Did he really have so many horses? Was his coat really made out of silk?* Carefully, skillfully she twisted and turned the conversation until she learned what she wanted and then with a gasp, exclaimed over the time. Her saikan suitor allowed her to escape to her home.

When she was several streets away from the promenade, the young woman carefully slipped in between two buildings and waited for her compatriots. In a few moments, she was joined by three other women.

"His father has three ships coming in which will bring men and weaponry," she said. "The ships are expected to reach here in two days, so, we ha time. Also, de ships carrying other, profitable cargo too."

"We'll pass de message," said one of the women. The young woman nodded and then watched as her fellow Dame Lorraines slinked out into the night. In a few more moments, her alluring figure had slimmed down into one with gentler curves and the aura of enticement faded. Still pretty but no longer unbelievably gorgeous, she shucked off the fine garments to reveal a simple under-dress. She tucked the discarded clothes over her arm and blew a kiss in the direction of her unknowing source of information in mocking thanks.

Sadika was out of her depth. There were many more men coming through from the other side and they had broken through the layer of illusions before both she and the Stickfighter had reached them.

She entered the fray in time to duck from a muzzle flash. The bullet whistled over her head and she had to stifle a noise of alarm. The Stickfighter was undaunted, moving through the men like there weren't guns firing at him and swords being whirled with deadly accuracy. But then he could heal far faster than she ever could, so he had less to fear.

Sadika ducked in the bush and drew her cutlass from her waist. She was no excessively trained fighter so she would have to attack strategically. She reached out for the spiderwebs surrounding them again and used one to spark a flash of light, distracting a man before she slashed at him, relieving him of his gun and knocking the hilt into his head. The man crumpled under the blow and then Sadika was diving for cover again. She was found almost instantly and had to fight her way out, receiving a nasty cut on her arm for her trouble. Then the Stickfighter was there, beating back her attackers.

He took her by the arm and pushed her further into the forest.

"Run!" He hissed at her. "Get out de way!"

So Sadika ran.

Khion had a bullet burn across his ribs and his arms were littered with sword slashes and even a stab from a bayonet. His lungs were heaving, muscles were burning, heart pounding hard in his chest; he had never felt better.

Under his feet Ierie was screaming with rage at the saikan' intrusion. Khion ignored it. He understood Ierie's rage but did not need it now. The beat though, the beat he would take. He ducked from a sword slash, danced away, and twirled his stick and then lashed out. Bones cracked, swords fell from limp fingers and men dropped to the ground unconscious.

Guns were reloaded and men were sighting down at him. Too bad for them. Khion was far faster than any person they had ever tried to shoot before. The first volley missed him.

Khion wasn't surprised. It wasn't like he'd been going as fast as he could while fighting them, so the speed of movement they had factored in for him was wrong.

Ierie's beat sounded under him, running up through his feet, echoing in his bones. Khion laughed at them and lunged in the space of time where they stopped to reload. He knocked more than one unconscious again, but then the group leader whipped out a pistol and shot it straight at him.

Khion's body jerked backwards, and pain blossomed. He staggered to a stop, assessed the wound and then grinned at the leader. Through and through, it would heal just fine. The man frowned at him, head tilted almost incredulously at him and then Khion was moving, darting through the forest to the false village the young woman had made.

The problem with running away from a fight, Sadika realized, was that people tended to run after you. As it was, she had three well-trained mercenaries on her heels. She was ever so glad she'd been in fights before. Small skirmishes it was true, but she had learned not to panic. She had also learned to deal with pain. The slash she'd received earlier was a searing, screaming gap in her skin that threatened to render her arm useless from sheer pain but she was able to push it away. She evaded pistol shots, took a headlong dive into a bush and scrambled for cobwebs. Her fingers only encountered mere wisps before she was forced to wiggle her way out of the bush and run for it again.

The men continued their headlong chase after her and Sadika heard the whistle of a ball as it flew past her ear. The first man caught up with her and Sadika desperately blocked with her cutlass, only barely managing to save herself from fatal wounds and gaining a myriad of non-fatal ones during the encounter.

She defended herself with increasingly frantic blows, sure she was going to die soon when the two other men chasing her suddenly gave a shout.

The man fighting her was distracted momentarily and Sadika took her chance, pushing away from him with the cutlass and running away as fast as she could.

When no footsteps followed her, she slowed and looked behind her, panic gradually receding. Then she smiled, slow and wicked. The men had seen her kalinag village and were now advancing on it.

The smart thing about the illusion, Khion realized, was that it looked farther away than it really was. He knew that the other dark thing was still alive, because the figures in her illusion were moving, appearing as if they had noticed the gunshots and either standing in defiance or quickly ushering children into huts.

Khion, when he had sufficient distance from the men chasing him, slipped into a thick wall of vines that were strangling some trees. As he guessed, the men following him quickly lost interest upon seeing the kalinag village in the distance.

They gathered into proper formation and advanced on the village, guns cocked. The kalinags stood strong, spears in hand; ready to repel the invaders from what little land remained to them.

The saikan continued to march forward until they were within range of the village. They marched straight into the webs.

There was much spluttering, flailing and someone's gun even went off. With the web discovered, the woman dropped the illusion, causing the saikan men to jerk back in surprise and disgust. There was much muttering about evil and strange things, but the leader, a hard-eyed man, shouted at them to be quiet.

"There's the real road gentlemen," he snapped. "Unless you'd like to go running back to your mothers, I suggest you continue following it.

They won't get away from us this time." With that the leader forged on, pushing his way through the sticky strands of cobweb, his men reluctantly following his lead.

Khion moved out from his hiding place and scanned the forest. After a moment, a dark shadow moved towards him.

"Ah should do something?" he asked, remembering her warning not to touch the webs of that particular illusion.

"Only if yuh want to dead too," the woman replied casually.

"It go kill them?"

"Some of dem, maybe," she shrugged. "Nuh everybody could take it. Buh it have to get through they blood for it to make a real difference."

"They kinda cut up," Khion observed. It's true, the forest at night is unforgiving. Branches cut far too easily and Khion was pretty sure he opened up some wicked cuts on all of them. He was also sure that in the confusion they all opened up some cuts on each other.

"Oh well," the woman said.

"What did you put?" Khion asked, honestly curious.

"Spider venom," she replied smugly. "An ah even didn't put the funnel-web spider one."

Khion gave her a look. "Lady, yuh scary," he said with heartfelt honesty.

She gave him her trickster's smile. "All ah we is."

There was shouting as men began to rub at their eyes.

"Liquid comes off a spider's web easily," the woman said. "With all they pulling they just sent up a mist of the stuff."

"It gone in they eyes," said Khion in sudden understanding.

"And they breathe it in."

She smiled at him again, slipped off her hat and veil and offered them to him. "They might need some help getting knock out," she explained. Khion blinked at her meeting her cool, nonchalant gaze and then laughed.

"They might," he agreed and took the hat and veil.

CHAPTER 11

When Sadika finally walked into her house both Reshma and her father cried out.

"What happen?" her father said, hurrying over to her.

"Encountered some rather motivated saikan," she said, feeling tiredness settle over her like a particularly heavy blanket. "What you still doing awake?" The last part was directed at Reshma.

"Ah tell you I cah sleep!" the little girl said angrily. But her anger was marred by the tears glittering in her eyes.

"Hey," says Sadika, stooping down, "I okay, and I'll heal," she added. "All I need is a bath, some bandages and a nice sleep." Reshma didn't look convinced. Sadika sighed and ran a hand over the child's hair. "No really, I'm fine. It's not the first time I get cut up like this," she looked pleadingly to her father for help.

He sighed and squeezed Reshma's shoulder reassuringly. "It's true, she'll be okay. Your aunt is a lot tougher than you think."

"How about you?" Sadika said, standing.

"No trouble," said her father. "They must have decided to test the borders with your village first."

Sadika nodded. "I guess. Good thing though. If it was you alone…"

"I wasn't alone," said her father. "Is more dan me guarding the villages."

"Which village?" says Reshma, frustrated. "Wha happening?"

"Nuh for you to worry yuh head about," Sadika said firmly. "Nuh right now. An doh argue!" she added as Reshma opened her mouth, "Is big people thing and you doh want to get involved. If you do and yuh mess up something, is the jumbie and the robber I dragging in here to deal with you eh!"

Reshma shrank back but nodded.

"Good," said Sadika. She reached down and hefted the child in her arms. "Let's get you to sleep so I can get my bath." The child sniffed a little and buried her head in Sadika's neck.

"Doh die like mommy!"

Sadika jerked to a stop and then said, "Oh Reshma." She ruffled the hair on the tiny head gently. "Don't worry gurl. I here to stay, okay?"

Reshma sniffed again but nodded.

"Good girl," Sadika said. She dropped a kiss on the child's head and then carried her upstairs.

Amrika is exhausted by the time midnight comes. It is, she thinks, entirely unfair that Kirish is not winded at all. A light sheen of sweat covers his skin but he is fine, can probably continue this all night but Amrika is currently struggling to get up from the ground.

She staggers to her feet and raises her stick again. Her brother laughs at her.

"Put dong de stick chile," he says. "You cah swat a mosquito rite now."

Amrika might have listened; her arms are shaking, but the statement is said with the Robber's condescension. She attacks and Kirish steps out the way, deflects her stick with his knives, whirls and hits the butt of his blade into her back, sending her sprawling into the dirt again. She scrambles up, even though her back screams. The pain will fade soon enough with her Stickfighter healing.

She doesn't quite make it upright before her brother hooks a leg around her feet and yanks. She falls again but instead of hitting dirt, a hand snatches her arm and hauls her upright.

"Okay gyul," Kirish laughs, "Dais enough now." His voice is amused but it lacks any mocking and so Amrika allows her body to slump.

Kirish props her up on him, tugs the stick out her hand and half-carries her over to the back porch. Amrika gratefully sits and even more gratefully sips the water her brother brings her. Kirish collapses next to her and they sit in companionable silence for a while as they both rest.

"Wha yuh think ma and dad go tink ah we now?" Amrika asks him after a moment.

Kirish huffs out a laugh. "Ma go tell me all the things ah did wrong in growing you up fuh yuh to turn out dis way."

Amrika smacks halfheartedly at her brother and he laughs again. "She woulda be happy fuh you ah tink," he adds. "She didn't wah yuh to be a Robber either."

"And dad?"

Kirish gives a fond chuckle. "Daddy did like being ah Robber eh?"

Amrika snorts. "I know. Dais why we have some oriental jar that worth more dan we whole house, collecting dust inna corner."

Kirish snorts as well. "Yes. Disappointed maybe, dais yuh not a Robber. Buh he ent go mind dat yuh is a Stickfighter." He is silent for a moment. "We survived 'Rika," he says. "I think they woulda be proud ah we jus fuh dat."

Amrika sighs and wishes she had clearer memories of her mother. What she had left faded a little each year. Memories of her father were much stronger but all were always coloured by the last time she'd seen him; seen his body. Even Midnight Robbers can be overpowered. She found it ironic his death had come for him the one time he'd openly been doing something for good.

Her father had not been a good man, but none of their extended family ever went into debt, ever wanted for the simple things like food and shelter. He may not have given as generously to the village but he took care of his family. And more than once, Amrika knew of instances where medication only saikans had access to were mysteriously dropped by doorsteps or hidden on windowsills after her father had heard of a need for them. He never took credit for it, always clicked his tongue in derision if he heard of the mysterious happenings. But Amrika knew, and so did Kirish. He had not been a good man but he was good enough.

She blinks and banishes the surge of memory. Kirish as if sensing her mood quiets too.

The silence is broken a little while later when a Robber's whistle sounds through the night. Wind rushes, darkness floods and the clock strikes twelve. The whistle sounds again and Kirish tilts his head up to the sky and grins. She never gets accustomed to the joy that lights up his face at the thought of being the Robber. For the first time though, she thinks she truly understands it.

"Yuh going out tonight?" she asks, sipping from her glass

"Not tonight," he says. "Tomorrow maybe, we go see how to divide weself up. Come now. Whistle blow chile. Leh we get you inside." When she gives him a look, he laughs. "Rika you cah hurt nobody now. Nuh even yuhself 'cause you so beat up you ent feeling anything." He hauls her to her feet and ushers her inside even as she protests.

CHAPTER 12

Lord Ainsley, profitable merchant, noble even among the saikan class, was not having a good day. Or so Jamal surmises from the amount of shouting that was coming out of the house.

He carefully trims the hedges, being sure not to draw any attention to himself.

It had been a good night's work for the dark things as far as Jamal could tell. The kalinag villages were safe, the men sent to destroy them were all ill and half of them were babbling about monsters. Most of them currently could not see. Those that were not affected by spider venom had enough injuries to make anyone cringe. And that had only been the work of two of the dark things.

Jamal doesn't want to know what it would have been like if the men had made it to the village only to discover the four other Stickfighters who had been stationed there that night. Actually, he does want to know. The men who were attacking would not have shown mercy to the kalinags. Jamal may not be particularly close to any of the kalinag but he was firmly against mass murder.

When his master finally leaves the house in a fit of fury and sets off to have a comforting ride around his estate, Jamal drops his pruning knives into the hedge and grabs his stilts from where they lay, not so hidden in the grass.

He kicks off his shoes, straps his feet into the stilts and then rises into the air. He is tall enough now to reach the window of Ainsley's study and he grabs the edge, sits on the sill, tugs his feet out of the stilts and swings his legs into the study.

He heads for the letters first, shuffling through them. One is a letter from the captain of ship, saying that he had met some of Ainsley's ships out at sea and that if the ships continued at their current rate, they should reach Ierie in a week's time.

Another letter was from the governor of the Port of Gold, thanking Ainsley for his support in expanding their holdings and gently encouraging him to give even more support. Jamal interprets that as 'thanks for putting money towards killing out the kalinags, we would appreciate more.'

The third he reads is a half-finished letter from Ainsley himself, giving permission for a certain man to have access to goods in one of his private warehouses. Jamal notes the address of the warehouse and then moves on.

The safe is not difficult to find, although it is rather cleverly placed in the floor. Jamal supposes he could rip open the door if he tries hard enough but he doesn't want his employer to know anyone has been here, so he resolves to pass the message on to one of the Robbers and then hastily exits the room before one of the other workers happens to notice his stilts standing outside the window.

As it is, he has barely pushed the stilts behind the hedge when one of the yard foremen comes around the corner. He pretends as if he has just lost his grip on his pruning knives, retrieves them from the hedge and continues with his job.

"Where are you going?" Jessica asks curiously. They are standing in a field far away from the village.

Jamal pauses in strapping on his stilts. "Dere's a few jotlin who are also contributing to the governor's schemes. We going to convince them to stop."

"Convince," says Jessica with raised eyebrows.

Jamal smiles. "Convince," he says innocently. "You was jotlin Jess. You knew about us."

"We thought you were stories," Jessica says. "Mostly stories anyway. Just good stories built on exploits of normal people. We didn't know, didn't know you were... this."

Jamal laughs. "Well that will help. Is always best to keep people in de dark. It does make things seem scarier."

"What if they don't believe you are, well, real?"

Jamal grins at her. "We have our ways of convincing people."

"Convincing," says Jessica, with an amused air. "I'm beginning to be afraid of that word."

Jamal laughs again and finishes strapping on his stilts. The wood becomes flesh and he pushes himself up into the air, towering over the world.

He looks down and sees the young woman staring up at him. He kneels down and bends to come closer to her. The girl he calls sister has her arms wrapped around her, but she is not scared of him. Not even when he pushes his face close to hers.

"Go Jumbie," she says with a wry twist of her mouth. "You have people to convince." She gives him a quick smile and then playfully pushes at his head.

Jamal quickly stands aloft again. One by one the others rise from where they had been getting ready and together they form a forest of dark trees in the flat field. The sun slips beneath the horizon sending the night on its way and with it, the dark things that live within.

"Huh," says the Midnight Robber who is rifling through the contents of Ainsley's secret safe. "Dis man could be a Robber in ah nex life."

"Is that 'cause' he does steal or something else?" the other Robber asks.

"Is 'cause' he heart black like thick molasses," the first replies. "You know wha it have in dis safe?"

"Obviously not," says the second dryly.

"Blackmail," says the first smiling. "Dis man have proof of some nasty secrets about fellow saikan. I bet he does use it to geh favours done fuh he."

"Huh," says the second. "Nice buh it so cowardly. If yuh wah a man thing jus take it."

"Some men doh like to get dey hands dirty," replies the first. "Dey think they too good for blood to get on dey hands."

The second Robber laughs darkly. "If yuh cah get yuh hands dirty, keep yuh heart clean," he says.

Across town, outside a certain warehouse, three other Midnight Robbers crouched and scoped out the building.

Kirish narrowed his eyes and let the Robber's sight drag the building into sharper focus. There didn't seem to be any windows, not even small ones. The roof was also well sealed to the walls. He twisted his head and found a narrow side door, a lock hung from it. He took in a deep breath and leaned back.

"Rotating guards," reported Surish. "Five of them, constantly patrolling. They doh let a single area be without a guard."

"All carry pistols, rifles and swords," said the third Robber, Trevon. "Along with whistles to signal the others."

"So... no problem den?" says Kirish.

"Nope," Surish agrees.

They're inside the warehouse in less than a minute with none of the guards aware of their trespass.

"Dais rel guns," Trevon says conversationally.

"Rite," agrees Surish. "De man only have two hand, how much gun he really need?"

"Leh we relieve them of dey guns nah," says Kirish surveying the horde of guns around him. "Why, with dis much, a man can afford to share."

Trevon gives a sidelong glance at the others. "Should we leave two for de man two han?"

"Nah," says Kirish, as the Robber's miasma of darkness begins to flood the warehouse, and numb the senses of the men outside, "Someday soon we go relieve 'im of he hands too."

CHAPTER 13

The first of the jotlin whom they visited was working hard in his study. It was a pity that he should work so hard and put so much money to such terrible ventures. It was time to set him straight, Jamal decided.

The Moko Jumbie casually leaned his forearms on the windowsill and waited. When the businessman did not look up for five minutes, Jamal sighed.

"Ay!"

The man jumped, ink went everywhere, and the feather skittered across the page. Jamal blinked. The jotlin stared down at the mess for a blank second before turning to see who dared interrupt him. This time the book went flying and the chair scraped back as the man leapt to his feet and darted away from the window.

"Siddong!" Jamal snapped. The harsh tone seemed to bring the man to his senses.

"Who are you!" he snapped in return. "What are you doing climbing up to my window?"

"I come to chat," Jamal said pleasantly, waiting for the man to realize that he was not hanging on to the windowsill.

"I will not speak with filth like you!" the man said.

Jamal had a sudden understanding about why this jotlin was working with the saikan. He smiled and said, "Den watch," and Jamal moved away from the windowsill. The man blinked as he realized that Jamal hadn't been clinging to the side of his house, his face grew hard.

"Is the fact that you're on stilts supposed to scare me?"

Jamal laughed, then his voice turned deeper, menacing. "No, I am a Moko Jumbie, I is already everything you should fear."

But the jotlin wasn't listening, he had already placed him in the category of stilt walker and refused to believe he was anything else. No matter. Jamal took a deep breath of the air and breathed in the evil that surrounded the house. It was not strong, which is why he thought there was a chance of saving this one. But there was still a stench here, strong enough to hover on the grounds and that, that he had to cut out. So, Jamal leaned forward again and showed him why people were afraid when a Moko Jumbie looked in their windows.

The jotlin man froze, eyes locked in Jamal's unrelenting gaze, unable to move now. Everything he ever feared was dragged forward in his mind, every frightening scenario played over and over in painful detail until it was almost too much to bear. The man's heartbeat rocketed up, Jamal could see his pulse beating rapidly in his throat. His face was white with terror. Then Jamal switched it up a little. The images became everything he had ever done that had caused others to fear, every evil thing he had visited on others. The Moko Jumbie brought it up without mercy and slung it at his now vulnerable mind. The man cried out, fighting to get away from what he'd done, his previous fear magnifying everything to him. When Jamal judged that sufficient time had passed, he released the man.

The jotlin staggered back and fell heavily on the floor, taking great sobbing breaths. When he finally calmed, he half-looked at Jamal.

"What do you want?" His voice was shaking.

"Leave the kalinag alone," said Jamal, "or something much worse than me will come. An yuh should probably stop trying to be a saikan. You doh play de part good."

The man looked up at him properly, revealing tear-streaked cheeks. "Are... is that all?"

"Dais all," said Jamal. The man blinked and then shakily rubbed the tears from his face. "If I do this, will you leave me alone?"

"Sure," said Jamal, "unless ah need to visit you again buh ah sure you go make sure I doh have to."

After a moment the man nodded jerkily. "Now get out of here!" he ordered with as much courage as he could muster. It wasn't a lot, making the command sound like a warbling request. Jamal snorted.

"A Moko Jumbie does go where dey please. Ierie is ours to wander." He turned and left anyway. He had others to visit tonight.

The three Midnight Robbers stared at their stash of weapons, stolen from the warehouse.

"So," said Surish. He looked at the carriages now pulling up in front of the warehouse. "I think dais the men coming to get dese guns." He put a hand to his waist and tilted his head. "Should we leh dem see all de guns gone? Or distract them?"

"Distraction would be better," Kirish replied, eyeing the men. The less the saikan knew about the movements of the dark things, the better. It would give them a little advantage and advantages are always helpful in a war.

"We doh ha time fuh anything fancy," warned Trevon.

"Jus blow de whistles den," Surish said.

Kirish studied the the carriages for a moment and then he smiled slow and dark under the brim of his hat.

"Actually, I have a better idea, let's thief dem too."

The others paused and cocked their heads at him.

"It doh matter if dey notice de warehouse empty if dey gone too," Kirish pointed out. "And dey people go focus on finding them and not on de guns they was supposed to be getting." Trevon and Surish glanced at each other and then matching smiles crossed their faces. Three whistles blew simultaneously, shattering the night's silence and the three Midnight Robbers were gone, focused on their next target.

CHAPTER 14

The saikan were spitting mad. Amrika went about her chores in the house, still confined by her brother's orders but the gossip flew among the boerin.

The saikan weren't pleased to not only have one of their warehouses raided but some of their men were missing too. It hadn't given them as much of an edge as the dark things would have liked but it had allowed any trail left behind to run cold. Besides, there was still some vigorous debate among certain saikan as to whether the disappearing men had done so involuntarily or if they had chosen to run of with the stash of weapons. All in all, it was a nice bit of confusion. Her brother had headed off to work in the smithy he was apprenticing at, but there had been a happy, crooked smile on his face. She resolved to get him to tell her what he had done.

However, the incident had added fuel to the fire. The dark things had poked at the saikan and they had poked hard. For the first time, they were becoming more than nuisances. They were beginning to be a real threat. She had a feeling that very soon the saikan in charge of the plan would begin to put the pieces together, and would realize that those being targeted were the persons in charge of the plot to rid Ierie of the kalinag.

Amrika piled the washing into the large tub and began scrubbing at them when a small voice went

"Hello? Hello?"

"Hol' on!" Amrika called. She washed off her soapy hands and went to the front door. When she pulled it open, she found the little kalinag girl she had saved, staring up at her.

"Hey," said Amrika, surprised. "Wha you doing here?"

"Ah come to say thanks," said the little girl. She paused and then said, "Thanks."

Amrika snorted with laughter. "Welcome," she replied. "Yuh by yuhself still?"

"Nah," the girl turned and pointed to the older girl across the road. "Meh cousin come wit me."

"Good," said Amrika. "Little girls shouldn't wander de streets of Ierie alone even if dey is kalinag."

The child huffed but nodded reluctantly.

"And what you was doing theifin from a saikan eh?"

The girl shrugged. "One ah meh cousins dare meh to."

Amrika sighed and shook her head. Children apparently would always be children.

"Yuh ent gone home?" Amrika asked. "It dangerous for you to stay here yuh know."

"Ah going jus now," the child said, kicking at the dirt floor. "It nuh safe in de villages either."

"It is safer," said Amrika. "People protecting you there. Over here the saikan can find you easy, and over there yuh have yuh parents. If push come to shove, the kalinag will save deyself."

The child paused and then nodded solemnly. "We will." But then her head bowed. "But you might not survive," she added softly. "I don't want you to die."

"Ierie will survive," said Amrika, lightly. "You will; the kalinag will. Doh worry about we, don't worry 'bout me, adopted chirren easy to find."

The little girl glared at her. "Life is nuh to throw way so!" she snapped. "Yuh supposed to respect it!"

"True," said Amrika stooping down to the child's level. "But we are the dark things, little kalinag. We are Ierie's temper. Ierie knows that to save lives sometimes you have to lose others. Even ours, the children of Ierie's heart. We respect the sacrifice of those lives when they are necessary."

The girl swallowed. "You can't fin dat easy, you can't jus accept dat."

"Little sister," she says, stooping down and holding the child's hands in her own. "We stubborn and Ierie harsh. But stubborn as we is, we doh leave family behind. We not fighting simply cause Ierie ask and threaten we yuh know. We fighting because this is wrong. We fighting because allowing dis to happen is not who we are. Is nuh in we nature to allow those we care about to die. It is not in we nature to condone genocide. It is not and has never been in we nature to allow the oppression ah we people."

At the little girl's pleading silence, she says softly:

"It not like us to let de people we care about die."

She takes a deep breath, draws on memories that seem so far away and yet have imprinted on her too sharply for time to ever scrub it away. "Lil sister. I've spent too many days on the side of the river with the kalinag. I've spent too much time under de mangrove trees and in de bamboo, searching for oysters and de best fishing rod. I too know de peace of de wind through de trees and de water underfoot. I spent too much time with de kalinag to not know how you draw peace from de land and how much it is a part ah yuh. I spent too much time with you and yuh people, to ever want you to disappear. The dark things? We wasn't quite born then, when the saikan came and made de land run red with your blood. But we here now. We here now."

The child nodded slowly and sighed. "Ah know, big sister, I know de dark things and their honour even though dey doh walk to the laws of men." She paused and then asked timidly, "The men who went missing, they dead?"

Amrika laughed, shattering the somber mood. "No chile, they probably being kept somewhere embarrassing They will be free soon. We are tryin not to have the saikan descending on the whole town and killing all ah we."

The child smiled and then moved away, running across the road to her cousin. Amrika stood up, waved to her and then returned to her chores.

Protect the first born!

"Where dey dey?" Amrika asked her brother when he came home. Kirish laughed. It was the Robber's laugh.

"Yuh go find out nah," he said, grinning.

Amrika shook her head. "Can I go out now?"

Kirish sobered and shook his head. "No. Not tonight."

"What happening tonight?" asked Amrika. She was out of the loop due to her enforced convalescence.

"Ships," said Kirish. "Ships are coming in tonight. With ammunition and men."

"Okay," said Amrika still puzzled. Then she paused, and her eyes widened. "Oh," she said. "Oh."

Kirish grinned.

"Are the Robbers going?"

Kirish snorted. "Not us, we geh vote out."

"Who den?" demanded Amrika.

Her brother's smile was full of glee.

CHAPTER 15

Tamara glanced sidelong at their companions for the night's work and then shuffled closer to her twin Vishal. Jab Jabs were scary no matter who you were. Their blue skin was barely visible in the moonlight but somehow that made them more frightening. One of them saw her looking and smiled widely, flashing his razor teeth at her and she turned away from him.

"Yuh okay?" her brother asked her.

"I good," she murmured. "I jus doh like them is all."

"Nobody like dem," her twin replied with his perpetual cheer. He was shuffling anxiously, ready for the night to begin. Tamara was not so excited. There was an element of danger here. If she and her brother were not so fast, they wouldn't be here. The older members of the families had made the executive decision to keep the younger ones out of the problem, no matter what the other dark things of Ierie had decided to do. But the younger ones were agile and quick, and they needed some of that just in case things went south. Tamara, cautious by nature, did not like to have the fate of her people laying on her shoulders. Vishal on the other hand didn't seem to understand the implications at all. Still, there was no one else she would rather have at her back for this.

After what seemed like forever waiting in the cold, breathing in the salt breeze from off the ocean, one of the Jab Jabs gave the signal. Tamara and her people waited until the Jab Jabs were slipping across the docks and scrambling up the rigging hanging over the sides of the ships in harbour, and then they began to move.

Tamara let the long loose dress she wore flutter to the ground and in the moonlight, the tight brown costume she wore underneath looked like her own dark skin. Beside her, Vishal had shed his shirt and trousers and was rolling his shoulders, muscles rippling under the black sheath he wore. He twisted his head and grinned at her. He rolled his shoulders again, once, twice and then his wings burst out.

They stretched behind him, high and tightly strung between the narrow bone frames. His ears were sloping now into a more slender shape and his canines were sharper than they had been before, when he grinned at her again.

"Wha yuh waiting for?"

Tamara laughed and then rolled her own shoulders, wings flowing out while the rest of her bones hollowed. She grinned back at her twin.

"Nutting!" she replied and took to the sky. Behind her the rest of the Bats followed, a fluttering black flock that would soon rain destruction down on the saikan ships.

Come children of my heart!

Tamara soared high in the night, threading her way through the wind currents, as she carved and slid her way through the sky. There was nothing like flying over Ierie. It wasn't just the spectacular view that the moonlight gave of the wild land she called home; it was what she could hear. Her ears, tuned for hearing frequencies that no one who was not a dark thing could hear, heard nearly everything. The trembling of the trees, the humming of the masses of people, moving, living, breathing beneath her. She could hear fires crackling and feet stomping and the wind rushing over the dips and hollows in the land. Most of all she could hear Ierie itself.

The land's beat thrummed through the sky from the ground, its song flowing through the air, twanging the breezes like plucked strings. The kalinag with their connection to land sounded different, the villages were an earthier sound, something wild and bright but still so oddly serene. The dark things were rich low notes, but they echoed faster, a pleasing harmony to the kalinag's melody but still part of the same song. The boerin were another part of the harmony, but they were a repeating rhythm, a steady sound in the wild song that was always in play. The jotlin, some of them, were staccato beats, the sharp raps of tamboo bamboo on the ground pushing the melody forward, wrapping it together somehow. The saikan, whenever they managed to make an appearance in the sounds of Ierie, were high delicate notes, small silver bells that rang just out of sync with everything else. They were not part of Ierie's song. Not these at least. Tamara had heard bells, deeper, somber, wiser bells in Ierie's song before.

But this was not the time to be lost in Ierie's song. That was for later. They had a job to do. The Bats circled around the three target ships and then, without warning, they dropped.

The sailors, still on deck, let out startled shouts as black shapes plummeted from the sky and then even more shouts occurred when the Bats screamed.

A wave of sound hit the boats, hit the water and then reflected. The Bats, already titling back in the sky caught the rebound and quickly translated. Small crew, guns and ammunition confirmed aboard. The hired men already ashore.

The Bats let out another scream, this time to the sky and then the Jab Jabs got to work. Whips cracked, and men shouted again, this time far more panicked than before. Pistols cracked open the night and the Bats were diving again. Tamara threaded her way through rigging and brought her claws to bear against the sails. Metal gleamed in the light and then the sailcloth was giving way.

She didn't wait to get tangled, moving away soon. It was a good thing too because a bullet whistled through the air past her cheek. Vishal, more daring, snapped a rope holding the sail and then tilted away from the rope's recoil.

Sailors shouted at them and then Tamara was twisting down this time, into the space between the ships. A Jab Jab on the rigging grinned at them and signaled them closer. She and Vishal grabbed the Jab Jab under his arms and pulled, lifting him free of the net and carrying him up and over the ship. They dropped him in the crow's nest and then twisted away to avoid the rifles shooting at them.

Beside her Vishal screamed, the sharp sound disorienting the sailors for a second and giving the Jab Jabs time to advance again. Only this time the Jab Jabs didn't bother using their whips to shred the men. The whips cracked, sparked and then the Jab Jabs breathed. Flame spilled out, clothes caught fire and men dived over the railings. Good.

The Jab Jabs breathed again, and the remaining men on deck made for the ocean. The few stragglers who attempted to fight, were put down with cracking whips or picked up in the Bats' clawed feet and evacuated to the ocean.

On the other two ships, the men were putting up more of a fight. She saw a sailor catch a Jab Jab's whip around his sword and then used it to pull the Jab Jab closer while aiming at him with a pistol. A Bat screamed, disorienting the sailor for a moment and the Jab Jab managed to twist away before he was shot.

Rifles shattered the night, shots following so closely together they would have been indistinguishable from each other, had she not been a dark thing. One of the Bats jerked in the air and then plummeted. Tamara dived after them, working her wings to speed up the rate of her descent. She caught up to the wounded one in seconds and dragged them back upwards. It wasn't easy; she was fighting against the drag of the wind and gravity, but she managed to pull them out of the dive that could prove fatal for both of them. In another second, Vishal was somehow at her side, taking the burden of the shot Bat and stabilizing her flight.

Now that they were out of immediate danger, Tamara could see that it was just the wing that had been hurt.

"Drop meh in de water," their companion ordered. "I can swim just fine." Tamara and Vishal shared a look and then reluctantly swooped close to the water's surface and dropped the wounded Bat there. Then they were curving up into the sky and back to the fight.

On the docks, the night guards were running up to help defend the ships, three small platoons of them, armed with rifles and far better trained that the sailors on the ship. Ierie's song was fast paced now, the beat thundering over the land. Tamara glanced at the soldiers who were heading towards them and then glanced at Vishal.

Her careless but brave twin gave her a wide, reckless smile that reminded her that he, that both of them, were of the dark things of Ierie and the night was theirs. She matched his reckless smile and they tilted in the air, headed straight for the soldiers who were now aiming their rifles.

The tempo of the land danced along their wings and Tamara collected every note, every sound, every little snatch of melody. She cupped it in the fluttering of her wings and when she was close enough, she twirled through the air, wings tucked in tight, and unleashed Ierie's song on the men. The line of soldiers was tossed back from the force of the song and Tamara unfurled her wings, checked herself mid-flight, changed direction and headed back towards the stars, far out of the range of the remaining rifles. Next to her, Vishal laughed and then they were tucking down again, closing in from another angle.

Vishal made the first pass, taking care of the remaining group and Tamara came in opposite to him, knocking down those who had started to regain their stance. Behind them, other Bats came in, snatching the dropped rifles of the men, sinking them beneath the waves. Tamara arced back toward the ships and used her claws to snap through some rigging. The boom groaned and began to swing helplessly. Vishal raked through some of the sail and then ducked the swinging boom.

Tamara knocked a sailor overboard and then pushed another Bat out of the way. The bullet burned a path as it skimmed across her skin, but no real harm came from it. The Jab Jabs breathed again, and the wooden ship finally began to surrender to the flames.

On the other ship a Jab Jab clung to the mast with one hand and with the other he cracked his whip, sending sparks flying. He breathed, and the sails of that ship lit up, flames running up the cloth like waves scrambling to shore. The Jab Jab pushed off from the mast and Vishal caught him and lowered him to the deck.

Just then, another loud scream came from one of the Bats. This time the scream was held for a count of five before tapering off. At the signal most of the Jab Jabs made for the sides of the ships. They jumped and the Bats caught them, carrying them away. A Jab Jab, one on each of the three ships cut the ropes tethering the ships to the shore and then also cut the anchor ropes.

Another group of Bats swung around and came towards the ships from the shore. They unleashed Ierie's song on the ships and the great structures groaned and slowly began to move. The Bats made several passes until the ships were well away from the port and sailing off into the night. When they were sure that the ships were far away enough, the rest of the Bats peeled off into the night. Tamara, Vishal and a third Bat, the fastest of the older ones, remained behind, hovering some distance from the ship. They screamed together giving the signal to show they were ready.

There was a pause before they began their descent towards the ships at breakneck speed. As they approached, the Jab Jabs left behind on each ship appeared from the ships' hold at a run. They made for the railing and jumped without hesitation.

Tamara caught one, Vishal grabbed the other and the other Bat caught the third. Together they quickly flew away from the ship. They were not a moment too late. They had barely cleared the danger zone when the gunpowder stores of the ships, lit by the Jab Jabs, exploded. The blast still rippled through the air, enough to make her flight path wobbly but she corrected in a second and then she, Vishal, the third Bat and the Jab Jabs they held, were all laughing helplessly. They angled back to the shore, Ierie's song thrumming in satisfaction against Tamara's wings.

Chapter 16

There was a complete uproar all over the villages as the news passed down. Three of the saikan ships had been destroyed in the night. The governor was furious. The saikan, on the whole, were furious. The governor's men were searching for the perpetrators whom they were sure came from the boerin.

"I thought we were trying to keep the saikan from descending on de boerin," Amrika said to her brother when she heard the news.

"Ah, yeah," he said. "We was hoping they woulda be a little more spooked. Relax, they watching we buh dey not going and do anything jus yet."

"Why not?" asked Amrika, worried.

"Because dey is saikan," said Kirish. "They pretty sure is us, but they all have dey own enemies among themselves. It could be a ploy to throw them off the scent of their real enemies. When they done work through all their own internal enemies first, then they'll come for us."

"They could not though," said Amrika.

"We have people listening just in case," assured Kirish. "Now, is time you meet some people today."

"Stickfighters?" asked Amrika.

Kirish nodded. "Yeah."

"Good grief," said Sadika as she helped her father down the stairs in the morning. "Did they have to blow up the ships?"

"It was ah warning, child," said her father placidly. "Besides, if they focused on us and de boerin, they not going and focus on the kalinag."

"So, it was a diversion," said Sadika.

"Just so," nodded her father.

"A dangerous one," said Sadika. "They will put the pieces together soon."

"They was going to do it soon enough anyway," said her father.

"Hmm."

Sadika settled her father in his chair and then called up the stairs for Reshma.

"Reshma. Yuh done yet chile!"

"Coming!" Reshma called down.

"Doh make meh come up that stairs fuh yuh you know!"

"Ah coming!" Reshma yelled back.

Moments later, small feet started to clatter down the stairs. Sadika took her place at the table and then asked,

"How did the saikan take the presence of the Bats?"

Her father smiled. "They did not mention them at all. None of de rumours from the saikan talk about de Bats. There was only men with torches and painted blue skin."

"Surely the governor didn't believe that," said Sadika, amused.

"They aren't telling any other story," said her father. "Dey probably think dey going mad. At any rate none of dem want anybody else to say dey mad. The jotlin though," he continued. "The jotlin getting scared. Dey know de stories. De Bats are de the least of the dark things to parade de night but the jotlin know dem and docks are hardly ever empty. They could pass off the Jab Jab as costumes but de Bats? Nah. Dey know dat was real. I think the saikan are going to find it hard to get support from the jotlin again."

"Aren't the Moko Jumbies helping in dat too?" asked Sadika.

"Yep," said her father.

Just then Reshma came into the dining room. "Morning!" she said.

"Morning," replied Sadika.

Reshma took her seat and then said casually, "Um, de spider web talk to me this morning."

Sadika choked on her water.

"What?"

"It say 'protect the first born?'"

Sadika and her father both looked at each other and then Sadika said gently. "Ignore it chile, eat yuh food."

"But!"

"No buts! Eat yuh food!"

Reshma gave her a sulky look but commenced eating her breakfast.

Amrika found herself staring at a bland-looking house backed far into the edge of the plantations. Despite the frequent use of the plantation road, it could still be considered off the beaten track. The one strange thing about it was that it had a fence. Most boerin houses did not have fences, at least not fences this tall and made completely of thick slabs of board. The gate was open, allowing Amrika a view of the house.

Kirish nudged her. "Go, I hadda get to work."

Amrika gave him a look. "Yuh not coming?"

Her brother snorted. "No. I look like a Stickfighter to you? Go, introduce yuhself." Then he was gone, leaving Amrika glaring at his back.

She turned back to the house, squared her shoulders, and walked in.

"Morning!" she called out as she walked through the gate.

"Morning!" called back a male voice. The speaker was leaning on the porch of the house, grinning at her. "You look like de new Stickfighter."

"I am," confirmed Amrika.

The young man grinned at her. "Thought so, thought you might end up here sometime soon."

"Looks like I did," Amrika replied.

"Markus," he said hopping off the porch and holding out a hand.

"Amrika," she said as she took his hand. Then she fought a gasp because Markus had just squeezed her hand with enough force to make her bones grind together.

"Nice," he said grinning, letting go of her hand. "Yuh really is one."

Amrika snorted. "If ah wasn't ah go done be dead."

Markus laughed. "Come nah!" he said with a jerk of his head. "Leh we introduce you."

"Introduce me?" asked Amrika, raising an eyebrow, but she followed him into the house anyway.

They walked straight through the house to the backyard, which was considerably larger than the average backyard. It was, Amrika realized, enough space for Stickfighters to practice.

Someone else was already there, stick in hand, moving slowly as if warming up.

"Look we have company," Markus said to the person.

The person shifted back into a normal stance and then moved forward with a smile.

"Jiang," she said, holding out a hand. "Most people call me Ji."

"Amrika," Amrika introduced herself for the second time. "If you squeeze meh hand too…"

Ji laughed. "Doh worry!" Amrika grinned at her and shook her hand.

"So," said Jiang. "Yuh now come out eh?"

"Yeah," said Amrika.

"Well you just so happen to be the best dark thing it have in Ierie," Ji grinned at her. "Come on. You ha real thing to learn."

If Amrika had thought sparring with Kirish was hard, it was nothing compared to sparring with Jiang and Markus. Her brother was strong and fast, but he was no Stickfighter. Their blows vibrated down her arms and would have cracked bones if they weren't skilled enough to keep from doing so.

She had been knocked to the ground so many times in the first hour, she began to contemplate why she even bothered to get back up.

Of course, they didn't just beat at her. They interspersed everything with a lesson. They showed her the proper way to hold her stick, then showed her why she should hold it that way by knocking it out her hands every time she didn't hold it right. They showed her how to block a strike and then reinforced it by attacking her over and over until she managed to block it. She learned to set her feet properly and how to actually move so that she didn't put herself in more danger.

They were relentless, pushing her far past her breaking point. She didn't get food or water for nearly eight hours and she had spent most of that time moving. When Jiang finally called a break, Amrika was shaking from pure exhaustion and didn't quite know how to move anymore.

Jiang carefully took her by the arm and sat her down on the wooden bench. Markus brought water for them all and Amrika drank mechanically until she revived a bit. Once she was more alert, she went for more water and then collapsed back on the bench.

"Doh worry," said Markus. "You'll get used to it. Yuh healing does kick in yuh see. So, you go find you can go on much longer than other people."

"But you still need to train, to... stretch dem abilities," Jiang continued the explanation. "So, if yuh ever need to go this long, and fight this hard, yuh can because yuh already did it."

"And without food and water," said Amrika in sudden understanding.

"Right," said Markus. "We is warriors Amrika, we doh geh breaks." Jiang nodded in agreement.

"Alright," said Ji. "Enough talk 'bout that for now." She smiled at Amrika. "What do you do?"

"I does work in a small shop for one of the jotlin," Amrika replied. "Right now, meh boss tink ah real sick."

Jiang laughed. "I work in meh father's shop too. Is it true yuh brother is a Midnight Robber?"

Amrika nodded. "Yeah."

"Huh," said Markus. "Allyuh have Stickfighter blood somewhere or what?"

"We doh know," said Amrika. "Maybe we do. Maybe I's a first line."

"Maybe," said Jiang. "I have mix up blood in me too."

Amrika laughed. "Really? I woulda think you was a Dame Lorraine if you didn't have a stick."

Jiang grinned. "My grandmother was one yes. But I take by meh grandfather side."

"Nice," said Amrika.

"Come on, leh we eat," said Markus. "I real hungry an we still hadda cook de food!"

CHAPTER 17

"What are the damages?" the governor asked his men.

"Three ships and full cargo lost. The ships' passengers however were all off the ship."

"So, we have the men, but we have no ammunition."

"The next shipment from Lord Ainsley will have ammunition," said the aide.

"But Ainsley has just lost an entire warehouse of ammunition. In addition, some of his men guarding that warehouse got captured," said the Governor silkily.

"Were they not released?" asked the aide.

"Yes," said Governor Archibald, "But they still failed to have picked up any useful information about their captors. We will store this incoming shipment in one of my own warehouses."

"Yes, sir," said the aide.

"Now," said the governor. "Bring me the head of the dock guards. I want to know, how exactly did these saboteurs get past them and manage to destroy not one, not two, but three ships in my port!"

"Yes sir!" said the aide. "I will have him fetched immediately."

"Well, get to it!" said the governor. The aide scuttled out, leaving the governor of Port of Gold fuming.

Lawrence Kit, mercenary of the Motherland, prised opened his burnt, abused eyes. The sunlight, always strong and bright in this accursed place instantly stung his eyes, causing them to water and burn even more. But Kit refused to close his eyes anymore. He struggled up from his bed into a sitting position.

The nurse in the infirmary instantly protested but Kit knocked her away when she tried to push him back down.

"Where's the doctor?" he snarled at her.

The nurse cowered but said, "I'll fetch him for you right now sir!" She hurried away and Kit swung his legs down to the floor. They hit the ground with a dull thump, still rubbery and almost lifeless. On closer inspection, through his still watering eyes, Kit noticed that they were swollen. He held up his hands to his face and realized that they too were swollen and red.

He stared at his hands for a moment more as they shook with rage and then he deliberately closed them into fists. He set his fists on the bed and pushed up. The sudden change in height left him reeling with nausea and his legs almost gave out on him. His body shook with the strain of being upright, but Kit fought the weakness, fought the insufferable pain that the natives, that the things, for they were not men, had brought upon him.

In that moment, the doctor came through the door. Surprised to find Kit standing, he said

"Well now my good man, it's best if you sit back down."

Kit's eyes were half-closed but he still managed a look that froze the doctor in place.

"I will remain standing," Kit hissed. "Tell me what happened to me."

The doctor nodded dumbly for a moment and then seemed to recover and walked forward. He sat on a stool and said, "From what I have been able to discover, you and your men were exposed to some nasty spider venom."

"Spider venom," said Kit flatly. Some little spider had done this to him?

"Oh yes," said the doctor. "It seemed as if someone had laced some... string I think one of your men said… with spider venom which then entered through your wounds and your eyes. You also breathed in quite a lot which did some damage to the insides of your body. Which is why I really would recommend some rest."

Kit glared at him and the doctor shrank back but continued valiantly.

"The thing is, that the signs and symptoms don't quite match a single spider. I think whoever laced this string with spider venom must have used several different types. Even if the venom were not fatal by itself, mixed in with others, well, some unusual effects occurred."

"What of my men?"

"All of them have survived, though two might be permanently blinded and quite a few of them sport broken bones."

There was silence as Kit took it all in and then he said harshly. "Leave." He turned to the nurse. "Get me my clothes."

The nurse quickly bobbed her head and dashed out of the room. The doctor hesitated but eventually he too left, leaving Kit alone with his thoughts.

Spider venom. He flexed his swollen hand. He would pay back that spider for the damage and humiliation it had caused him and his men. He did not care for the fighter, the man with the stick. Kit had shot him anyway, he would be easy to find, he might even already be dead from infection. No, he didn't want the fighter, excellent as he was, he wanted the other, the spider, that had spun out its webs so confident and clever. He was going to find the spider that had bested him, a mercenary with over twenty years of experience and the men he had trained to exacting standards so effortlessly. He would find the spider that had made him fail in his attempts to complete his job over and over again and belittled his competency. He would find it and crush its neck under his hands, watch the life leech out of its eyes. The spider would pay for daring to cross him.

Ainsley's fist crashed down on the desk in his study. He was a picture of rage as he eyed the politely-worded letter from the governor who had informed him that Ainsley's very own cargo would be held in the governor's warehouse, as a favour to his good friend. The letter commiserated with him on the loss of his ammunition from his warehouse and carefully stated that he was just providing assistance to Ainsley, a loyal subject under the governor, to get his feet back under him. But Ainsley, well versed in the machinations of court intrigue, knew that his goods were being co-opted because of his failure to keep his precious cargo safe. The governor was saying he did not trust Ainsley to keep the goods he had offered for the project safe and also suggested that Ainsley might go back on his contributions.

Ainsley ground his teeth together. Two hundred guns gone, almost that many boxes of ammunition, four guards and three men with whom he had been conducting business were all missing. There hadn't been a single sign of the thieves on the streets that night.

His new chief guardsman, Maple, had even condescended to paying the dirty street rats of the boerin for information. None had come up with results. No one had seen any sign of the thieves with two hundred guns, ammunition and six men, being carried away into the night.

They must be covering for them of course, Ainsley thought scornfully. Though why they would, even when being paid, was more than Ainsley could understand.

He scowled at the thought. He was already being far too generous, not rippling apart the boerin section of town where his men had been attacked. True, he had only restrained because the governor preferred to have the boerin held in dull submission. Destroying that part of town would certainly rile the pitiful creatures. They held no ability to do anything, of course, but the governor would have been displeased and he had power to make Ainsley's standing a little less than it was. One day, when they were done with the kalinag, Ainsley would destroy the boerin too.

Outside Ainsley's study, unbeknownst to him, a Moko Jumbie tended the yard and carefully measured just how much evil was emanating from Ainsley's window.

CHAPTER 18

"Sadika," said Reshma, standing in the doorway of Sadika's room.

"What child?" asked Sadika, busily embroidering.

"Why de spider talk to meh?" Reshma asked flatly.

Sadika paused and then sighed and set down her needlework. "Come here."

Reshma came over and Sadika sat the little girl down on her lap. "Look, it's a family thing," she said. "But we'll tell you about it later. But dis is something you must keep secret okay? You mustn't tell anyone about the spider speaking to you, okay?"

"Okay," said Reshma, "Why?"

"Because it's our secret and we don't want anyone else to have it," Sadika replied. "And because some people don't like people who can talk to spiders and they might hurt us. So, don't say anything."

The child blinked, unsure of why anyone would want to hurt another person because they heard spiders, but nodded.

"So, you can hear spiders too?"

Sadika smiled but nodded. "Me and granpa both," she told Reshma. "There's other things too but you'll learn when you're older. We'll teach you."

"Could my mommy hear de spiders too?"

Sadika swallowed hard at the unexpected mention of the sister she'd lost far, far too early, but nodded. "Yes, she could hear de spiders too. She was real good at de all the spider stuff yuh know. Maybe you will be too."

"Is spider stuff de thing you does leave at night to do?" Reshma asked and Sadika snorted because of course Reshma had figured it out.

"Yes," said Sadika.

"Can I do spider stuff with you when ah grow up?"

"Of course," Sadika laughed, "But fuh now, you hadda sleep early or the jumbie will come back fuh yuh!" She poked the little girl in her chest and the child squealed and then pouted at Sadika.

"No, he won't, is not my fault I cah sleep."

"Well you still have to try," Sadika said. "Now come on, you done with yuh spelling?"

"How was yuh day?" Kirish asked Amrika, grinning at her.

Amrika glared at him. "The only thing that not aching rite now is the air around me!" she snapped.

Kirish outright laughed at her. When he sobered, he said, "Please tell meh yuh learn something nah gyul."

"I learn something!" Amrika said scowling at him. She wearily walked into the house and contemplated falling asleep on the floor right there. Kirish seemed to guess what she was thinking and guided her to a chair.

"Doh worry," he said far too cheerfully for her liking. "It go get easier soon."

Amrika sighed but nodded. "It was fun though."

"Really?" asked Kirish.

"Really," nodded Amrika.

"Good," her brother said. "It always should be."

"So," said Amrika, stretching, "what we doing now? I still out de loop."

"Another ship coming in tomorrow with ammunitions and cargo," Kirish said.

"We blowing it up again?" Amrika asked through a yawn.

Kirish snorted. "No. De governor might really kill all ah we if we do dat. We just ambushing the carriages when they being transported to de warehouse."

"Are the Midnight Robbers going this time?"

"Yep," said Kirish grinning, "Though the Bats coming along too."

"De saikan figure out an explanation for de Bats yet?" Amrika asked curiously.

Kirish snorted. "No." Then he smiled wide and dark, "But the jotlin have."

Amrika cocked an eyebrow. "They realize is the stories?"

"Yeah," Kirish nodded, still smiling that slightly unsettling smile. "And de best thing is, dey 'fraid to tell the saikan 'cause de saikan eh go believe them and den de saikan go look down on dem."

Amrika giggled. "It's good to be a myth sometimes," she said cheerfully.

"Or a horror story," her brother rejoined, eyes alight with the Robber's glee.

"A folktale," Amrika rebutted and Kirish laughed.

"Or a folktale," he agreed. "We are de folk of this land and you will hear our tale." His voice dropped into the deep ringing tones that Midnight Robbers used to tell their speeches, "Buh is not one to tell when night stalks the land, cause yuh never know what walking under she cloak."

Short and sweet and the hair on Amrika's arms were already standing up in fright.

"Well I think we agree on folktale," she said to break the moment, and Kirish leaned back eyes gleaming with amusement. He knew he had scared her and took no end of joy in it because no matter how much he might love her, tormenting little sisters on occasion was an acceptable pastime for older brothers.

Amrika scowled at him to let him know she personally didn't think it was funny and then deliberately reached over and smacked him hard on the arm with Stickfighter strength. The startled gasp he made was worth it. She smiled at him sweetly and got up to go have a bath saying

"I feel strangely revived now."

"Haha," said her brother dryly.

The next night however, the dark things were in for a disappointment. The Bats and Midnight Robbers waited on the road for the carriages carrying the cargo to Lord Ainsley's private holdings but no carriages rumbled past.

When half an hour passed from the estimated time that the carriages would pass, the Bats took to the air to investigate.

Two hours later, the Bats fluttered down to a roof where the Midnight Robbers waited.

"Found the ship," a Bat told them. "They moved it over to a private dock and unloaded the cargo there."

"Did you see where they unload the cargo?"

The Bat shook his head. "Nah it was gone by the time we find de boat."

There was a hiss of dissatisfaction coming from the Midnight Robbers.

"Looks like it's time we start working for real," said Surish and the rest of the Robbers agreed. Shrill whistles burst from the group, causing the poor Bat to wince, and then the Robbers were gone, slipping off the edge of the roof. The Bat as well spiraled up in the air, riding the winds of the Caribbean Sea.

While the Bats and Midnight Robbers were waiting to ambush the carriages of cargo, Sadika was riding back to re-string illusions around the kalinag villages. The horse cantered to a stop upon nearing the Stickfighter who was standing guard over the village of Chagna.

"Stickfighter," said Sadika in greeting.

"Daughter of the spider," replied the Stickfighter. It was a woman this time, around Sadika's own age, with small almond-shaped eyes that gleamed in the moonlight. She too swayed slightly as she stood, her straight hair brushing her shoulders as she rocked back and forth to Ierie's song.

"May I start my work here?" Sadika asked.

The Stickfighter appraised her and nodded. "Here is good."

Sadika nodded and slipped off her horse, took her reel of spider's silk and began to string her illusions across the path.

It was a long night of work. She spent nearly three hours sealing the perimeter of Chagna and hiding escape routes through the forest and when she was done, she had to ride to the next village of Tarigua and do it all over again.

When she finally came upon the Stickfighter standing in the road to Tarigua, she pulled her horse to a halt and said, "I've come to help, Stickfighter."

"I know, dark neighbour," the Stickfighter replied, voice amused.

Sadika recognized him then. It was the same Stickfighter who had fought alongside her that night when the saikan attacked.

"Are you well?" she asked.

"Yeah man," the Stickfighter said shrugging a shoulder, "That done heal up. What 'bout' you?"

"I good," she replied simply. "I ent really get hurt."

"Well the front part of the village already have illusions," the Stickfighter told her. "It's just the rest of the perimeter yuh have to do."

Sadika nodded. "Thanks." With that she set to work, adding to the illusions already set in Tarigua by her father.

It was drawing to daybreak when she was finished. She swung back on her horse, which had made the most of the night by grazing peacefully, waved goodbye to the Stickfighter and galloped off towards her home.

Khion watched the scary lady gallop off before continuing on his patrol. He had only taken a few steps when Ierie's song shifted uneasily underneath him. Saikan, the land said, but only for a moment, as if they just made a single step over the boundary from which Ierie would warn him of their presence, before leaving. He stood still and waited to see if the saikan would dare come any closer but they didn't. Little did he know it wasn't him or the kalinag village that was the target but the dark thing that was fast riding home.

Lawrence Kit watched the progress of the spider that had dared try to trap him in her web, through a spyglass. The spider was on a black horse, face veiled. He could not follow her for the entire way. The distance he'd had to keep from alerting the other fighter of his presence made it impossible for him to keep up with her. Her horse did leave tracks though, and Lawrence Kit, mercenary of the Motherland, was an excellent tracker.

CHAPTER 19

Three days later, the young Dame Lorraine came back from a date with her saikan suitor. She quickly slipped through the streets until she came to the house in which the dark things were all gathered to find out what she had learned.

"I found the shipment," she announced when she entered.

"Where is it?" asked a Midnight Robber.

"In one of de governor's private residences," she said, "kept hidden in an old stable."

"Good," said the Midnight Robber, "We'll take care of it."

"Did you find out anything else?" asked a Stickfighter.

"I think," said the Dame Lorraine, "That dey might be going to attack de kalinag soon. He didn't say when. Is jus an impression I get."

"Well, we better move quickly then," the smooth voice of a Jab Jab interjected.

"Yes," agreed the Midnight Robber. "But not tonight. Tonight's almost over. Tomorrow. We'll geh it tomorrow."

Amrika's new routine was to go to Markus' house directly after work. She was learning pretty quickly but Jiang told her that that was to be expected, since she already had something of a background in protecting herself and scrambling around rooftops.

She had to learn how to adjust the things she already knew how to do, to her augmented strength and speed. She had broken three jars of jam in the shop yesterday because she had gripped them too hard.

Today, instead of just Markus and Jiang, along with the rest of Marcus's extended family, there was another guy practicing in the backyard.

"Amrika meet Khion. Khion, Amrika," Jiang introduced. They shook hands and then Amrika asked

"You come to practice today?"

"Not quite," Khion replied. "Here just a lil' bit closer to the kalinag village than meh house. Ah on patrol today and it have rumors that de saikan want to move to the villages soon, so all ah we going up earlier than usual."

"Right," said Amrika. She turned to Jiang, "Allyuh going too?"

"Yes," replied Jiang. She saw the thoughtful look on Amrika's face and apparently read it correctly because she said, "No Amrika, yuh not trained well enough yet."

"I doh have to be on the frontlines," Amrika protested. "Yuh need people to guard the escape routes, right?"

"Yeah and we have dem," Markus said firmly but kindly. "Saikan shoot to kill, Amrika."

"I know," Amrika said calmly. "They almost killed me and a kalinag child last week."

"Then yuh should know how dangerous it is," Jiang said.

"I'm not afraid."

"No but yuh might be chupid," Markus said.

Amrika scowled at him but before she could reply, Khion said, "Let her come."

Markus and Jiang tilted their heads at him. Khion shrugged. "Look, Ierie nuh going an' take de death of any kalinag well. They can protect themselves but that means putting them in the line of fire. I really doh want that. Another thing is dat the saikan have been getting serious about dis. One more Stickfighter won't hurt. Even half-trained she might hold off some men long enough for some of de kalinag to get way. So leh she come."

Markus and Jiang exchanged looks and then shrugged.

"Fine," Markus said.

"But," added Jiang, "You explaining to your Robber brother what you doing eh. We not dealing with dat if you get yuhself kill."

Amrika nodded. "I will."

Kirish was predictably angry at Amrika's predictability.

"Chile!" he snapped. "I tell you, yuh could go gallivanting in kalinag villages?"

"I not gallivanting," Amrika snapped back. "Look, I really not doing anything. I basically just there, jus in case!"

"There," enunciated Kirish carefully, voice shaking with rage, "is where saikan are coming to kill the kalinag and everyone in the villages!"

"I's a Stickfighter," Amrika snapped, "I have as much right as any one of you to be there!"

"Not if yuh chupid so!" he yelled back at her. "You think just 'cause you is a dark thing that you invincible? We die, Amrika! We can get killed. We're living without a father because Midnight Robber he was, but dat didn't stop him from deading!"

"I don't think I'm invincible!" she shouted back. "But I doh want to jus stand here and do nothing!"

"There'll be plenty fuh you to do if the other Stickfighters die in the first assault," he told her darkly.

"And how I reaching the kalinag villages after that?" she asked. "If all the Stickfighters die in the first assault, who going and keep the kalinag safe while they escaping and running from the saikan? Kirish, dais a job for Stickfighters, not Robbers or Jumbie or even Jab Jab. If this attack really going an be as bad as everybody think it is, and it going an be bad because everybody trying to hide thing from me, then you're going to need the people and yuh going and need the people right away."

Kirish stared at her, face hard and then turned away. "We doh know anything."

"Ierie does," Amrika said, simply. "We can all feel it. Something bad coming."

"'Rika," Kirish said, "Doh get yuhself kill eh chile." He spun and glared at her. "I mean it! Or I go bring yuh back an cut yuh tail."

"I doh really have plans to dead yuh know Kirish," Amrika told him, but smiled to let him know she understood.

Later that evening, however, she slipped out and went down a familiar but rarely used path. Kirish and the others were right, this was going to be dangerous. She might die. Kirish might die. If that were the case... well if that were the case, then she wanted to visit, one more time, before they set of on their tasks.

Amrika stares at the earth. There is little here to mark it for a grave but the spot is burned into her memory. Father, mother, uncle, two aunts, a niece that never breathed air; another who only saw two years before illness struck, a cousin, who'd been lost to the sea, another whose cause of death had never been revealed, but Amrika knew the danger that those with black blood put themselves in. She did not need to know, the silence regarding the cause was enough.

She doesn't remember her mother well. She was too young to have more than the impressions of brown and a faint floral scent. Her father however.... Amrika closed her eyes briefly.

He was not, she'd understood as she'd grown older, a very good man. Their home was littered with the spoils of his nighttime work, both from neighbors and saikan alike. But she remembered him working hard at his day job too. Putting in extra hours, coming home exhausted and hungry only to lift her into his arms and kiss the top of her head. He hadn't been the best of people, but he'd never failed to put food on the table, to get them what they needed, to fight through the grief of becoming a single parent so abruptly. He'd never failed to let her know that she was loved and cared for.

But as not-good as he'd been, when news of the ship carrying slaves came to them, his eyes had narrowed and he had volunteered to assist without hesitation.

All of the boerin had come here as slaves at some point in time. Never mind that they called it other, prettier words and paid them a pittance to save their conscience and obey their laws. They'd still toiled under the sun in conditions less than human, being driven by taskmasters without mercy.

Even a not-good man railed against such horror.

Amrika still remembers the wet thud that had roused her from sleep and sent her younger self to the door. She can remember seeing the wet footsteps leading away from their door, hearing the tapping of the fancy sailor's cane as he disappeared into the fog. She hadn't comprehended what he'd dropped at their doorway, seeing first only the hat, the sodden coat and then finally, her father's slack face under the dark brim.

She doesn't remember much after that. Only Kirish's voice, his hand tugging at her. The next thing she knows clearly is sitting trembling at their table, tears running down her face without effort, looking at the body, Kirish had dragged into their small living room.

She remembers Kirish's face; the anguish and agony. The despair, as he sank to one knee next to the corpse, trembling hands hovering and then resting on the face, one gloved hand.

She remembers, she remembers having the wake, remembers passing food to wide eyed, starving children, hustled into their home with the visiting crowds, remembers Kirish picking the locks of the shackles still clamped around wrists and ankles. She remembers wrapping her only shawl around a girl her age, cleaning out her cuts, taking time to comb through the tangled mess of her hair, before shuffling them out into the dark, into the waiting arms of others who would carry the newly freed slaves into the hidden, secret places, where the saikan would never find them and where no one would ever trace them.

No, her father was not a good man. But he'd still been one of the best people she'd ever known.

She stooped and patted the earth. "Doh worry," she said. "We go be okay."

CHAPTER 20

"Ready?" Vishal asked her. Tamara nodded and together they tilted off the tall mango tree. Their wings caught air and with a few powerful flaps they were soaring high over the land. Since the governor had three private residences, not including the one that came with the job, the Bats had volunteered to search them quickly and report to the Midnight Robbers which of the places was being used to hide the cargo. Ierie's song was not clear as it usually was. The land was roiling with tension and anger. Tamara knew she had to be especially careful if she used Ierie's song tonight because with the way the land was right now, she could easily kill people without meaning to.

She and Vishal angled towards the house they'd been assigned to search, matching their flight path to the dark clouds to keep themselves invisible from those looking up. It turned out to be a good decision. When they reached the governor's mansion, Vishal clicked to her and then said, "Look, spyglasses, dey scanning the sky."

"We have to time it den," she replied.

Together they made several lazy loops in the sky, under the cover of a dark bank of clouds until they got an idea of how the men were scanning the skies and then, when the spyglasses were pointed away from them, they folded their wings and fell into a steep dive.

Sadika was just about to send Reshma to bed when the men burst into the house, rifles cocked.

"What is the meaning of this!" Sadika's father thundered from the top of the stairs.

There was a pause and then a burst of sound as the rifles fired. Sadika shrieked and then covered her mouth, her other hand going to clamp over Reshma's.

"Sadika, run!" her father yelled.

"Dad!"

"I coming! You run!" Sadika froze for a second in indecision but then Reshma whimpered behind the hand Sadika still had over the child's mouth. Sadika's gaze snapped to her niece and she knew she could not let the child be harmed; she had to run. They had to run.

She threw open the window and swung a leg over the sill.

"Come Reshma!" she ordered.

The child's eyes widened, and she shook her head. Sadika didn't have time to be nice. She swung her leg back into the room, ran over and grabbed the child. Reshma shrieked in fear but Sadika paid her no mind. She hauled the child over to the window and shoved her through, holding on to her long enough that she could grab the sill.

Reshma shrieked as she dangled from the sill. "Sadika!" she yelled, tears running down her face.

"Look!" Sadika snapped, glancing behind her nervously, "Remember de spider thing?"

"What?" the tears momentarily abated with Reshma's confusion.

"The spider!" Sadika snapped.

"Y-Yeah," Reshma said.

"Well spiders can climb walls real good right?" said Sadika.

"Yes," agreed Reshma.

"That means we can too," Sadika told her. "Just trust your instincts. Your hands and feet will know what to do to get you down. Now climb!"

There was a terrible moment when Sadika thought Reshma wasn't going to be able to do it but then the child shifted, got her feet braced against the wall and one hand shifted from the sill. In a moment she was slipping down the side of the house. Sadika went out the window after her, catching a glimpse of her father as he came into the room, running. Sadika didn't wait for him. She slithered down the side of the house and as soon as her feet touched ground she grabbed Reshma in her arms and ran.

They flared their wings just before they made impact with the ground. The updraft stretched their wings hard, and the jolt of the sudden stop was terrible but it wasn't anything that Tamara hadn't experienced before. Their bumpy stop was turned into a smooth long glide, with their bellies barely scraping over the top of the lawn until they collapsed, very gently, to the ground.

They quickly flopped their wings over themselves, causing them to blend with the shadows on the grounds. After a few moments, Tamara peeked out from under her wings and noticed the guards were looking the other way. She clicked softly to Vishal and they began the long slow belly crawl across the grounds to the building that looked like it might house the cargo of weaponry they were searching for.

The men were close on her heels by the time Sadika made it into the cover of the trees behind her house. Bullets whizzed past her head and she felt something sting her arm. Reshma was weeping softly in her arms again, her little fingers digging into Sadika's forearms and back.

Sadika dodged behind the trees when she could but she dared not stop running. Whoever these men were, they were not here to capture them.

Her bare feet pounded on the earth as she did her best not to trip over the roots of the very trees that were currently saving their lives. Sadika risked a glance and saw the men behind her were far too close for comfort. Eventually they would get close enough for her erratic path not to matter much to their aim or for their swords to swipe across her ankles. She put on a burst of speed, brought on by the desperation she felt. But when she looked ahead of her, her heart sank. The trees were coming to an end. Before her, only bush stood. Tall bush, true, but easy enough to find a path through it. Their pursuers would have a better line of sight to them and probably wouldn't be hampered by the bush: enough to give her a significant lead. Her chances of surviving the night had just fallen. Sadika took a deep breath and plunged into the bush.

"Dis is de worse," Vishal grumbled as they inched their way across the grounds. "We cah just run?"

"And get shoot?" Tamara hissed back. "No thanks."

"I rather be shot," Vishal said. "We're not even halfway cross."

Tamara winced. She glanced behind them at the guards. "We'll never make it in one run."

"Stop an start," Vishal mumbled.

Tamara sighed. "Okay. On my mark we run for three seconds and then drop, okay?"

"Okay," Vishal said. They both peeked out from under their wings at the guards and when the men moved away, Tamara hissed:

"Go!"

The twins scrambled up from the ground, ran for three seconds and then collapsed back heavily. They waited with bated breath to see if they had been caught. When there was no uproar, they cautiously peeked out from under their wings. The guards carefully scanned the area they were hiding in, failed to spot them and then began to move on to the next area to patrol.

"Go!" hissed Vishal this time. The mad scramble repeated itself as did the next few seconds of heart-pounding fear.

"I think we'll make it on the next run," Vishal murmured.

Tamara craned her neck, measured the distance and nodded. "Me too," she said. They both eyed the guards again and then made a dash for the building. They reached it at top speed and a quick flap of their wings had both twins airborne enough to grab the rafters of the eaves, hauling themselves up under them. They waited and then grinned at each other when the guards remained blissfully unaware.

They couldn't scream to get a look inside the building or the guards would hear so they had to carefully unlock the door while letting themselves down from the rafters in short spurts and then jumping back up. They eventually managed to get the door open and to slip inside undetected.

They paused to let their eyes get adjusted, and then they froze for an entirely different reason.

"Um," said Vishal.

"Yeah," said Tamara.

"We should, we should probably tell somebody."

"Oh yeah. Leh we get outta here."

Kirish was waiting at the meeting point for the Bats to return. The first set of Bats returned, saying that their place was empty but there was evidence that something had been stored there recently. While he was pondering this information, a second set of Bats appeared on the horizon. They were younger than the first set, only a year or two younger than he was, and they appeared rattled.

"We found the weaponry," the guy said.

"It worse than we thought," the girl added.

"How worse?" Kirish demanded.

"Yuh know how we thought it was just bigger guns?" the girl asked.

"They brought cannons," the guy said. "A lot of cannons."

The third set of Bats came in, landed and said, "We have cannons in the house we check too. Along with wagons to transport dem."

The second set of Bats nodded. "There was wagons too, where we searched." The guy blinked and tilted his head. "And carriages were heading to de house when we was flying away."

"Men," said the girl. "They were probably bringing men."

The pieces fell together in Kirish's head. "It wasn't one residence. He stored them in all three residences so that they would be close to all three kalinag villages."

"But the first residence didn't have weapons," said the first set of Bats.

"Dais 'cause they already move it out," Kirish said. "That house is furthest from de village it's targeting. The saikan are striking tonight!"

The Bats froze. "What do we do?" asked the girl of the second set of Bats.

Kirish lifted his whistle and the Bats instinctively covered their ears. He let out a long blast on his whistle calling the Midnight Robbers to him, then he turned to the Bats.

"You can carry people, right?"

"Not for long, not unless two of us carry you," said one.

"Then do it," said Kirish. "Get de Robbers to the second and third residences and send some of yuh people along the road of the third. Knock out de wagons."

"We go send some people to warn the kalinag villages as well," said another Bat and took off.

Kirish nodded absently, already working on a plan to disable the cannons.

Sadika ploughed her way through the tall grass heading towards a lone tree in the distance. Behind her the men still came on and her only reprieve was that the brush hampered them too. Sadika took a moment to shift Reshma on her back. She crouched low and dashed through the grass, trying hard not to make noise as she moved. The long leaves of the grass caught on her arms and legs, slicing them as she moved. Lines of burning pain marked her body followed by the warmth of blood trickling across her skin. Reshma too caught her fair share of cuts from the grass but the child didn't make a sound, only clutched tighter to Sadika.

A rifle shot cracked from behind them and Sadika ducked on instinct. The ball whistled over their head and Reshma whimpered. Sadika took off on a zigzag path, still aiming for the tree in the distance. Another rifle cracked from the side of her and Sadika dropped like a stone. It saved their lives, the bullet whizzing over them.

"Crawl!" Sadika hissed to Reshma who had tumbled off her back. Both of them scrambled through the grass as fast as they could before Reshma clambered back onto Sadika, and Sadika began to run again.

The men were much faster than she was, and it was beginning to show. They were gaining on her, even with her erratic path. Three shots echoed through the night and Sadika bit back a cry as one of them ripped a bloody gash in her arm. She struggled not to let Reshma fall and the little girl helped with that by nearly strangling Sadika to death.

She regained her footing, but she had lost distance. The sounds of the rifles being reloaded gave her time and she struggled on, the almond tree just ahead of her.

Sadika gritted her teeth and pushed on despite the rubbery feeling in her legs. Men shouted, another rifle cocked behind her and Sadika stumbled to a fall, the shot once more whizzing over their heads. She staggered back up but stayed in a crouch and half-ran, half-stumbled towards the tree.

Finally, the tree was there, spread out in front of her. Sadika made one more desperate lunge towards it, put the tree between them and their attackers and scrambled at its bark, letting Reshma drop off her back.

"Come on! Come on!" she hissed. Then, "Yes!"

She spun, and the thin threads of spider web billowed into long sheets.

"Come here!" she told Reshma.

When the saikan men burst into the small clearing around the tree there was no one there. The men quickly checked the grass around the tree to see if their quarry had hidden, but there were no entry points in the brush and no sounds of anyone running through the grass.

The men looked around suspiciously, clearly having been told what to expect. One of them carefully poked around the tree to disturb any illusions that might have been set. Failing to find any illusions, the men casually shot into the branches of the tree, just in case they were hiding up there.

Sadika was very glad she had covered Reshma's mouth before the men started to shoot or the child might have given them away. The men grumbled and after a while continued onto the brush to see if they had somehow managed to sneak away. Sadika and Reshma watched them go from the same side of the clearing that they had entered, the side the men clearly hadn't thought to check because they hadn't expected them to double back.

The two of them remained crouched behind the web Sadika had strung up around them until the men made their way back and disappeared towards the house. Then and only then did Sadika drop the illusion. She tilted suddenly and crashed hard onto the dirt as exhaustion and shock from blood loss made itself known.

"Sadika!" Reshma hissed in alarm.

"I good," she said tiredly from where she lay. "I good."

CHAPTER 21

Tamara and Vishal powered through the air, struggling to keep a good grip on the Midnight Robber and maintain a good height. Beside them four more Bats, a Midnight Robber suspended between each pair, flapped hard. All of them were going as fast as they could because they needed to delay the attack on the kalinag villages as soon as possible.

The journey however, seemed to take forever. Bats were strong, but they were built light to be able to keep themselves aloft easier. Midnight Robbers were very far from light and they were not aerodynamic, with their large coats and hats. The wind drag was killing Tamara and she was afraid that she might drop their deadly passenger. From the quick glances Vishal was shooting her, it was killing him too. The fierce wing strokes and the slight angle he held while flying told her that he was worried that their passenger would throw off their flight far too much for them to make the complex aerial maneuvers required to get them all unseen into the govenor's private residence. But they persevered and then the governor's residence was beneath them.

"Doh scream," Vishal cautioned the Midnight Robber they held.

"Wha…?" the Robber started to say but Tamara and Vishal had already tilted downwards and snapped shut their wings. They dropped like a rock and the Midnight Robber clamped his mouth shut so hard she heard his teeth click. But he didn't scream as they free-fell from the sky.

Tamara and Vishal gave tiny flaps of their wings to correct their course as they dropped, each automatically working in tandem with each other to ensure that they didn't spiral out of control or into the sightlines of the many spyglasses that were aimed at the sky. Tamara was never so glad that she and Vishal knew each other so well, and had flown together all their lives. She could imagine how difficult this was for the other set of bats who were, no doubt, not as practiced at flying with another.

But their companions were older, more seasoned flyers and they held their own. All too soon the ground was looming up at them from the darkness and Tamara flared her wings and braced for the pain.

Kirish tumbled to the ground as the two Bats, a pair of twins, released him from their hold. He forcibly reminded himself not to scream. The twins didn't even land, just arced back to the sky before the guards caught sight of them. Next to him, Surish and Trevon landed, rolling on the grass to dispel the excess energy from the landing. The Bats fluttered up into the sky and then they were alone.

The three of them took refuge behind the building where the cannons were and took a few moments to calm their screaming nerves and let their rabbiting hearts slow. Dropping from the sky like that was the most terrifying thing all three of them had experienced.

Normally heights did not bother Kirish, but a couple hundred feet up was way, way too high. And dropping from such a height, while relying on someone else to save him from certain death, had not been pleasant in the slightest. It had been a long time since anyone had had control over his fate and he didn't like the reminder. He was quite certain the scream he'd been forced to contain was still rattling around in his lungs somewhere.

However, they were here now, and it was time to get to work. All around them were the sounds of men being marshalled.

"We hadda do this now!" said Surish, still breathing a little hard.

Kirish nodded and the three Midnight Robbers set off on the business of robbing.

With the Midnight Robbers dropped off, Tamara and Vishal headed over to the road leading to the kalinag village of Aria. Gunshots were heard far before they came up to the road.

"Whoa!" murmured Vishal as they came up to the scene. Tamara nodded dumbly. Two long lines of men were defending the wagons that were carrying the cannons. Bats were still attempting to take out the cannons, but the men had rifles and had set up a revolving group of shooters so that the Bats couldn't get close enough to cause any damage.

"How we going to stop them?" asked Vishal, "They still moving along the road. All we doing rite now is slowing them."

Tamara frantically racked her brains to come up with an idea. Before she could, Vishal half-paused in the air.

"What?" she asked.

"Torches," he said.

"What about dem?"

"Cannons needs gunpowder," her twin replied. "They'll be carrying de gunpowder in de wagons."

Tamara paused. "If the gunpowder blows... Vishal, a lot of men are going to die."

"And if we don't stop dem, a lot of kalinag will die. And then all of Ierie might die," her twin replied grimly.

Tamara swallowed hard and then nodded. "Okay. Leh we get some torches." They spun back from the road.

Amrika was sitting inside the kalinag village with her stick across her knees when a Bat landed in the center of the village.

"The saikan coming to attack tonight," the Bat announced without ceremony. "They coming with cannons. Be prepared to run." Then the Bat was gone in a gust of wings.

Amrika blinked and then froze for a second. Cannons?

"The other dark things trying to slow them down or stop dem," Jiang said, jogging into the village. "Buh we doh know if they go be able to stop dem."

"Any saikan reach yet?" Amrika asked.

"Nuh yet," said Jiang. She turned to the head of kalinag village, "Sir…"

"We will not run until there is no choice," the leader said firmly. "Dis is our home."

"Alright," said Jiang. "But we chose when there is no choice. Ierie tasked us with your protection."

The leader lifted his head but after a moment gave a stiff nod. Jiang nodded in reply and then said to Amrika:

"Be ready to get dem out. They survive, no matter what."

Amrika nodded seriously.

When the men in the governor's second private residence quickly went to put the cannons in the wagons, they were met by a peculiar sight. All the wheels of the cannons were gone, as were all the wheels of the wagons. Upon reporting the theft, the men were ordered to place the cannons in the carriages. When they went to do so, the carriages which, just minutes ago had been perfectly functioning, were all also lacking their wheels. All the horses were also gone for good measure.

"What we going to do with all dese wheels?" Surish asked, flipping a wheel in his hands.

"We go figure out something man," Kirish replied. He waved to a Bat that was fluttering up ahead. The Bat carefully landed and Kirish said, "We've slowed them down for now but they could still requisition carriages from anybody nearby. They'll get back on their feet soon enough."

"Why didn't you just steal the cannons?" the Bat asked.

"Seriously?" said Surish. "We're good but we can't tote several hundred pounds of cannon away with us. Not unless we have a lot more Robbers than it have available right now."

Several riders pounded down the road and Trevon said, "They're already going to get more wagons."

"I could stop the riders," the Bat said.

"Do dat," Kirish said.

"What now?" Surish asked, when the Bat had left.

"We leave," said Kirish. "It doh have anything else we could do. Dey watching everything too close now for we to get in and out. We good buh we cah survive being shot."

The others grumbled but they understood. With a twirl of their coats the three Robbers were gone, striding through the darkness.

CHAPTER 22

Tamara and Vishal hovered nervously in the air, far out of reach of the rifles' range. Around them the air was filled with Bats, all of whom were also carrying torches. The flames flickered in the hard wind but the oil that was soaked into the rags kept them lit.

Below the flame-carrying Bats, another wave of Bats awaited. They were the vanguard, the ones opening the path for the torches to reach their targets. They were also the ones who would take the hits, if any came. Tamara's insides roiled unhappily. This plan of theirs was dangerous, far too dangerous, but they had to stop those cannons.

Protect the first born!!!

Ierie's words howled through the air, the land's song a thundering yet oddly jaunty tempest of hair-raising melody.

Tamara looked to her brother and Vishal gave her a little nod. She nodded back and then tilted her head back and screamed.

Below her the first wave of Bats folded their wings and dived towards the cannons, unlit falling stars streaking towards the earth. Then the wings came back out to play, short, sharp snaps, driving them closer and closer to the earth at astonishing speed. Tamara could hear Ierie's song muting as the Bats caught the sound in their wings. She screamed again and then the second wave of Bats began their journey down, streams of fire trailing through the sky.

Below her the first set of Bats unleashed Ierie's songs just as rifles fired into the sky. The bullets fired, twisted, blown off course by Ierie's song. The second line of the first wave unleashed Ierie's song as the first line curved away. The second volley of rounds were scattered again. By the time the third line unleashed Ierie's song, Tamara and Vishal's wave arrived. This time, they were close enough to drop the torches onto the stores of gunpowder. Torches were flung frantically to the stores and on top whatever else could burn, and then the Bats left. There were no waves of Bats to protect their backs. The saikan rifles could fire at their leisure; the only thing the Bats had going for them was their speed.

It wasn't enough. In those moments before the gunpowder exploded, four Bats went down, pitching out of the sky. Then the night ignited and Tamara was flung through the sky. She spun haphazardly through the air, unable to control herself, heat blazing along her back.

She barely managed to wrest control of her descent in order not to crash. She landed hard, wrenching her ankle and picking up a couple hundred bruises. She staggered to her feet, ears ringing, calling frantically for her brother.

"Vishal! Vishal!"

"Tamara!" she heard at last, a tiny voice coming from far away. She spotted her brother in the distance, now staggering to his feet. She ran over to him and he promptly grabbed her by the face, examining her for any serious injury.

"Ah good! Ah good!" she reassured him frantically. "You?"

"I good," he said. Then he jerked his head to the road behind them. Tamara turned to look and then gasped. The road was still alight but there was barely anything there. Soft, tortured moans drifted through the night from the unlucky survivors.

"I..." her voice trailed off. "What do we do?"

"Save who we can, I guess." Her brother's voice sounded as sick as hers. They did this. Tamara covered her mouth with a hand and breathed helplessly. *They did this.*

Sadika stayed crouched in the grass as she watched the saikan men ride away, her father slumped unconscious on the back of a horse. It appeared as if all the men had pulled away but Sadika knew that someone must be left behind to watch the house. It was a trap and Sadika had no intention of stepping into that trap. She crept back to where she had stashed Reshma and took the child's hand.

"Come now."

"We going back home?"

Sadika shook her head. "We cah do dat, it not safe. We hadda hide now chile, and we have a long way to walk."

Reshma looked up at her with watering eyes but she nodded solemnly and let Sadika pull her through the bush, away from the house.

Khion felt the change in Ierie's song even before the Bat landed to tell them that the mercenaries were coming.

"The Robbers managed to par them down to four cannons but dais enough," the Bat said.

"What about Aria?" Markus asked.

"Safe fuh now," said the Bat. "But a lot of Bats got hurt in that and they trying to keep whoever of de saikan that survived, alive. So we numbers down. We cah help a lot now."

"Dais fine," said Markus. "Dis is we kinda thing anyway."

The Bat gave Markus a look that clearly said he disbelieved him. Then the Bat shrugged and said. "Ah going an warn the village."

Khion waited until the Bat was out of earshot and said. "Par them down to four cannons? How much dey had before?"

"I real doh know," said Jiang. "And I doh want to know."

Mass amounts of men do not move quickly. It was another hour before the column of men appeared on the road. The men halted at the sight of the illusions woven by the Child of Anansi, which made it appear as if the road dead-ended.

There was a debate and then a man came striding to the fore. His face was set in a rictus of pain but there was a deep burning anger in him. Khion recognized him as the leader of the men who had shot him a few nights ago. The fact that the man had been poisoned by the venom in the spiderwebs clearly hadn't stopped him. In fact, it only seemed to have infuriated him more.

The man grabbed a lighted stick, ordered a cannon to the front of the line and then touched the wick to the cannon.

Khion, Markus and Jiang all dived to the side. The cannonball blew past them with a terrifying bang, crashing through the webs and tearing through the illusions. The three Stickfighters got to their feet and surveyed the damage.

"Well dats dat," said Khion.

"Dat's dat," agreed Jiang.

Gripping their sticks, the Stickfighters stepped back into the middle of the road. Ierie's beat swelled and throbbed beneath their feet, resonating all the way through their bones. They took their stances, feet spread, sticks held over their heads and wide grins on their faces. On the other side, men cocked their guns and aimed at them. It was an execution at best but the three Stickfighters never wavered. The beat of Ierie picked up pace and their bones vibrated, the sound reverberating through them.

"Fire!" the saikan leader called and the guns went off in a cacophony of sound. When the smoke cleared there was no one left in the road. The saikan blinked in confusion but then men screamed.

Khion laughed as he dashed in from the side of the saikan forces and quickly picked off the men there. Jiang and Markus appeared on the other side, whirling through the ranks of men with a speed that was fuelled by Ierie's beat. Khion's stick crashed into guns, deflected swords and redirected shots into their own men. The suddenness of the attack, by people who were supposed to be dead a few seconds ago, caused mass confusion and the men scrambled to respond properly to it. Just when the men began to arrange themselves, Khion and the others disappeared back into the forest bordering the road.

The leader clearly wanted to follow them, but his orders were to destroy the kalinag village so the order was given to move forward.

Khion glanced at Markus. "We go hadda face dem head on, jus now."

"Ah know," said Markus. He grinned at him. "Buh not yet."

They harassed the saikan three more times on their journey to the kalinag village, but each time they took down less and less men. On their final attack, one of the men finally got a shot that hit Jiang through her left side and both Khion and Markus had to drag her away to safety.

It was this that allowed the saikan to make the final stretch within cannon range of the village.

"Shit!" hissed Khion.

"Go!" Jiang snapped at them. "Allyuh have to stop dem cannons!"

"How?" Markus said. "There's too many men covering dem, we didn't take out enough."

Jiang gave them a bloody grin and then said to Khion. "You ever feel like playing cricket with a cannon ball?"

There was a pause while Jiang grinned at him and Markus' jaw dropped.

"Yuh, know," said Khion, "I've suddenly conceived a desire to try."

"Yuh go dead," Markus said flatly. He sighed and stood up. "We both go dead."

Khion laughed. "But we go take them dong with we!" With that, both Stickfighters sprinted through the forest until they caught back up to the front of the saikan lines where the cannons were being rolled out.

"Ah real hope they evacuate the village by now," Khion huffed as he darted through the undergrowth.

"If dey haven't, they crazy," Markus replied breathlessly.

Khion slowed as he was now ahead of the saikan lines. He grinned at Markus and then dashed out in the middle of the road between the saikan and Chagna. Markus stepped out behind him and the two of them faced down the line of men. They were out of easy rifle range but not out of cannon range.

"Come on, doh shoot we with guns," muttered Khion. Bullets would make this a very short last stand. Not that what he was planning to do probably wasn't going to kill him either, and sooner than the bullets too.

"Seriously, no guns," Markus agreed as he readied himself. Markus stood further back and to the side of Khion so that if this killed Khion, Markus would be left to protect Chagna.

The saikan let out sharp growls when they noticed Khion and Markus standing in their way. Many of them lifted their guns but the leader, the man who had survived the venom, stopped them.

"Later," he growled. "When the village is in ruins you can kill these. Ready the cannons."

Khion dug his feet into the dirt and let his stick slip down until he was holding one end like a bat. Ierie's beat thrummed through him and he couldn't help but smile. His heartbeat slowed and matched the rhythm of the land and Khion began to sway, feet dancing lightly in the Stickfighter's quick steps. From the forest a hollow thump came, Jiang knocking her stick against a tree, following Ierie's beat. The rhythm was beautiful, wild and real and it scared them, scared those saikan who were used to the wildness and cruelty of men but not the wildness and sheer life of lands that did not follow the rules of men.

Khion swung his stick back and forth in front of them and let them see, let them feel what stood in front of them.

Stickfighter.

Warrior. Guardian. Dark Thing of Ierie.

Stickfighter.

He was a dark thing of Ierie and they should be afraid. They should be very, very afraid.

CHAPTER 23

The leader, realizing that his men were halted by the figure in front of them, angrily grabbed the wick away for a second time that night and jammed it into the cannon. The cannon ball exploded out the cannon and Khion stepped up using Stickfighter speed. He swung as hard as he could. There was loud crack, and a wave of sheer force rattled down his arms. His whole body shook, his spine screamed, his legs burned and dug into the dirt whilst his head vibrated so hard his brain felt scrambled for a bit. He heard bones fracture, felt pinching lines of pain running through his body as the force was redistributed through him. The world blanked out for a moment.

When the world swam back into focus, Khion found that he was still on his feet, bent over, stick propped up on the ground, teeth clenched so tightly together he was surprised his jaw didn't crack. But in front of him, only three cannons were lined up. Three where there used to be four.

Silver wreckage was scattered back from the line. It appeared to have taken a chunk of men with it. Khion straightened up and was pleasantly surprised to realize that his stick was still intact. There was silence as the saikan absorbed what had happened.

"Yuh alive?" Markus asked softly.

"Pretty sure meh han break," Khion replied.

"Good thing yuh have two han then."

Khion laughed, half-hysterical, half-triumphant.

The laugh broke the horror-filled tableau and the saikan quickly fired the three remaining cannons.

Khion knocked back one, Markus took care of the second one but the third was going to go past both of them and crash straight into Chagna. A bone-shattering crack sounded through the air and the third cannon ball went flying off to the side. Jiang stood there, blood spilling out her mouth, but she was grinning, stick held firm in her hands.

"One fuh each ah we?"

"Sure," said Markus and all three of them turned to face the saikan men. "I tink we could manage to share."

There was nothing quite so terrifying as the sounds of cannons booming through the night, Amrika thought. It was equally frightening that none of the cannon balls made it through to the village. It's not that she wanted them to hit the village, but she knew that if they're weren't making it through then the Stickfighters must be doing something they might not survive, to stop the cannon balls.

She gritted her teeth and ignored the cannons, making sure that everyone in the village had made it out onto the planned escape routes. The village leader was the last to go and Amrika nodded to let him know that all the people were gone.

"Yuh coming gyul?" One of the Stickfighters who was covering the escape routes asked her. Amrika shook her head.

"No! Allyuh get them out, I go cover dem when they come in."

The Stickfighter paused and Amrika said, "I'll run if dey ain't make it out." He gave her a grim nod and then he was gone, disappearing into the illusioned paths made by the Child of Anansi.

Amrika stood in the middle of the village, stick at the ready, waiting for the others to come in.

All but one of the cannons were gone, destroyed by their own cannon balls. Lawrence Kit was infuriated. In front of him stood three figures of terror, doing impossible things. All he wanted to do was kill them. He didn't care that they had batted cannon balls away like they were mere fruit. He would kill them. He had shot one of the figures before; they could be shot again, shot and killed.

"Advance!" he shouted to the men. When they hesitated he snarled at them. "They are men! You have already shot one of them. They can be killed so kill them! Or so help me I will kill the next man who hesitates! Advance!"

The mercenaries hardened their faces and advanced.

"And dais we cue to leave," Khion gasped.

"But!" began Jiang.

"Ji, we can barely hold onto we sticks anymore," Markus told her. "Time to get!"

Jiang hesitated but the men were advancing. She nodded and the three of them turned and ran into the village.

Amrika gripped her stick tighter as figures emerged out of the darkness, heading to the village. Then she recognized them. They ran up to her and bent over, breathing hard.

"Wha you still doing here?" Markus gasped.

"Covering allyuh," she said, eyeing them. The three Stickfighters were trembling from exhaustion, fingers only barely holding onto their sticks. Jiang was bleeding badly, her face pale, eyes ringed with black circles. Markus and Khion were littered with cuts and looked like they were barely staying on their feet. All three had dark bruises blooming under their skin, a garden that covered their entire bodies. Ierie had given them power to save the first born but the Stickfighters would have to pay the price. Fractured bones and destroyed blood vessels. Amrika couldn't fathom how any of them were standing because they should all be dead. They still could be.

"We good!" Khion told her. Amrika gave him a look and said flatly,

"I learn early how to tell when someone lying, all ah allyuh could barely walk, come on, everybody done gone. Leh we get out from here."

The three Stickfighters looked at each other and then nodded.

"Alright," said Khion. "Leh we go."

They had just disappeared out from the village when the saikan arrived.

CHAPTER 24

The remaining cannon roared behind them, the saikan taking out their frustration. The sounds of Chagna being destroyed echoed through the night.

Amrika had Jiang's arm slung over her shoulder as she half-carried the woman down the path. She tried not to gag at the feeling of broken bone shifting under her hand.

"They going an come soon," Jiang rasped.

"Not yuh problem," Amrika retorted.

"Is my problem."

"Not anymore," Amrika told her. Still they sped up their pace, hoping to keep ahead of the saikan. A few minutes later, the sound of men crashing through the trees broke through the night. The sound of shots followed, bullets whistling on their path through the forest.

"What are they shooting at?" Amrika asked. "They cah see us."

"Exactly," groaned Khion, "They know we ha' something that can make illusions so dey just shooting in a line. Eventually dey go hit the illusion an break it, or they go hit us."

"Well dat cah happen," said Amrika.

"You cah survive fightin so much men," Markus said.

"And none ah allyuh could survive more dan walking," Amrika replied flatly.

"I go help," a new voice broke in. It was the Stickfighter from earlier.

"Raj, yuh supposed to be covering the kalinag," Jiang said.

"Wha yuh tink I doing chile?" he said. "De three ah allyuh go. Come new gyul, leh we go distract some saikan here."

Amrika carefully handed Jiang over to Markus and Khion, neither of whom looked much better, and followed the strange Stickfighter back down the path.

They didn't go very far down, just enough to put some distance between them and the three injured ones. They crouched within the path made by the Child of Anansi and when they were sure no saikan was about to run into them, they carefully ducked between the webs holding the illusion and found themselves in plain sight.

They crouched once more, keeping themselves hidden in the undergrowth of the forest and waited for the men to appear.

"I thought it woulda be better if de Children of Anansi was here," Amrika muttered.

"Dey was supposed to be here," Raj replied. "They didn't reach," he added grimly.

"Yuh think de saikan…?"

"Well ah certainly doh think dey did abandon the kalinag," he said.

Just then the first figures of the saikan appeared through the trees.

"Careful now," Raj told Amrika, "Dey done fight Stickfighters already tonight. Dey will have learn how to deal wit we. Yuh hear meh? Dem is professionals, so yuh hadda be real fast and real precise. Doh do nothing fancy. We is ah distraction. Nothing more. Doh try to knock out people an thing. Jus keep dem in one place until the kalinag safely away."

Amrika nodded, nerves already pooling in her stomach. Raj gave her a grounding squeeze on her shoulder and then glided away in the night, moving to get to the other side of the men.

Amrika moved then too, shifting closer and trying to get a handle of how to move quietly in the forest. Urban areas were more her setting, streets and roofs and people too distracted to know that you had robbed them. Here there was growth everywhere, and the men were scanning the woods with a sharp intensity.

But she was a Stickfighter and Ierie's beat hummed under her feet, telling her where the saikan were. A sharp wind blew through the forest, riling leaves and tossing back her hair.

Protect the first born.

It was a whisper and a command and a request.

The wind blew again bringing with it the sharp scents of greenery, the acrid tang of smoke and even a light hint of ocean salt.

Protect the children of my womb.

The next time the wind blew, there was ozone crackling through the air and moisture lingering on the wind. Caribbean weather at its finest. Amrika smiled as the breeze picked up, ruffling trees and composures. She could feel Raj moving somewhere on her left, his Stickfighter's aura penetrating the night. She mirrored his movements, waiting for him to give the signal.

It came soon enough. One moment, Raj was creeping through the brush, the next he was exploding into motion. Bones cracked, the saikan cried out and men whipped around, firing rapidly into the spot where the skirmish had taken place. All they really managed to accomplish was pepper their own man with shots. Amrika winced even while she was moving, using Raj's distraction to attack the men at their backs.

She took a page out of Raj's book and didn't try to be nice about it. She whacked hard enough to shatter a man's upper arm and then spun down, stick arcing to crash into someone's lower leg, before making a full body lunge away from the spot, landing on her belly and rolling away.

It was just in time. Bullets lanced through the air where she'd been, one missing her by inches. She scrambled along her belly and then took cover behind a tree.

Raj used her distraction to attack again, this time taking down two men and rendering the rifle of the third unusable.

Amrika moved out from behind her tree, using her stick to give a man a short sharp blow under his chin. She took cover again in a second and then dashed away from tree to tree. She whirled behind another tree and almost got skewered by a sword. She blocked just in time to stop herself from being eviscerated. The sword flashed again and Amrika stepped back to avoid the blow. A bullet burned its way across her shoulders. She cried out and stumbled forward into the sword-wielding saikan. The man leered at her and stabbed forward. Amrika twisted to the side, letting the sword rip a bloody gash in her left arm, using her right elbow to whack him in the face. The man staggered back, giving her enough leverage to use her stick. He crashed down hard, unconscious.

But she'd been exposed for too long. Rifles shots smacked into the tree she was behind, sending splinters flying into the air. She shielded her face and dashed away. Someone came up parallel to her and she dropped flat onto her stomach again, rolling to the side until she found cover behind a small fern.

Somewhere behind her Raj was harassing the saikan but they had split up into two groups now, to hunt the both of them. She got a moment of reprieve as the men quickly reformed into larger groups to prevent the Stickfighters from picking them off. Amrika changed position again, managing to get far away enough that she could stop crawling and crouch behind a tree. She peeked out from behind her tree and eyed the men. They were grouped in a circle now, moving carefully, rifles pointing outwards in all directions and cutting off any area she might choose to attack from.

Amrika frowned, trying to figure out how to plan her next attack when a silhouette darted over her for a moment. Amrika snapped her head up in time to see a dark figure land in a tree. From where she crouched, she could see the sharp, silver claws on their feet and the feathered mask of the Bats. The Bat tilted its head at her, smiled and then tilted its head at the circle of men. Amrika grinned at the Bat and nodded. Without further ceremony, the Bat launched itself from the tree, soaring above the treeline. Amrika quickly moved forward, creeping up on the men until she was close enough. The Bat burst through the treetops a moment later, unleashing Ierie's song on the unsuspecting men below.

The circle of men was scattered, many of them being knocked flat. Amrika stepped into the midst of the confusion, whirling her stick on downed bodies, ensuring that they stayed down.

The Bat screamed into the night, the piercing sound a battle cry. Rifles fired in response to the cry and Amrika gave a savage grin.

"Leh we dance nah!" she thought fiercely.

CHAPTER 25

Khion twisted his head at the sound of the shrill cry that echoed through the night.

"De Bat," he said.

"Good," gasped Markus, "Dey go get some help."

Between them Jiang stumbled hard. Khion kept her upright but his bones screamed and his eyes watered. They were all dead men walking right now.

Up ahead, they could see the tail end of the evacuees. The kalinag were moving through the forest with the ease of long practice, not making a sound as they navigated the forest pathway. Another Stickfighter, Shawn, was guarding the rear. He glanced back at them sympathetically but didn't move from his position to help them. Khion was glad.

Behind them, the forest seemed to explode in a mess of sound; rifles and pistols were going off. Swords clanged through the night. The Bat screamed again, men cried out in rage, in pain, and beyond that there were the sounds of sticks thumping into things, sharp cracks of broken bone or snapped metal.

There was a quick shuffle of motion up ahead and then the crowd of kalinag were speeding up, running almost flat out, no longer trying to conserve strength. Khion looked at them dismally, knowing they would never catch up. Still he and Markus shuffled along behind them, Jiang now hanging limply between them, having passed out at some point in time.

Footsteps thumping behind them caused him to turn sharply.

"Is we!" Amrika hissed at him. She and Raj emerged from the gloom, bloody and scraped up, the Bat just behind them. None of them paused in their headlong flight, simply grabbing Khion, Markus and Jiang as they passed, hooking arms around their necks and hauling the three of them down the road.

"We geh the first wave but the second wave coming and dey done find one of de illusioned pathways," Raj informed them with a gasp. Khion didn't bother to reply. Though they were being as gentle as they could while hauling him along, his body was screaming with pain.

"We break down de rest of de illusions for dat path so they doh follow it to a safe place," the newest Stickfighter added. "Buh is too much for we now."

"Running is de best option fuh now," the Bat huffed out, struggling under Markus' weight.

"Wasn't arguing," Khion replied through gritted teeth.

With the three, less-injured persons dragging them along at a punishing speed, they soon caught up with the back of the column. Several of the kalinag noticed them and they quickly paused to hack several branches off a tree. A cloth appeared from somewhere and before Khion comprehended what had happened, a rough stretcher was on the ground and Raj was lowering Jiang's unconscious form onto it.

"Thank you," Raj told the two kalinag who hefted the stretcher up. They nodded in response and then ran off with it. Raj took Markus from the Bat who released him gratefully.

"What now?" asked the Bat.

"We hadda stop dem from coming on somehow," said the new Stickfighter. Her name was Amrika, Khion remembered belatedly.

"How?" asked Markus, voice strained. "I don't think we ever planned for this. The cannons were new." He hissed with pain as he was jostled by a tree branch.

"I doh know," said Amrika adjusting her grip on Marcus. "Buh we have to think of something."

"I told de other dark things, when I last left you all," the Bat said, "buh ah doh know if dey coming. I doh know how they reaching we if they are."

Search fire began again, slow methodical shots, designed to pierce the illusions that hid them from view.

"Well right now, we hadda move," Khion said decisively, ruthlessly pushing the pain away. "Or we go dead before we save anybody." The five of them quickly began to hobble behind the disappearing group of people.

The wind blew again, the weather really starting to pick up now. Amrika was glad. The sound of the wind and the trees would cover their trek through the forest. The illusions hid them from view but did not stop sound. If they made too much noise the saikan would easily figure out where they were.

Dark clouds began to scuttle over the sky, driven by the wind. What light that came from the sliver of moon dimmed and the forest itself seemed to mute with the expectation of rain. The wind lashed through the trees again, causing Amrika's cuts to sting and she held back a little gasp. Behind them the sounds of the saikan coming through the forest were getting louder. They were gaining on them and from the grim faces surrounding her, everybody knew.

Just then Amrika felt a familiar miasma of darkness rush over her. She froze and then said frantically

"Wha time is it?"

"What?" the other Stickfighters asked.

But the Bat said, "Midnight I think."

Amrika's eyes widened and then the night was broken by the haunting sound of the Midnight Robbers' whistle.

The Bat clamped his hands over his ears and Amrika said, "I tink de other dark things reach."

Kirish had literally just stepped foot in the town again, having returned from the governor's residence when a Dame Lorraine smacked into him.

"Dey need help in Chagna," she told him. "Four cannons almost there already. De Stickfighters go slow dem down but dey cah stop them."

"And ah suppose you wah we to help?" Surish interjected smoothly, the Robber's darkness in his voice daring her.

"Yes," she snapped, not caring. "We done soften some ah dem up for allyuh buh it go take time to work."

Kirish tilted his head in curiosity but then decided not to press.

"I will go," he said.

"What?" said Surish.

"Meh dear hot-headed sister in Chagna," he said lightly though his heart clenched in his chest. He scanned the area he was in and shrugged gracefully. It would be easy to steal a horse.

Protect the first born! Ierie's words tugged under his skin. Behind him Surish let out a harsh sigh at Ierie's demand and sped up to match his stride with Kirish's.

CHAPTER 26

Chagna was a smoking ruin. Kirish, Surish, Trevon and Sonny all pulled up to a stop at the sight of the village. There was silence as the four Midnight Robbers surveyed the scene. Surish tilted his head and eyed Kirish from under the brim of his hat.

"We thiefin they life too, tonight?"

"Nuh yet," Kirish replied after a considering pause. "Dey ain't shed kalinag blood yet."

"And if they have?" Trevon asked.

"Den we robbin all ah dem tonight," Kirish answered darkly.

They left the horses in what remained of Chagna, choosing to continue on foot in the thick forest. They moved fast, not knowing how far ahead the saikan were. They slinked around patches of downed men who were being treated by one or two of their comrades left behind to ensure they didn't die. They weren't after them just yet and anyways it looked like the Stickfighters had done enough damage to them already.

They heard the main group before they saw them, methodically firing shots into the greenery.

"Dey better not be executing people," Trevon said lowly.

"No," said Sonny. "Is searching fire, they looking for dem through the illusions."

"Good," said Kirish feeling relief flood him, "Dey ain't find them yet."

They calmly wove their way through the trees towards the unsuspecting men who were standing in a curved line now, backs to them.

Even as they watched, some of the men seemed to waver on their feet. Others shook their heads, as if trying to clear their vision. In a few moments they were staggering heavily, and one man even went tumbling down.

"What really happening here?" Sonny asked, lifting the brim of his hat as if to see better.

"Never trust a beautiful woman," Kirish replied. "Especially if she's a Dame Lorraine."

"Ahh," said the others in sudden understanding.

"It seemed like ah good time to hit dem, ent?" said Kirish grinning. He lifted his whistle to his mouth and blew hard, letting the Robber's dark miasma flood the night.

The men who were already drugged by the Dame Lorraines were easiest to steal from. The Robber's darkness numbed sober men's minds; drugged, they were no match for them. Not all the men were drugged of course, but enough were so as to a leave a hole in their defenses.

Since they hadn't seen any kalinag bodies on their way in, the Robbers didn't kill the men. Instead, they targeted the men's weaponry, snatching rifles, pistols and swords away from them in that second when the Robber's darkness numbed their brain so much, they just didn't think.

It wasn't easy. To keep the darkness that concentrated meant that they had less range. Which then meant that the people out of range were shooting at them. Surish lost his hat to a well-aimed rifle shot and thereafter proceeded to snatch the guns of a good chunk of men in pure rage alone, using his knife to keep the more skilled men at bay.

Kirish soon found himself pulling his knife as well, batting away swords and the occasional muzzle, even while damping the minds of the men around him. Trevon blew his whistle again, the sound sending men for cover even if they didn't know why and giving them a breather.

Before the men recovered from their sudden caution, the Dame Lorraines' poison went to work on a couple more men, dropping the number of the saikan and making their job easier. Sonny blew his whistle, sending men scuttling away and giving them much needed space to slide into their ranks, snatching their guns and swords.

All in all, it didn't actually take them very long. It was a lot of men, but there were four of them, all they had to do was literally snatch stuff out of the men's hands and the Dame Lorraine's poison had made quite a dent. Once they'd relieved all the men of their weapons, they vanished with a blast on their whistles. Their miasma of darkness numbed the minds of the men from noticing how they'd left.

"Where now?" asked Surish.

"I guess we better go dump these with the Stickfighters," said Kirish, hefting his cape which was acting as a sack for all the stolen weapons. The others shrugged, and they threaded their way through the trees in search of the hidden paths where the kalinag were.

The Midnight Robbers slid through the webs like they had known where they were the whole time. They did it without breaking any which was quite a feat, considering they had their capes slung over their shoulders like large sacks, bulging with pointy things.

The foremost of the Midnight Robbers eyed her and Amrika recognized her brother's visage from under his wide-brimmed hat.

"Robbers," said Raj in cautious greeting.

"Stickfighters," said Kirish in reply.

"You get meh message?" asked the Bat.

"We did," replied another Robber. Surish, if Amrika had to bet.

"Well we better get going," said Raj. "Dey still coming?"

"Nah," said Surish, "We thief all dey weapons and de Dame Lorraines do something to dem. They retreating to regroup. Ah doubt dey go try anything tonight."

"Good," said Khion. Amrika was alarmed at the weakness in his voice.

"We have to go an get somewhere allyuh could heal," she said to Khion, who merely grunted. He was swaying on his feet and the bruises looked worse than ever. Markus wasn't much better. Her eyes met Raj, who gave her a grim nod.

"Alright," said Raj, "De two ah allyuh getting on we back here."

The two injured Stickfighters promptly revived at those words and tried to protest but Kirish's cool voice cut through their protestations.

"Yuh slowing us down." The words held warning and both Khion and Markus glared at him but then grudgingly let Amrika and Raj carry them down the path. Crossing a Midnight Robber right now wasn't very smart, especially when he was right.

CHAPTER 27

It was somewhere around four in the morning when they finally reached the safe spot for the kalinag. It was a clearing, protected on three sides by thick forest and bordered by a river on the fourth. By the time Amrika and the others staggered in, the kalinag had already set up tents and built small fires. Markus and Khion had both been unconscious for almost two hours.

Upon seeing them, the kalinags hurried over and relieved them of their living burdens. Markus and Khion were carried over to where hammocks were strung up and laid into them. The kalinag elders quickly went to work on them, bringing out medicines made from various herbs and other things Amrika was far too tired to identify. In another hammock, Jiang lay, also unconscious, but she'd already been attended to. It looked like her rest was peaceful. Amrika felt a surge of relief thrum through her at the sight.

The Midnight Robbers sat on the edge of camp, their coats at their feet, while they peered out from under the brim of their hats at the proceedings. None of them looked like they'd walked for four hours in the forest; they didn't look tired in the slightest and they didn't seem to have collected any leaves or dirt on them. The kalinag, like the rest of the dark things, avoided them beyond initial greetings and thanks.

Amrika half nodded at her brother, drank a cup of some tea or the other and promptly fell asleep where she was.

When she awoke later that day, she found Kirish sitting next to her. He was using his hat to lazily fan mosquitoes away from her. When she stirred and sat up, he gave her a look.

"What?" she said, "I told you ah was coming. You knew what it meant."

He shook his head at her.

"You were hurt," he said in a not-quite change of subject.

Amrika inspected her arm where the saikan's sword had gashed it. There was only a thin slice left. She couldn't see the bullet wound on her back but Kirish said:

"It's almost healed."

"Good," said Amrika. "What happen last night? With de other villages?"

"We not sure yet. Aria was safe, I think. Buh ah not sure about Tarigua. De Moko Jumbies went there though, and the Dame Lorraines probably poison dem saikan there too."

"Wha happened to the Children of Anansi?"

Kirish frowned. "Someting happen to dem?"

"Dey didn't show up," said Amrika.

"Oh rite," said a new voice. It was one of the Robbers who had come in with her brother last night. He too had his hat off, slung on his back, and he wore a jovial grin. "Sonny," he said, holding out his hand.

"Amrika," she said taking it, even managing to smile despite the fact the Midnight Robbers in their full getup were strangely more terrifying in daylight than they were at night.

"So," said Sonny, "Word came dat de saikan shoot up the house of the Children of Anansi."

"What?" said Amrika, startled.

"Anybody living?" asked Kirish.

"Doh know," said Sonny. "Ah tink the Dame Lorraines trying an find out what going on."

"Good," said Kirish. "Well dey go find out if is anybody."

Amrika nodded in agreement and then noticed the hammocks in which Jiang, Khion and Markus lay.

"Ah going an see wha happen wit dem," she said standing, jerking her head to indicate who she meant. She dusted off her clothes and strode over to where her fellow Stickfighters lay.

They looked worse and not just because she was seeing them in daylight. But still, they were alive and that was more than she had thought she'd have when she had fallen asleep earlier. Out of them Jiang still looked the worst; pale and fragile, frightening blue-black splotches marring her skin, with nothing of the powerful fighter she'd been yesterday. Amrika swallowed, finding it surprisingly hard to see her in such a state.

"They're healing," Kirish said gently from behind her.

"What?" she asked.

"Ah know dey looking bad but healing does look worse than if it wasn't at dis point."

"So dey might be okay?"

"Is too early to tell," a kalinag woman replied, having heard her question. "Buh de Robber is correct. Dey healing. Is de only reason any of dem survive to de camp."

"Thanks for yuh help," Amrika said to the kalinag who waved it off with a motherly hand.

"Allyuh helping we. Allyuh putting allyuh self in a lot ah risk for we. This is the least we could do. Now doh worry 'bout dem. Dem strong. If dey could make it, dey go make it. You go an geh something to eat before you fall down. You too, Robber." With that, she strode off leaving Amrika and Kirish giving each other slight grins at her no-nonsense manner.

"Come leh we go eat," Amrika said. "I starving."

"Okay chile," said Sadika, "We goin in town buh we cah go as weself ok?"

"How we doing dat?" asked Reshma. She looked like she was about to cry. Sadika didn't blame her. It had been a trying night.

"I'll teach you," Sadika told her gently. "I jus need you to be a big girl for a lil bit more okay?"

Reshma's lower lip trembled but she nodded.

"Good girl," said Sadika. She pulled out a little ball of spider web and carefully netted some over her face. Then she put a spiral of the stuff from her shoulders all the way down to the edge of her dress. She did the same thing for Reshma.

"Now," said Sadika, "Spiders are tricksters. They can weave a web of lies as easily as they can weave a normal web. What we're going to do next, is ah trick. We're going to trick people into thinking we look different."

"How?" asked Reshma scrunching up her face underneath the spider webs.

"Dais what the webs are for," Sadika told her. "You and I are Children of Anansi, brethren of spiders and one of the dark things of Ierie, just like the Moko Jumbies. Okay? So just like how yuh climb down the house yesterday, yuh going an use these webs to make ah illusion."

"Ah what?"

"Ah picture," said Sadika, "A picture on top of your face. Just imagine what yuh want to look like and draw it on the webs."

Reshma closed her eyes and scrunched up her face as she tried hard, but nothing happened. She opened her eyes, realized that nothing had changed and then closed them back and tried again. She even tried to use her hand to physically draw on the webs when it didn't work and Sadika had to hurriedly pull her fingers away from her face.

"Okay," said Sadika, "Let's try this a different way. Um, ink. Picture your thoughts like ink, filling the webs and as the ink pours over your face, it forms the image you want."

Reshma gave her the classic child look that plainly said, 'You're going over my head.'

Sadika threw up her hands in despair.

"Can't you do it?" Reshma asked.

"Yes," said Sadika, "but you need to learn in case we get separated."

Reshma startled at that, hands reaching out and gripping Sadika's dress tightly.

"We aren't going to be," said Sadika soothingly, "But this is just in case. Yuh need to learn and I'm sorry yuh hadda learn so fast buh yuh hadda try chile."

Reshma nodded.

"Okay. So this time, just picture the image you want. Pretend it's a mask made of ink, hanging over your face. Then just splash the ink on your face and let it stick to webs."

Reshma nodded and closed her eyes again. After a moment, she made a little jerking back motion, like she'd actually been splashed with something and for a second, an illusion flickered but disappeared.

"Good!" said Sadika. "You almost got it! Try again!"

Reshma grinned in delight and closed her eyes again.

An hour later, a plain boerin woman with an unusually beautiful boerin child entered the town. Sadika and Reshma both held illusions over their clothes which were grass-stained and smeared with dirt, to prevent unwanted questions. Sadika would have preferred if Reshma had chosen a plain face to go with their plain clothes but had been unable to persuade the child to do so.

"Whey we going?" asked Reshma in an undertone.

"To ah friend," said Sadika. "Hopefully she go hide we."

"And if she don't?"

"Well," said Sadika, "Ah go hadda come up with a new plan."

Reshma gave her a look that was still perfectly understandable despite the foreign face that wore it.

"Hush you," said Sadika.

She tugged the child into the first alley way they came into and then carefully threaded her way through the back street until she came upon a vividly beautiful woman, just about to close her door behind her.

"Miss!" called out Sadika.

The woman paused, eyed Sadika and then said. "What yuh want?"

Sadika smiled and went up to the door. "Ma-dame," she said pointedly.

The woman's expression cooled even as a smile bloomed on her face. "Yes?"

"If yuh doh mind, can we geh some water?"

"And who asking?" asked the Dame Lorraine.

"Jus two loss chirren," Sadika replied smoothly.

The woman's eyes widened and then she said, "Come in. Fas!"

Sadika quickly ushered Reshma in and stepped through the doorway. The Dame Lorraine closed it sharply behind them.

"Anansi?" she asked.

"Yes," said Sadika, letting the illusion drop for a moment before pulling it back up.

"Yuh survive?"

"Yes. But dey take meh father."

"Oh shucks," said the Dame Lorraine. She quickly hustled around the house and brought them back cups of water. Reshma gulped hers down gratefully and Sadika had to restrain herself from doing the same.

"Yuh alright chile?" asked the Dame Lorraine. "Yuh want to sit down?" Reshma nodded wearily. The Dame Lorraine guided her to a comfy chair and settled her down there.

"I'm Sheryl," the Dame Lorraine introduced herself.

"Sadika," said Sadika. "Thank you. Dais Reshma over there." Reshma gave a sleepy wave.

"Wha happen? We hear de saikan did attack allyuh house. We was trying to find out if any ah allyuh survive."

"We all alive," said Sadika tiredly. "But dey capture meh father. Ah doh know how dey find we. We geh way by climbing out ah window. But Sheryl, dey definitely knew what it was we could do."

"Well we wasn't trying for subtle," said Sheryl dryly. Sadika gave a little shrug of agreement.

"True."

"What yuh going an do now?"

"Ah going by Eliza," said Sadika.

The Dame Lorraine's eyebrows lifted. "Eliza? But she right next to where de saikan living. Dem is high class jotlin."

"Exactly," said Sadika. "No saikan would expect to find us there."

"Risky, is what I say," Sheryl told her.

Sadika shrugged. "Ah have meh reasons. Besides, the boerin part of town is not going an be safe at all. Watch just now they go come and lock it down. Speaking of, what happened with de villages? From what ah see dis morning, they didn't get de kalinag buh…"

"They didn't," said Sheryl, "All the villages got away but the saikan definitely know we out there and they realize we protecting them."

"What you think bout dat?"

"I think," said Sheryl, "We have given dem reason to fraid and dey will. Which means saikan will do what they do to things dey fraid. They go try and kill all ah we. Dey done start with you. We dark things hadda watch we backs. But even if we do, they go take it out on the boerin." Her mouth twisted unhappily.

Sadika understood. They were dark things, but they were also born out of the boerin. Some of the boerin were their friends. Some of them were family.

"They'll be fine," said Sadika. "We're the dark things remember? We doh like when people touch we stuff."

Sheryl laughed. "We are rather possessive on occasion, aren't we?"

"Specially when is the saikan who tryin to take we stuff," Sadika agreed.

CHAPTER 28

Tamara scrubbed at the clothes in the basin.

"If yuh rub dem dat hard they going an rip," said her mother, "And den people wouldn't pay we."

"Sorry," Tamara muttered.

Her mother sighed. "Wha wrong chile?"

Tamara pushed the clothes back in the tub and sighed herself.

"Last night."

"Oh chile," her mother said. "Look…"

"People died," Tamara interrupted. "Vishal and I killed people. Four of our people are dead. And people... the ones who lived? They were suffering. I never seen anybody burn alive before and I didn't ever want to! The ships… We did make sure everybody did get off before we blow them up. We even push them away to save the docks. But last night we killed people."

"Last night you killed murderers," her mother interjected. "Now I know it doesn't really make yuh feel better, but those men were mercenaries, Tammy. Dey were hired to come and kill de kalinag. Dey had no other purpose than to kill innocent people okay? Out of all the people yuh could have killed, dey was probably de best. You know yuh had to choose between the men and de kalinag and yuh know yuh had to save the kalinag."

"I wish I didn't have to choose!" Tamara said bitterly. "Why? Ierie didn't care when de saikan came and killed kalinag for de first time. Ierie didn't care when dey enslaved dem. Why does Ierie care now?"

"Because in truth, little of the kalinag were killed in the initial altercation and little of the population were enslaved. It was disease dat kill dem out. If they had slaughtered all ah dem with dey own hands, Ierie would have gotten rid of the saikan a long time ago. Ierie cares now because there are so little of dem left."

Her mother sat down next to her and pulled Tamara's head against her shoulder. "If Ierie had cared you would have grown up in the lands we came from. You would have never known what it was like to smell the ocean, you would have never taken flight or hear Ierie's song. If Ierie had killed everyone for killing the firstborn the first time, there would have never been any children of Ierie's heart. There wouldn't have been any dark things, any boerin. You would have grown up in a place that was definitely cultured and well-worn by the feet of men. You and me, we live in a land that isn't ruled by people. Our home rules itself and it's not human and it asked you to do something very, very difficult. And you have every right to be angry if you want. But Tamara, those men were coming to kill its children. If anybody was coming to kill you I would have slaughtered anybody who tried. I would do anything to keep you safe. Those saikan? If they hadn't come to kill innocent people, women, little children, then you wouldn't have had to do what you did. You're right, that Ierie didn't kill them de first time they shed kalinag blood, but it will kill them if they try to shed de last of it."

She took Tamara's face in her hands. "You may have killed people Tamara, but you did it to save lives. You can feel pain for that but never regret it."

"Ah not sure ah could do that," Tamara said hoarsely.

"Well at least doh let it eat you up inside," her mother said.

Tamara gave a grudging smile. "Maybe I could do dat."

Jamal had never been so happy to get home.

"What happened? asked Jessica. She sounded very worried.

"Tarigua ok," Jamal said, before collapsing on his bed. He was tired in way he had never been before.

"Jamal get up!" said Jessica. "Tell me what happened. No one else has come back home yet!"

"Saikan came," said Jamal. "We stopped them. Us and de Stickfighters. De village gone though. De kalinag in de bush hiding. Buh we stopped dem. Ah think de Dame Lorraines did do something to de men. De other villages okay?"

"Yes," said Jessica. "But you have to go to work."

"Is ten in de morning," said Jamal. "De saikan gone to a meeting 'bout last night. Dey ain't going an notice I wasn't there."

"And if dey do?"

"Den ah was sick. With... something."

"That's a terrible lie," said Jessica.

"Meh ears ringing," Jamal groaned. "Cannons are loud!"

"No but really, what going an happen now?"

"Now we wait," said Jamal. "Buh brace yuhself. Dey know something strange but ah don't think de saikan will want to quite accept it yet. They go blame ordinary people. They go blame the boerin," he added sleepily.

"But the dark things are from the boerin," said Jessica.

"Yeah," said Jamal, "But we can defend ourselves. De boerin can't."

"I mean, if dey try and torture people to talk, de dark things can handle it better. De boerin can't."

"Torture?" asked Jessica in surprise.

"What?" said Jamal. "Yuh really think after spending all dis money on men and weapons dey going an take being set back so easily? Dey doing this to kill out a civilization. Yuh think dey go be bothered by a lil bit ah torture to find out how we doing wha we doing and where we have de kalinag?"

"Torture is a lot more deliberate than shooting someone," said Jessica in a small voice.

"Yuh doh destroy a people suddenly," said Jamal, falling asleep. "Yuh have to plan it, carefully. I've been to some ah dey meetings Jess. They plan this real careful." He settled down to sleep adding one last thing. "Doh worry, we nuh going an leave allyuh alone."

CHAPTER 29

"What happened!" yelled the governor.

"Well sir," said one of the men leading the attack against the villages, "I told you…"

"I don't want stories!" snapped the governor. "I want facts." He straightened his coat and regained a little more composure. "Now surely one of you men can explain what really happened."

Lawrence Kit said with a calmness he was not feeling on the inside,

"We have lost almost a third of our men. Around a third of our weapons and ammunition and one of twelve cannons, bought for the purpose, remain. A quarter of the remaining men are ill, struck down by some illness or poison."

"And how did this occur?"

"They had superior fighters and either we accept they had some sort of illusion-creating capabilities, or that they had some very powerful hallucinogen released into the forest somehow."

"This drug, it would explain this?" asked the governor, clearly latching onto something that would make sense.

Lawrence Kit wanted to tell him that it wouldn't, that even hallucinations were not solid enough to carry torches into the sky and drop them on gunpowder. But telling the mayor that wouldn't suit his agenda. Besides, the mayor would insist the men had imagined it and really someone had just snuck right in and lit the stores afire. Lawrence didn't care. He wanted to tear these creatures apart for the humiliation they had caused him to suffer a second time in a row, for the blow they had dealt to his professional pride. And to top it all off, the woman, the spider, hadn't even been caught. But, but, he had her father. And daughters do love their fathers so. The spider would come to him and he would have her in a trap and from them he would tear the plans of these creatures, these fighters who could fly, recover from bullet wounds far, far too fast and steal a gun straight out your hand without you knowing they were ever there.

"Yes governor," said Lawrence Kit, "This drug would explain it. We would take precautions against it for the next attack. But we'll need more men to supplement the ones we lost."

Lord Ainsley was seething from the news. The mercenaries had not managed to rid the land of its disgusting inhabitants, failing to clear the area for its betters. Now this venture was being strung out and Ainsley would have to pump more capital into this if he didn't want to back out. But if he did back out, he would gain nothing. The governor would simply thank him for his contribution in the name of the Motherland and gift him with nothing in exchange. He stood to lose a lot of money and most importantly, influence, if this did not pan out.

He needed more money, but his trusted avenues for getting cash quickly and putting together favours were also being shut down. Many men on whom he had destructive information were turning their backs on him, not heeding his threats. One had even laughed in his face when he threatened to show his proof of a very sordid business scandal.

Ainsley was infuriated and puzzled. Never before had blackmail failed him when he had needed favours or cash. He couldn't understand why this was happening now.

He stormed into his house and went up into his study, tearing at his floor safe. He opened the safe and stared inside in disbelief. None of his documents that facilitated his habit of blackmail were there. He blinked in shock and then rage roared up in him.

Someone had stolen from him! Someone had given his victims back their freedom. No doubt his documents had already been burned by their prospective owners. Either one of his saikan enemies... but no. Not that they wouldn't have given the chance but if they had stolen the documents, they wouldn't have given them back to everyone. No, they would have kept the documents for themselves, so they could blackmail the others. No, this was the work of someone else. As he stared down into his empty safe, the pieces came together.

Ainsley needed the documents for money to kill the kalinag. Therefore, the people who were doing this, the impossible stories frightened mercenaries were jabbing about, had done this. The boerin had done this. The stupid, mindless creatures had dared to cross him, dared to take what was his and make a fool of him. Ainsley would remind them why the saikan ruled and why the boerin obeyed them.

CHAPTER 30

Sadika slipped up to the back door of the large house and knocked. When the door opened, she triggered her illusions to make it look like no one was there. The confused servant peered around and then shook her head and made to close the door. Sadika gently yanked the door from her hand and the woman made a surprised noise and lunged for the door. Sadika quickly slipped in through the opening and dashed down the hallway lest the woman see her when she came back in.

It took some maneuvering to avoid all the people in the house but eventually Sadika managed to make it to Eliza's room. She slipped through the door and shut it behind her.

"Who is it?" asked Eliza, half-angry at the forward intruder.

"Eliza, it's me," said Sadika quickly.

There was a pause and then Eliza said, "What are you doing here?"

"Did you hear?"

"I heard," Eliza replied shortly. "What are you doing here though? This is the last place you should be."

"Exactly," said Sadika.

"No, not 'exactly'," snapped Eliza.

"Yes," refuted Sadika. "Look it have no one else I trust well enough for this and de boerin section will be searched. I have my niece with me Eliza. Please."

Eliza looked away and then back and sighed. "Alright. Alright. But you have to stay low. The people who work here are boerin too, so they won't talk."

"Your parents?"

"Know what I am," she said, "They won't sell either of us out. Go get your niece."

Sadika nodded and turned to the door. She paused before she stepped out and said, "Thank you."

Eliza gave her a wry smile. "What are friends for?"

The sounds of commotion filtered into Jamal's mind and woke him from his well-earned sleep.

"Wha happening?" he asked groggily.

"Soldiers," said Jessica. "They gathering around the boerin section."

Jamal sat up quickly, all traces of sleep abandoning him. "What?"

He scrambled over to a window and saw that Jessica was right. Soldiers were gathering around the boerin village that adjoined the town. He studied the approaching figures and then gave a sigh of relief.

"Proclamation," he said. He quickly ran back to his room and got dressed and then hurried outside to hear what the proclamation was.

When a suitable crowd had gathered, the speaker stood in front of them, opened his little scroll and began to read aloud in a carrying voice.

"By order of the governor of Port of Gold, protector of Ierie under the monarchs of the Motherland, all boerin class members are hereby ordered to give up any information on the criminals who have destroyed saikan life and stolen saikan property. The perpetrators are ordered to give themselves up to the justice of the saikan courts to pay for their crimes against the Motherland. Persons failing to comply will be punished for obstructing justice.

Until the perpetrators are caught, the boerin class of Ierie will be restricted in their movements. The town of Port of Gold is off-limits to any boerin class member. Any boerin class member found outside their homes after the hour of seven o'clock will be arrested. So orders the governor."

The speaker stepped back, ignoring the loud protests of the boerin and the soldiers stepped forward. They pushed back the protesting boerin and quickly set up a line between the village and the town area and marched off to bar the other main exits of the village.

Sadika looked out of Eliza's window at the soldiers surrounding the boerin section in the distance.

"Do dey really think that de boerin will tell anything?" asked Sadika.

"As far as they know the boerin knows what's going on. Also, they've cut off the boerin from the town. Food the boerin has in supply, but things like medication…" Eliza trailed off.

"I'm curious as to how this is going to work," said Sadika. "Many boerin work for the saikan."

Eliza snorted. "They'll let them in on some system or the other. The saikan would never stoop to getting their hands dirtied with menial work."

"One ting for sure," said Sadika, "Our jobs jus get harder."

"Much harder," said Eliza.

Protect the first born!!

"What now?" asked Jessica.

"Now," said Jamal, "We be real careful."

"Is dad okay?" She asked.

"As far as I know," Jamal told her. "He was in Aria and they din geh attack dere so he should be good."

Jessica nodded.

"How are you going to get out de village?"

Jamal smiled softly. "We have we ways. Doh worry chile. Besides, the saikan cah cut we off entirely. Dey too dependent on the boerin."

"And the kalinag?"

"They have people dere with them," said Jamal. "And they're hidden. They're fine."

"You don't think the saikan will try to kill them again?"

"Of course they will," said Jamal. "But they in de forest and ah doh think the saikan realize just how at home in de forest the kalinag are.

But they have the dark things protecting them and we have some tricks up we sleeves."

"If those tricks don't work, would the kalinag use their power?"

"Probably," said Jamal. He smiled at his adopted sister. "Doh worry. It won't come to that."

"Um," said Jessica. "A lot of terrible things are happening. The whole situation seems to be getting worse. I'm worried and I know a lot of other people are too."

"We know it woulda be worse," said Jamal shrugging.

"What?" said Jessica.

"Yeah. Yuh didn't think it would geh worse? We going against the saikan. We actively preventing dem from getting something dey want. Dey going an hit back hard because ah dat. We knew, but we going an win anyway. We have to."

CHAPTER 31

It was quiet for a few days. Amrika stayed with the kalinag in their hiding spot while they waited for the next development of the saikan's plans. Her brother and the other Midnight Robbers had left the morning after the attack, heading back to the town to keep up appearances. He had given her a fond but firm 'Be careful!' before slipping off with the others.

The Bats had brought them news of the governor's proclamation but also the news that boerin were being allowed in to work so long as they received letters of allowance from their employers. The boerin section was still locked down, leaving all the boerin feeling antsy.

On the brighter side, Khion, Markus and Jiang were all still alive and well on the mend. Whatever herbs and medication the kalinag had applied had saved their lives. None of them were quite awake yet, rising to consciousness only for a few moments, but she and the other Stickfighters were assured that they'd be okay.

She was profoundly grateful. She had tried to imagine telling Markus' large, extended family that he'd died and the thought had made her sick to her stomach. She didn't know Khion but she imagined that he had family that were no doubt worrying about him. Jiang, she knew, had a little sister. The thought of someone telling her that Kirish was dead was world-shattering. She had not wanted to shatter Jiang's sister's world.

She'd spent the last few days patrolling and being given a crash course in all things Stickfighter. Raj and the others quickly built on whatever training Markus and Jiang had given her, each one bringing their own area of expertise. It wasn't easy, the training, but she stuck it through because she knew very vividly now, how it would save her life.

They were all on edge, because they knew the saikan would attack again and they had no idea when.

Kirish crouched on the roof inside the boerin section, careful not to let the roof creak or to step on any of the termite-eaten parts of it. A squadron of soldiers marched down the street looking for people who were breaking the curfew. Kirish calmly laid down flat on the roof until they passed and then got up again.

A soft whisper of sound had alerted him to the presence of one of his fellow Robbers. Trevon crouched next to him.

"Dis messing up some ah we plans," Trevon murmured. "The Dame Lorraines cah do nothing."

Kirish said nothing, simply tilting his head as he eyed the soldiers. A flicker of motion across the road caught his eye and he looked to see a Jab Jab grinning at him from the space between the houses before melting back into the darkness.

"Tomorrow will be the fifth day since de proclamation," Kirish said. "That will be long enough for the governor to get impatient."

"And then?" asked Trevon.

"Then he'll come for the boerin," Kirish said.

"Wouldn't he go for de kalinag?" asked Trevon.

Kirish shook his head. "Nah. Whoever we is, we disturb dem de first time. Dey go come for the boerin. Threaten them to stop we from helping de kalinag when dey go fuh dem again." He shrugged. "Is a good strategy," he acknowledged. "An if any of dem sell we out, all fuh de better."

"Wha 'bout de Child of Anansi, de one dey capture?" Trevon asked. "Are we stealing him out?"

Kirish smiled. "Actually de Jab Jabs asked to do it. I tink dey like de old man."

"Where granpa?" Reshma asked Sadika as she combed the child's hair before she went to bed.

"The saikan took him to a jail," Sadika said calmly.

"Why?" asked Reshma.

"Because they doh like him," she said simply. "Dey fraid what we can do."

"Are dey going to let him go?" Reshma asked.

"Yes," said Sadika calmly. She carefully failed to add that it was going to be entirely involuntary.

"When asked Reshma.

"Soon," Sadika told her. "Soon."

"You can't get him out by yourself," Eliza told her when Reshma had left the room.

"I know," said Sadika. "I have help. Dey volunteered."

Eliza cocked her head at her inquisitively. "Robbers?"

Sadika smiled. "Actually, no."

Eliza blinked and then said. "Jab Jabs?"

"I think daddy made an impression on dem," said Sadika, shrugging.

"Huh," said Eliza. Then after a pause she added. "Yuh need any help?"

Sadika blinked and then smiled. "I would love your help."

Chapter 32

The saikan marched into the boerin section of town around ten in the morning. There was no speaker this morning, just a captain and extra men.

"Come round!" the captain ordered. When people reluctantly left their work and shuffled around the men in the clearing that could, possibly, pass for a village square, the captain said coldly:

"The governor gave an order for the persons involved in the crimes committed against the saikan to step up. Failing that, those with information of these criminals were supposed to come. It has been four days and none of you have obeyed the governor's orders. I am here to ask again. Any of you involved in the crimes step up now. Anyone with information step up now."

When after ten minutes no one in the fidgeting crowd moved, the captain's eyes narrowed.

"Very well," he said. "I will find out myself."

Tamara and Vishal, both of whom had been hidden in the back of the crowd, watched in surprise and horror as the captain's men pulled a random man from the crowd. When the people went to protect him, a line of soldiers aimed their guns at them. The people in front of the crowd shrank back.

Two of the captain's men held the boerin man between them while a third jammed the stock of his rifle into the man's stomach. The crowd gasped and instinctively tried to move forward again but were stopped by a reminder of the rifles pointed at them.

The third soldier hit the man a few more times, ignoring the cries of the crowd, and then the captain walked up to the poor man. He lifted the man's chin and said calmly,

"Who are the perpetrators?"

"I doh know!" the man groaned out.

"Hmm," said the captain. He backhanded the man brutally and then grabbed his chin and yanked his head to face him.

"Who are the perpetrators?"

"Ah doh know!" the man wailed.

He earned another hit with the rifle's butt, this time across his face. Blood splattered from a broken nose. His wife in the crowd cried out and finally broke into tears, one of her neighbours holding onto her.

Tamara realized that she was shaking but not with fear. She was shaking with anger. Vishal had alternatively gone very calm and still. He was a cool statue of hatred and rage.

At the next hit, she reached out and grabbed Vishal's hand. Her brother squeezed her hand back hard enough to make it hurt but she didn't care. She was probably squeezing him just as hard.

"He has children," she said, voice trembling with suppressed rage. "They will kill him."

"Not yet," said a new voice. The man was standing next to her, eyeing the beating and questioning, with an aura that was almost detached. Tamara wanted to hit him for appearing so aloof from the situation.

"They go keep him alive 'cause it'll make people more willing to come forward with information. Or," he added warningly, "To give themselves up to free him."

He knew who they were, she suddenly realized. Or at any rate, he knew what they were.

"He won't survive," she said tightly, looking at the man who was more bloody mess than human at this stage.

"He will," said the man. "It just looking worse than it is. But," he tilted sideways towards her, whispering in her ear, "If you and yuh brother up fuh a rescue mission tonight, I'm pretty good at stealing things." The darkness that flooded his voice in the last few words told her what he was. Midnight Robber.

She leaned back startled and then felt Vishal squeeze her hand.

'Yes' the squeeze said.

Up ahead the soldiers tied the man to a pole they had brought and stuck in the ground. The man slumped on his knees, hands tied to the pole in front of him. His wife wailed from the crowd, being held back by neighbors and friends.

Tamara turned and smiled grimly at the Midnight Robber.

"See you tonight," she said.

"Dis is a trap ent?" said the girl twin.

"Allyuh have names?" Kirish asked instead of answering her. "I cah keep calling allyuh girl twin and boy twin."

Both Bats who were lying on the roof next to him turned their heads to look at him. Granted he couldn't actually see much of their faces, the mask they wore making that difficult, but even so he was pretty sure he knew what the expression was.

"Tamara," said the girl.

"Vishal," said the boy.

"Kirish," he said.

"Is it a trap, Robber?" Vishal asked.

"Probably," said Kirish. He grinned at them, face mostly shadowed by his hat so all they could see was the grin. "Leh we go spring it nah?"

"What dey doin?" asked Shamika from the roof they lay on. She was looking at the three figures which were lying on the roof on the street across from them. One of the figures, lifted its head and smiled at them.

The hat gave it away.

"Midnight Robber," said Shamika.

"Guess we is not de only ones who came to rescue," Jamal said.

"No," said Shamika, still looking at the Midnight Robber, who pointedly turned his head to another alleyway. He watched as she strained to see something and caught a glimpse of motion. "Ah doh think we are."

"Dere's a lot ah soldiers hidden out in between the houses," said Jamal. "Is ah trap I think."

"But fuh who?" said Shamika. She looked at him. "Ah doh think soldiers is all it have hidden in dem spaces between de house an dem."

Jamal blinked at her, then mentally ran down all who was likely to be lurking in alleyways and felt profoundly sorry for the soldiers who hid there. There were two sets of dark things that might frequent an alley: Dame Lorraines and Jab Jabs.

"Dis going an be interesting," said Shamika. Jamal couldn't help but agree. It certainly was going to be.

Kirish waited for the Dame Lorraines and Jab Jabs to clear the alleyway of the soldiers. He had to admit, that even for him, it was pretty scary how silently they had done it. When the alleyways were clear, he nodded to the two figures lying across the roof from him. From the long bundles resting next to them on the roof he had surmised that they were Moko Jumbies and therefore, a perfect distraction for the ring of guards who were surrounding the man.

The two figures carefully slid backwards, grabbing their stilts, and went to sit on the opposite side of the roof from the street. They were busy for a few moments, strapping their stilts on, but then he saw the change, the way their bodies reformed into the lanky shapes of the Moko Jumbies even though they were still sitting. Beside him he heard the two Bats give little intakes of breath, clearly never having seen a Moko Jumbie change before.

The two Jumbies twisted to face him and gave a solemn nod. They were ready.

"Be ready," he said to the Bats, "Allyuh gehing him outta here okay?"

The twin nodded somberly and he could see the way they crouched a little, muscles tensing as they prepared for a fast dive off the roof.

Kirish darted looks to ensure that Surish and Trevon were where they were supposed to be and then nodded to the two Moko Jumbies.

The jumbies simply stood, tall figures that just rose out of the darkness, towering over everyone. The saikan didn't fail to see them. The men yelled in surprise and aimed their rifles at them. Before they could shoot, the Moko Jumbies hit them with all their evil deeds.

Kirish didn't have to signal Surish and Trevon. The Robbers' dark miasma flooded the area and dampened the mind of the men who were also locked in a recital of their evil deeds. It was child's play to free the man. He dragged the man out of the circle of guards and signalled to the Bats who quickly swooped off the roof and picked up the man between them. With a powerful flap of their wings, they were gone, heading off into the night with their precious cargo. The Moko Jumbies let up and the Robbers waited for a few moments to let them get away before letting out a shrill blast on their whistles.

The blast sent the men cowering even as it cleared their minds. After a few moments, there were confused shouts. Soldiers ran around trying to find out where their prisoner was and what happened to the men who were supposed to ambush any rescuers. Kirish looked at the confused mass of men below him and laughed.

CHAPTER 33

"What?" said the governor softly.

The captain swallowed hard. "The prisoner escaped," he said. "It appears he was rescued."

"It was my understanding that you laid a trap for these possible rescuers," said the governor, still very calm.

"We did," said the captain. "But all the men were all incapacitated by the, uh, rescuers. Clearly, they were more organized and dangerous than we anticipated. It won't happen again."

"Get out," said the governor.

"Sir?"

"Get out!" snapped the governor. The captain turned and hurriedly left.

"Problems my dear governor?" asked Lord Ainsley from where he rested against the doorjamb.

The governor looked up, eyes hooded. "You do not want to trifle with me today Ainsley," he warned.

"Of course not," said Ainsley. "I'm here to help you."

"Help?" said the governor disbelievingly. "These boerin have somehow concocted a drug that meddles with the minds of my soldiers. They've struck against my men and won. I dislike the discontent and malicious seeds of revolution that these petty victories have sown."

"Well, instead of beating up one poor fool a day, why not a drug for a drug?" said Ainsley.

"What?" asked the governor.

"The boerin draw their water from a well outside their section. I have in my possession a… certain substance. It incapacitates but it does so over a couple of days and there's an antidote. Surely if their brats lie dying, they will be motivated to give up their brethren? And if they don't, well, you've incapacitated your enemies anyway. Then you can rid the land of the kalinag once and for all and the boerin will know your power."

The governor stared at him and then said coolly. "The boerin are still citizens of Ierie and under my rule, Lord Ainsley. The Motherland expects that I protect all those under my care. Incapacitating my workforce for days is also not a plan I intend to be a part of until drastic measures are really called for."

"And what of the kalinag? You'd rid the land of them but not of the boerin?"

"The kalinag do not belong to the Motherland, the boerin do. I hold those things belonging to the monarchy and use them as the monarchy will. The kalinag do not belong to the Motherland and never will. Good day, Lord Ainsley."

Ainsley gave the governor a cool look but knew when not to press his luck. "Good day Governor. You know where to find me."

Tamara winced as soldiers ripped through the houses of the boerin searching for the missing man. Failing to find him, they dragged random persons into the street and beat them.

"Who are the criminals!" roared the captain from the day before. He obviously didn't like having his prisoner rescued. "Who rescued the man and where is he? Answer me!"

The boerin cowered but no one replied. Those who would have said something clearly knew nothing and those who did wouldn't sell out their families. The dark things were born out of them after all. It still ached Tamara to see the violence done on her neighbours.

"Very well then," said the Captain. "Every hour that the criminals do not come forward, one of your innocents will pay the price."

Soldiers aimed at the crowd which had instantly begun to protest. The people backed away.

"Remember," said the captain. "I am not doing this to you. It is you who have chosen your own fates. All you have to do is give up the people who have broken the law to rightfully receive their punishment."

Tamara turned away, knowing her face would give away too much.

"Doh do anything chupid," said a familiar voice.

Tamara looked up to find Kirish next to her.

"They going an hurt them," she said in a fierce whisper.

"And we go save them if we can buh if not we have to leave dem."

"What!" she hissed.

"What going an happen if the kalinag die?" he asked harshly, and it was the first bit of real emotion he had shown. "We all go dead," he answered his question. "Yuh have to remember what at stake here."

"I know de rest of de dark things doh really care," said Tamara angrily. "You all steal from and scare the boerin just like you do to de jotlin and the saikan. But we born from the boerin. And we Bats never hurt them. I cah just let dem suffer like this."

"So wha yuh go do? Rescue them by yuhself? Either you go dead or yuh go hadda kill people to get out."

"I killed for kalinag," Tamara said, "You think I can't kill for boerin?"

"I think you shouldn't kill at all. You said it yourself. Killing isn't a Bat's temperament." He leaned towards her. "That belongs to other dark things." His voice made her shiver. "And even so, we weren't made to be killers. Not you, not me, not even de Jab Jab. We were made as another layer of defense for Ierie. Every dark thing knows it. We're the land's weapons and dais why Ierie call we to protect the kalinag."

"Weapons kill," pointed out Tamara.

"You doh want to kill."

Tamara's jaw trembled. "I don't," she allowed. "But I doh want to see dem like this."

"Den be a shield," Kirish told her, gripping her arm lightly. "But also understand, that sometimes there are sacrifices yuh have to make, that all ah we have to make. I was born out of the boerin too. Eventually all our families could end up in de han ah de soldiers. Buh if we want to save dem, we have to make sure Ierie doh kill dem too."

Tamara hesitated and then nodded slowly.

The Midnight Robber gave her a surprisingly kind smile and then said, "Besides, watch carefully. The boerin are already choosing who gets taken, so the people who can bear it best gets hurt."

Tamara whipped her head around and sure enough, there were subtle signals given by the men to each other. Then one of the boerin looked straight at her and gave a little nod.

'We have this,' it said.

Tamara wanted to cry.

"Dey braver than we," she said softly.

Kirish smiled. "True."

Jamal watched the boerin being captured and beaten by the hour. So far none of the dark things had been captured, the boerin men's strategy working out. Still, it could only last so long. They would have to stage another rescue sometime soon. But if they did, Jamal knew the saikan would up the ante. If beating didn't work then as a last resort they would threaten to kill and that, that they couldn't allow.

"Can you break him out?" asked Eliza. Sadika looked up from where she was mending clothes with Eliza.

"Maybe," she said. "They doh have him in ah official jail. Is ah dungeon I guess, under somebody house. Which really scary when yuh think about de fact dat they have ah dungeon under dey house."

Eliza conceded her point. "How many people are guarding him?"

"About ten," said Sadika. "But that's all we could see from the outside. May have more on de inside."

"I see," said Eliza. "Yuh need inside information then?"

"Can you get that?" Sadika asked.

Eliza smiled. "I think I could manage."

"Look!" an excited child's voice interrupted them. When both Sadika and Eliza looked it was to see a tiny child's figure but wearing an incredibly old face.

"I made an old lady face!" Reshma said happily. Sadika snickered.

"Yes, you did,' she said amused. "You're getting better." Reshma grinned and the illusion flickered and disappeared.

"Really?" she asked.

"Really," Sadika confirmed. The child beamed and danced out the door.

"How is she?" asked Eliza.

"Dealing," said Sadika with a sigh. "We both are."

"Lawrence Kit," said the governor, "You requested a meeting with me."

"I did," said Mr. Kit. "Thank you for making the time. I know it's been incredibly busy for you these last few days."

"I make time for what's important," said the governor. "What brings you to me? Is the number of men sufficient?"

"They are," said Kit. "That leads me to my second point. I know you want to use the boerin to capture these upstarts, but I propose that we march tonight. At best the boerin have figured out what you're doing and are using it to buy time. But even if they haven't, giving them less time to prepare defenses and recover from injuries seems wise."

"Tonight?" asked the governor. "Do you even know where they are hidden?"

"When studying the maps to figure out a plan of attack, I realized something," Lawrence Kit said. "All the kalinag villages are close to rivers. I believe that wherever they are hidden they will stay close to the river, perhaps even on the banks. They will need the water you see, not only for basic needs but also to fish since fish seems to make up a lot of their diet."

"So what are you proposing exactly?" the governor said.

"I'm proposing we go upriver," said Kit. "We will find them, and they will be prepared for an attack from land. Once we stay in the boats, they should find it reasonably difficult to attack us."

The governor was silent for some time and then finally nodded. "Very well, let me get you those boats you need."

Late that night Sadika waited in anticipation for Eliza to return. She was sitting very still in an alleyway in town. A Jab Jab lounged on the wall next to her. A few moments later, a figure slipped into the alleyway, all curves and feline grace. Eliza's hair was loose, tumbling down her back and she held a smart little bonnet in her hands. Sadika could never get over how different she looked as a Dame Lorraine. It's not that her face really changed, but somehow you could still never pick her out as the same person. All dark things have their tricks, she supposed.

"Well?" Sadika asked.

"He spilled all his secrets," said Eliza cheerfully. "There are only four extra men on the inside guarding because they don't think allyuh know where dey keeping yuh father."

The Jab Jab tilted his head and said sweetly, "What a terrible mistake." He looked to Sadika. "Tomorrow night then, Daughter of Anansi. Dame Lorraine," he said to Eliza and then he was gone.

"They always scare me," said Eliza with a suppressed shudder.

"They scare everybody," said Sadika.

CHAPTER 34

Amrika was patrolling her section of the perimeter when she felt something change in the beat of Ierie. She cocked her head and tried to understand what was going on, because she had never felt this change before.

Frowning, she stooped on the ground and closed her eyes, attempting to puzzle out the unfamiliar feeling.

Saikan.

It was the first thing she realized. Saikan were coming but it wasn't how she had felt the saikan before. It was somewhat nebulous, drifting, hovering in some odd way. Flying? Were the saikan flying somehow?

She concentrated harder, putting a hand on the earth as she sought to pinpoint the location of the intrusion. She managed to narrow it down and stood looking towards the area. It was a strange direction of intrusion because if they were coming from that direction, they would have to cross the river. Then she froze, eyes widening. They wouldn't have to cross the river if they were coming up the river itself. That was why Ierie's beat was strange; the saikan were coming up the river! She had to stop them from reaching the kalinag.

She turned and pelted down to the river bank, turning when she reached it, to follow it downstream. After a while she became aware of someone catching up to her. She turned and saw Raj. She slowed slightly, only picking back up her pace when he caught up.

"Dey on de river," she said, between breaths.

"Ah know," he said.

"How we stopping dem?"

"Girl I doh know," he said honestly. "We go figure something out."

Sadika was on her way back to Eliza's home when she spotted the torches at the boerin section. She stopped hard. She'd been so focused on her father she'd not bothered about what was happening with the boerin. But they were suffering. They were suffering because of them. Sure, the dark things had no choice but the boerin were caught in the crossfire and they did not deserve to be abandoned.

"What?" asked Eliza.

"The boerin," she said.

"You can't do anything," said Eliza.

"But I can," said Sadika. "And ah won't be alone. Ah real sure of dat."

"So you're going over there?" asked Eliza.

Sadika nodded.

"What about Reshma?" asked Eliza. "Yuh could get killed!"

"Take care of her," said Sadika, already moving down the road.

"Sadika!" hissed Eliza. "Sadika come back!" But Sadika ignored her.

Protect the children of my womb!

Ierie's word tugged under her skin. Tamara tried not to squirm uncomfortably as Ierie's call pulled and tugged at her. She knew why it was harder than usual. The saikan were attacking the kalinag again tonight. Bats had finally spotted them on the river and had flown ahead to warn the kalinag while the other dark things attempted to slow them down. Meanwhile, she and the other Bats were in the village square, prepping for another rescue mission. There were around twenty men in the village square, surrounded by even more soldiers. Those soldiers were then surrounded by other soldiers who were in turn surrounded by a squadron of hidden soldiers. They really didn't want anyone escaping.

"Please tell me allyuh have ah plan," said a new voice. Everyone who was in the hideout house swivelled their heads to see who had spoken. It turned out to be a young woman dressed in black, a heavy veil over her face.

"Child of Anansi," said one of the Midnight Robbers in surprise. "Wha you doing here?"

"I thought it had ah rescue mission going on?" she asked, head cocked, seeming amused.

"It does," said the Robber.

"Well. I thought ah woulda help. If dais okay?"

The Robber smiled. "We would appreciate it miss."

The Daughter of Anansi returned the smile, a hint of mischief oozing from it.

"I thought yuh might."

Protect the first born! Ierie roared.

"We trying!" Amrika huffed. Running on a river bank wasn't exactly easy. Everywhere that one could possibly find small trees with hard prickly branches, one found them. Amrika usually found them by running full tilt into them. And since this was a forest, the grass on the river bank was almost as tall as she was and on occasion the ground was really muddy. On more than one occasion she'd almost slipped into the river which had done nothing good to her already racing heartbeat.

She was pretty sure they were making enough noise to alert anyone coming upriver because they were not being quiet. She wasn't even sure they could be quiet with this amount of bush. Grass wrapped around her at the worst times, slicing into her skin when she pulled them away.

"I hate razor grass!" she hissed.

"Ah doh know who likes it," said Raj. Amrika hated that he didn't sound as out of breath as she did.

Suddenly Raj stopped.

"What?" she asked.

"I think I see something," he said. He crouched down, then he began to thread his way very carefully though the grass. Amrika crouched down too and followed in his footsteps, being sure not to make any noise. Ierie's beat was thrumming harshly under her feet, telling her and Raj the saikan were near.

Sure enough, when they rounded a slight bend in the river they found themselves facing several boats being swiftly but quietly paddled up the river, loaded with soldiers.

"Where are de Bats when yuh need dem?" asked Amrika.

"Up there," said Raj, he was looking up. Amrika looked up too and found several tiny specks circling in the sky.

"Why they not attacking?"

"Probably too dangerous," said Raj. "They'll jus make theyself a target."

"Buh we cah stop them," said Amrika.

"We go hadda try," said Raj. He turned to her. "How well can you swim?"

She gave him a disbelieving look but answered nonetheless. "Good enough for whatever yuh planning."

"Good," he said, and began creeping forward towards the river's edge.

Amrika sighed and began to follow him.

Just before Raj reached the water, he stopped and looked around to ensure none of the saikans were looking at them. Satisfied, he was about to continue when he froze and whipped his head back to the direction of the saikan. He stared at them for a moment and then said,

"Amrika, get back."

"What?" she asked confused.

"Now!" he snapped. "Girl geh back now!"

Amrika scrambled back through the bush and Raj followed her quickly, urging her to go on until they were well and truly buried in the grass, about ten feet from the river.

"Wha happening?" she asked.

"It ha fog on de river," he said, glancing anxiously at the river.

"So?" she said.

"Is nuh cold enough fuh fog," he said frantically.

"What?" she asked confused. "Den how is dere fog?"

He gave her a look. "Wha is the one dark thing tha is associated with water?"

Amrika blinked at him and then froze. "Oh," she said. "Oh no."

The soldiers were wearing cloths around their mouths and noses. Sadika thought it was rather funny.

"Why they wearing dat?" she asked.

"Ah not sure," said a Midnight Robber.

"Is 'cause dey think is ah drug," said a Dame Lorraine. "Dat we is hallucinations."

"Dat is funny," said Sadika. She turned to a Midnight Robber and smiled. "Would you be averse to assisting me?"

The Midnight Robber smiled, lips curling into a frightening expression. "Not at all."

It took some skill to do. The soldiers were much more alert than the last set, glancing up at the roofs as they scanned their surroundings. The Robber's dark miasma helped dull their minds and with a quick flick of his wrists, he tossed tiny knives across the alleyway to land on the other roof. Sadika checked that the spider webs wrapped around the hilt of the knives hadn't burst. Luckily none had, which was great since they really only had one shot at it. When each of the alleyways had a thin line of spider web stretched across the mouth of it, she carefully connected each of those lines to each other.

"What is it yuh doing?" asked the Robber, curious.

"We want the illusions to happen all at the same time, right?" she asked.

The Robber nodded.

"Well for this to work, I need to be touching the webs. Connecting them like this allows me to be 'touching' all of them."

"Ahh," said the Robber.

When she was ready, Sadika looked up. "Is everyone else ready?"

The Midnight Robber carefully used his Robber's sight to look at the places where the others were hidden. After a moment he turned to her and nodded.

"Good," she said. She gripped her spider web in one hand and concentrated, eyes falling shut. She could feel the thin, cool line of spidersilk stretching out from where she held it. She could feel the flex of the weave, the trickery buried in it. She could feel Ierie humming through the webs, hear the echo of a mischievous laugh. She grinned and snapped open her eyes. From the thin spider webs she had strung across the alleyways, more cobwebs unravelled, dropping like a curtain on the final act of a play. Illusions rippled across the surfaces as they fell, making them invisible to those soldiers facing the alley, and then settling to show what they expected to see, an alleyway of soldiers waiting to pounce on the dark things. Little did they know that the ones waiting to ambush were now about to be ambushed.

Sadika's wicked grin stretched wider as the dark things surged out of their hiding spots and into the dark alleyways.

CHAPTER 35

The fog crept up behind the unsuspecting boats.

"Cover your ears," Raj told her, hands already clamping over his.

Amrika dropped her stick and pressed her hands over her ears.

Protect the firstborn!

Ierie's song thrummed under her feet, beat vibrating through her bones. The pace of the music was picking up as the fog began to draw closer. There was a small stirring as the saikan noticed the fog but they eventually settled, having decided that it was a natural phenomenon. Silly, silly men. Fog would not come on a night like this, not confined to the river and its banks, the way this was.

Soon the fog whispered its way over the boats and continued down the river, following the winding path of the water. Amrika and Raj shivered violently as the cold fog rolled over them, hands still clasped over their ears.

Protect the firstborn!

The first strains of the music reached them then. Soft and echoing as it glanced off the surface of the water, it didn't seem like much. But eventually it grew closer and closer, increasing in volume and clarity. Amrika squeezed her hands over her ears tighter and ducked her head as if that would allow her to escape the sound.

Sounds of rifles being cocked made it through the fragile barrier of her palms. The saikan had heard the music too.

"Get ready!" a voice commanded.

The fog billowed over them, so thick now you could choke on the stuff. In contrast, the music was almost strangely clear, a jangling tune, worthy of a road march. Amrika had never been so afraid to hear music in her life.

Soon, voices were heard, singing along, the sound just coming in suddenly. The voices were loud and rowdy, a group of people clearly enjoying themselves. Feet slapped water as the revellers danced their way across the surface of the river. Amrika was suddenly filled with a desire to join them, to get up and dance. She half-stood, only to be dragged back down by Raj.

He shook his head wildly at her, clamping back his hand over his ears.

"Don't!" he mouthed frantically at her. Amrika blinked at him wondering why he would not want her to join them. Why shouldn't she get up and dance and enjoy herself? She tried to get up again and Raj grimaced and punched her hard across the jaw. Her hands flew away from her ears as she pitched to the side, but the blow jolted her mind away from the lure of the music. She nodded in thanks and then tightened her hands over her ears.

Rifles cracked through the fog but only one volley was let off. Amrika squinted through the fog and caught a brief glimpse of the revellers. Men in sailors' uniforms were dancing as they continued their trek on the river, waving canes and swords in the air. The mercenaries who had been on the boats were also dancing on the water now, caught up in the revelry of the fancy sailors.

Raj bumped her shoulder in warning and Amrika dropped her eyes, closing them tightly and grinding her teeth together as she fought against the pull of the music. It took far too long for the fancy sailors to pass.

Even with the sound muted, the lure was powerful. She dug her feet into the earth to stop herself from going after the sailors. Ierie's beat was strangely grounding but she wasn't about to complain. Raj was a mass of stiff muscle as he too fought against the pull of the sailor's revelry. Finally, the sound began to fade away.

When they could no longer be heard, Amrika slumped in the grass feeling like she'd just fought another Stickfighter for an entire day. Beside her, Raj let out a sigh of relief and sprawled out on the ground.

"You okay?" he asked, voice sounding hoarse.

Amrika tried to answer and found that her throat was dry. She swallowed a few times and then said, "Yes. You?"

"Yeah," he said. "Buh I not sure I might go carnival dis year."

"Yeah," she said, "Me either."

Protect the firstborn!!!

Tamara watched from a height as the dark things carefully knocked out the soldiers in the alleyways. With the alleyways clear of soldiers, the dark things flattened themselves against the walls. Bats came in then, swooping low, collecting Ierie's song with their wings.

Tamara winced a little. Ierie's song was particularly harsh tonight. The soldiers were not going to be able to recover very well. The Bats barrelled through the alleyways in a perfectly timed motion and then burst through the web of illusions, unleashing Ierie's song.

The song hit the soldiers in a devastating wave. The rows of men were practically flattened by the force of it. Before they could get to their feet, Jab Jabs, Dame Lorraines and Moko Jumbies were upon them.

Whips cracked, and knives flashed into those vulnerable spots in between armour, piercing painfully but not fatally. Moko Jumbies simply kicked men out of the way and stomped on them to keep them down. The Midnight Robbers ignored the soldiers entirely, heading straight for the captives. In a few seconds they had cut the ropes tying the men to the poles.

It was then that Tamara and the other Bats dropped from the sky. They reached the ground in record time, snatching up the recently freed men and then taking to the sky again.

Soon all the men were freed and the Robbers' dark miasma rolled over the square. The dark things retreated, and in a few moments, there was no trace of them left, save for downed soldiers and a severe lack of prisoners.

The Robbers' whistles sounded sharply in the night and then all was silent.

Amrika and Raj didn't move from where they sat on the river bank until morning cleared. The sun's rays washed away the fog from the sailors' passage and turned the river into a shining ribbon. Amrika and Raj struggled to their feet, legs having gone numb from sitting so long in the cold.

"Well," said Raj, "Back."

Amrika nodded and they began the run back to where the kalinag were camping. Just before they reached the village encampment, they found the remnants of the sailors' revelry. Amrika saw it first. She stopped suddenly spotting something odd in the river. Raj ran a few steps more before realizing that she wasn't behind him.

"Wha?" he asked.

She pointed. "Is that...?"

He looked towards the river and shaded his eyes as he focused on the odd blobs she had seen. After a moment he nodded.

"Yeah. Dais dem."

Amrika shaded her eyes as well and grimaced. The bodies of the saikan mercenaries were floating face down in the river. When she squinted, she could make out a red tinge to the water, darker where blood still streamed from the bodies. The sailors were devastatingly effective.

She felt a little sick. Then her stomach roiled as she realized that if had Raj not been there she would have been in the water too.

"Thanks," she said.

"Fuh what?"

"For keeping me out ah de revelry."

Raj snorted. "Girl. Wha ah was supposed to do? Leh yuh geh kill?" He waved a hand. "Dais nothing. Come on."

They resumed their trek to the encampment and soon came up to it. The camp itself was ringed by the remaining Stickfighters who all were looking very strained. When they saw that it was Amrika and Raj, they relaxed a bit.

"Dey gone?" one of the Stickfighters, Biyu, asked.

"We didn't see them when we was coming," Raj said. At his words the Stickfighters relaxed fully.

"Well," said Khion from where he was sitting up in his hammock. "We real have a problem."

Lawrence Kit dragged himself on through the forest. He was still damp from his dip in the river when he had jumped out the boat to avoid the strange people that had been dancing up the river. He had just managed to make it to shore before the people had hit the boats. It was only due to luck, that his ears had gotten filled with water, rendering their mesmerizing music ineffective. Having realized that the music was what was causing him to want to join the strange men, he had clamped his hands over his ears and then, when further away, had used his belt to tie himself to a tree. It was completely undignified, but Lawrence Kit was not above doing anything to survive.

He had known that it hadn't been a drug, unlike the poor buggers who had followed him, but he'd thought that he had seen all of these things that were attacking them. How much more of them were there? Never mind. He was going to kill them all, no matter what tricks they had.

Lawrence Kit stomped on through the forest on his way back to Port of Gold. He was going to destroy all these impossible things and he was going to kill the kalinag. They had all caused him enough failure and pain and humiliation for a lifetime!

CHAPTER 36

"Whey yuh was?!" demanded Reshma, shrilly.

"What?" asked Sadika as she tried to understand what had happened.

"Whey yuh was?!" the little girl demanded again. "Yuh was supposed to come back early last night and yuh didn't!"

Sadika woke up enough to realize that the child was on the verge of tears. She sat up and hugged the little girl.

"I'm fine. Ah was in the boerin section. We was helping free de people."

"Humph!" Eliza said as she entered the room. She held a tray in her hands. "You're lucky you weren't caught!"

"Yuh was hurt?!" Reshma cried out.

"No! No!" said Sadika. "I wasn't hurt at all. I'm fine, see?" She let the child inspect her and then gave a little frown at Eliza for scaring the girl. Eliza gave her an unrepentant look, clearly still not pleased about her actions last night.

"How did you get in without being caught?" Eliza asked. "The boerin section is sealed off."

"Child of Anansi,' said Sadika in explanation. "Father and I made ways in and out of town quite some time ago. Didn't you know? I thought all the dark things knew of them."

"Clearly not all," said Eliza.

"You is ah dark thing too?" asked Reshma.

"Yes," Eliza replied.

"Wha is you?"

"I am a Dame Lorraine," Eliza told her.

Reshma blinked. "Rely?"

"Really," assured Eliza. "But I don't go out often. Unlike your aunt here."

Sadika laughed. "I didn't used to go out a lot either. But Ierie called."

Eliza sighed. "Yes. Ierie called. But what happened last night has the governor very angry. I think he's starting to not believe the drug and hallucination theory. Also no one came back from the ventures last night, to report to him."

"What ventures?" asked Sadika.

"They went for the kalinag again last night," said Eliza. "One of the other Dame Lorraines told me this morning. But no one came back to report to the governor whether or not it was a success or failure."

Sadika felt strangely cold. "Eliza, if it was a success, someone would have reported back."

"And if…" Eliza paused, glanced at Reshma and then amended her statement, "If it was a complete failure, they still would have reported back."

Sadika paled even more. "Did dey attack all de villages?"

"Yes," said Eliza. "Yes they did."

Far away from Port of Gold and the ensuing war, south of the land, in a place where there wasn't much civilization yet, two Bats and a Jab Jab were standing at the foot of a bubbling cone of mud.

"See," said a Bat to the Jab Jab as the mud volcano bubbled. "It bubbling."

"It only bubbling though," said the Jab Jab. Just then, the mud volcano spewed out a large splatter of mud and hot steam rose from the cone of the volcano.

The two Bats turned to the Jab Jab.

"Why me?" said the Jab Jab.

"Because fire wouldn't hurt you," said the Bats.

The Jab Jab sighed and cautiously went up the side of the volcano, hesitantly peering into it. After a moment, he dropped back down to ground level.

"Please tell me that it isn't what ah thought it was," said the Bat.

"Is nuh wha yuh thought it was," the Jab Jab said promptly.

"Rely?"

"No!" said the Jab Jab. "Is exactly what yuh thought it was."

"Dais trouble," said the Bat.

The Jab Jab grinned. "Trouble is only one way of looking at it."

"Real sure trouble is de only way of looking at it," the other Bat retorted. "And you know it too!"

"What shall we do, sir?" the captain asked, warily.

"Nothing!" the governor said. He folded his hands on the desk in front of him. "Nothing for now. Not until I have heard what became of the men I sent out to the villages. Just keep the boerin contained until then. And send out riders to find out what happened!"

"Yes sir!" the captain said and hurriedly left the room.

CHAPTER 37

They all met halfway, in a cleverly hidden field that the Moko Jumbies knew of.

"It used to be an old estate," one of the Bats who were flying them out told Amrika, when she asked. "Dais wha the Jumbies said anyway."

The Bat dropped her off in the clearing where the ruins of a house stood crumbling into the ground. The other Stickfighters, Raj and Khion dropped down next to her. Khion was still wincing slightly. When she was about to ask if he was okay, he gave her a warning look.

"Yuh okay?" she asked pointedly which made Raj laugh and Khion frown at her for a moment before his humour reasserted itself and he gave a reluctant grin. Amrika didn't blame him. Lying injured wasn't fun for anybody and probably especially worse for a Stickfighter who was accustomed to moving.

"'Rika!" said a voice.

Amrika looked up to see Kirish leaning against the ruins of the house. A sharp feeling of relief washed over her and she realized just how much she had been missing her brother and how worried she'd been for him. She quickly padded over to him and then held still while he scanned her for injuries.

"Yuh good?" he asked.

"Yeah," she said. "'Lil spooked, buh good. Wha 'bout you?"

"I fine," he said.

"Ah hear something 'bout allyuh rescuing people?"

He grinned. "Is ah good set ah we. We have de boerin we rescue in a next place like dis. Most ah de Moko Jumbies protecting dem there rite now." He frowned then. "Yuh sure yuh okay? Yuh was near dem when dey pass?"

"Yeah," said Amrika, "buh I wasn't alone. Raj help meh so ah didn't get caught up in de revelry."

Kirish shook his head. "Ah tell yuh one day yuh would be too close. Yuh real lucky yuh know." He bopped her shoulder for emphasis.

"I know," Amrika admitted and then laughed at the look of surprise on her older brother's face. She reached out then and gave him a hug which he half-shied away from in the manner of older brothers all around the world.

"Doh worry. I good though!" she told him cheerfully.

He snorted in exasperation. "Of course, you are." A motion behind her caught her brother's gaze. Amrika turned to see what it was and saw one of the Bats who been ferrying people to the meeting place, a young woman looking only a year or two older than herself, landing in the clearing.

The young woman caught sight of Kirish and after a moment gave a nod to him. Amrika swung her head back around to catch her brother returning the nod. Something about the slight interaction awoke her sisterly and feminine instincts. She grinned at her brother and said,

"Ah going to walk around a bit," and promptly whooshed off, meandering her way around the ruins.

Soon enough she made her way to where the young woman was shrugging on a dress over the tight-fitted clothing of the Bat. Next to her was a young man, also shrugging on clothes and looking alike enough to the girl to only be her twin.

Amrika waited until the brother left his sister who was still tying the belt of her dress.

"Hey," she introduced herself.

The young woman looked up and smiled pleasantly, if a little confusedly. "Hi," she said.

"I'm Amrika," Amrika said, holding out a hand. "I think you know my brother?"

"I'm Tamara," said the young woman taking her hand. "Your brother?"

"Kirish," explained Amrika.

Tamara's eyes lit up with recognition and... maybe something more?

"Oh, yes," said Tamara. "I didn't know he had a sister. Are you a Midnight Robber too? I've never heard of a girl Robber."

Amrika laughed. "Dey exist but dey rare," she said. "Buh I'm not a Midnight Robber. I is ah Stickfighter."

Tamara blinked. "Really?"

"Yeah," Amrika laughed. "Maybe we had some Stickfighter blood in we, maybe I is ah first line." She shrugged. "So how do you know my brother?"

"Oh, um. We've been helping him rescue de boerin." She gave a wry smile. "If it wasn't for him me and Vishal, dais meh brother, woulda get ketch. We woulda be too hot headed, I guess. Yuh brother stopped we." she gave another little smile. "He's been... kind I guess?"

"Probably kind," said Amrika, "for a Midnight Robber anyway."

"Exactly," laughed Tamara.

Just then, Tamara's brother appeared and called to her.

"Ah hadda go," Tamara told her. "Nice meeting you!"

"Good to meet yuh too!" Amrika called back.

Amrika quickly walked back to her brother who was still leaning on the ruins and watching the rest of dark things gather. She propped up next to him and then lightly bumped his shoulder with hers.

He frowned at her, taking in her grin and said, "What?"

"I spoke to Tamara just now," she said casually.

Kirish stiffened slightly but said, "So wha?"

"She said," Amrika continued still grinning, "that you were kind."

Kirish shrugged. "And?"

Amrika gave her brother a look. "Midnight Robbers aren't kind," she said.

"I'm not only a Midnight Robber," he retorted.

"I'm sure yuh not," she said laughing at him.

"Wha is yuh point?" he asked her.

"You like her," said Amrika.

"No, I don't!" he defended.

"Fine. Yuh interested."

"I am not," he said.

Amrika gave him a disbelieving look.

"And even if I was," he added grudgingly, "is none ah your business."

"I's yuh little sister," Amrika told him, "Of course is my business." She grinned at him. "So you do like her."

"Shut up," her brother told her, which only caused her to laugh.

"You know she is only two years older than me."

"Hush yuh mouth!" Kirish told her, poking her in the arm warningly.

"Or what?" But she raised her hands and walked away, still laughing teasingly at him.

Sadika was flown to the meeting of the dark things by a Bat. She had ridden out of town until she'd gotten to a place that she could be flown from without the saikan spotting them. Eliza had opted to stay at home and watch Reshma for her. And at any rate her disappearance might have drawn some attention, so it was best for her to stay behind. As the only representative of the Children of Anansi, Sadika had to go.

She and the Bat who had laboriously carried her were the last to reach the meeting place. Upon her arrival, the people who were gathered in the ruins came together in a circle.

"So," said a Dame Lorraine. "Everybody here?"

When everyone had answered in the affirmative, the Dame Lorraine nodded and then said, "Well apparently we have a problem." She gestured to one of the Stickfighters, a young man who looked like he'd been ill but was recovering. No, not ill, Sadika decided upon closer inspection, injured and badly so. It took a moment to place him as the Stickfighter she had fought with when the saikan had attacked the first time. When she did, she was promptly horrified at how he looked now as opposed to the strong, powerful warrior he'd been. Still he moved with a sure-footed grace that Sadika could probably never gain her lifetime as he stepped into the middle of the ring.

"De Sailors came up the rivers last night an kill out de mercenaries," the Stickfighter said without preamble. There were sudden shocked reactions from those who hadn't known. Sadika herself felt her face pale.

"Now," said the Stickfighter, "ah assuming dat none ah allyuh did tell any of dem." Various heads shook in denial. "So dat mean dat Ierie call dem. Which means we kinda runnin outta time here. Dis plan of waiting for the saikan to give up. Dat hadda done. Ierie nuh waiting no more."

"And on dat note," interjected a Jab Jab smoothly, "The Bats and I also have some news." He waited until he was sure that everybody was paying attention and then said, "The mud volcano started having minor eruptions but they not natural. So we really doh have any time at all."

At that revelation, the entire group grew silent. Sadika's breath caught in her throat as she realized what it meant, and a slight shiver ran down her back.

"So," said a Midnight Robber, the same she thought, who had led the rescue mission the night before. "We doh really have any time at all. We hadda find a way to end dis and we hadda do it real fast."

"How bad was de eruptions?" a Stickfighter asked.

"Not bad," said the Jab Jab. "Buh since the Fancy Sailors appeared without warning, ah doh think we should think we ha plenty time."

"Not much," said Sadika, her own voice sounding a little strange to her ears. "But we should have enough time."

"Enough time for what?" asked the Midnight Robber.

"Enough to create and execute a plan," said Sadika. She focused on him. "Ierie came to us because the land didn't want so much destruction. Ah doh think it would do dat lightly. So I think we go have some time. Anyhow, the boerin cah take more ah dis either. We hadda end this soon."

CHAPTER 38

"What do you mean?" said the governor when one of the men who had gone to discover what had happened returned.

"All the men are gone sir," the soldier reported. He was young, clearly a new recruit and he was still bloodless beneath his naturally pale skin from whatever he'd seen.

"Explain 'gone' for me," the mayor said softly.

"D-Dead sir," said the soldier. "We found the bodies in the river, where they had boarded the boats."

"Dead," repeated the governor. He swallowed and then said, "All of them?"

"Yes sir," said the soldier.

"And what of the boats?"

"We found those floating downriver, sir," said the soldier. "They were empty. There was no damage done to them, sir."

"I see," said the governor. "Thank you, soldier. Dismissed." When the young soldier went out, the governor steepled his fingers in thought.

He remembered the day he'd been given his posting to this land, this colony of his beloved Motherland. His wife had been so proud, so pleased.

"I knew they'd choose you," She'd whispered to him, "Who else could they have picked?"

Like all governors, he'd been given the posting by the Monarchs themselves. They'd personally entrusted him to ensure that this colony of theirs, this little fraction of their kingdom and home would be given it's due. They had entrusted him to raise it to their standards and to make it a valuable part of their country. He had no interest in failing them. He would not! He would do his duty. No matter what obstacles came his way!

His wife's proud, sly eyes, twinkled in approval from the depths of his memory. A light knock soon interrupted him from his contemplation.

"Come in," the governor said. The door opened to reveal Lord Ainsley. The governor's eyes narrowed. "Lord Ainsley," he said with hostility.

"My dear governor," Ainsley said, "I heard the tragic news."

"How surprising," the governor said acidly, "when I have only just heard it myself. Have you been bribing my scouts?"

"Me?" said Ainsley, the very picture of disbelief. "I would never."

"Of course not," said the governor. "What do you want?"

"I have come to help as always," said Ainsley. "These things, they flout your authority. Kill your men. Is saikan life worth so little that you will not retaliate in kind?"

"They were men hired for a job they didn't complete. Not soldiers of the royal army," said the governor coolly. "Nor did they take the job thinking that there wasn't any risks."

"But still you allow these miscreants to think that they can cross you," Ainsley said.

"What would you have me do?!" snapped the governor.

"I have given you a solution," Ainsley reminded him.

"Get out!" said the governor. "When I want your solution, I will ask for it. Good day."

"Good day governor," said Ainsley. "I look forward to hearing from you soon."

Lawrence Kit slugged his way through the forest as he fought to reach the road back to Port of Gold. Which each step his hatred of the... things, that had dared to defy him, grew. In fact, his hatred for the whole island was growing. What did any of it matter? Why did any luxury on this place really matter? This little island was nothing, nothing to the Motherland. It did not even register on the scale of the conquests that the Motherland had made.

The mosquitoes buzzing around him and feasting his flesh did not help to mollify him any. He slapped futilely at the little beasts and finally spotted the road. He broke in a jog until he finally reached the road back to town. He eyed the distant capital, gritted his teeth and began walking. He had a governor to report to.

"Mr. Kit," said the governor in greeting. He sounded surprised. "I am surprised to see you. I had heard that all the men on the venture hadn't survived. How is it that you are here?"

Was that suspicion in his voice? Kit wondered. He ignored it.

"Luck," he said, "And the ability to make a rapid decision."

"I see," said the governor smoothly. "Come sit. Here, have some brandy." The governor pulled out a bottle, uncorked it and poured out two glass of the bitter, amber liquid. Lawrence Kit took the glass gratefully and shot it back. The liquid burned down his throat and left a pleasant warmth in his body that chased away the lingering coldness of his wet trek through the forest. When he replaced his glass on the desk the governor refilled it.

"Now," said the governor, "Tell me what happened."

When he finished telling his story, with a little embellishment of him telling his men to jump overboard with him, the governor leaned back in his seat.

"How can you explain what happened?" he asked. "The men were protected against the drug. They wore cloths to prevent them from breathing in the drug and yet they seemed to be affected worse than ever."

"I can't explain it," said Lawrence Kit. "I have never encountered any drug like this before."

"Can't explain?" asked the governor, "Or won't?"

Lawrence Kit sat up. "What are you implying?" he asked, his voice hard.

"Just that these natives seem to be making some miraculous victories. These untrained people are beating your trained men. It seems a little farfetched to me. Unless of course, someone was helping. After all, the longer this job goes on the more you get paid."

Rage boiled up in Lawrence Kit's breast. His jaw tightened even as he clenched his fists.

"You think I'm doing this? That I am in league with these, these things!" he roared.

"I'm simply saying," the governor said calmly, "That it's probably time I found someone who is better suited for the job. Good day, Mr. Kit. Your services are no longer required. You will still be paid, of course. Enjoy your trip back to the Motherland."

Kit stared at the governor in complete shock. "You would fire me?" he asked slowly. "You would stop me from taking my revenge on these things?"

The governor eyed him and then said calmly. "I thought I already had."

It was too much. The defeat at the hands of the boerin, the humiliation, the loss of his men, the loss of his reputation, the long trek through the inhospitable forest, and now being denied his revenge all caused the rage to boil over and Lawrence Kit launched himself at the governor.

He had gotten over the desk and had his hands around the bureaucrat's throat when a shot sounded. His body jerked and something hot and tangy flooded the back of his throat. Lawrence Kit looked down to where a red splotch was growing over his heart and then at the pistol the governor held. He blinked bemusedly at the governor's calm face and tried to tighten his hands around the man's throat but his fingers didn't seem to want to listen to him. He coughed once, and blood dripped out his mouth. His legs lost feeling and his body half-sagged to the floor as the governor pushed back his chair.

"Guards," the governor called, mildly. "Please get rid of this man." He glanced at Lawrence Kit who was staring at him. "Sorry," amended the governor, "Please get rid of this corpse."

Lawrence Kit felt a flare of defiance. He was not dead yet! He was not going to die! He tried to push himself up but only managed to move a few inches before dropping heavily back to the floor. His eyes drooped, and his breathing stuttered. The last thing he saw was the governor, picking up a sheaf of papers and settling down to read them.

By the time the guards came in, Lawrence Kit, mercenary of the Motherland, was quite dead.

"Captain," said the governor looking up as the captain entered the room. "Good. Come, I have an interesting dilemma. I would like your input."

"Yes sir," said the captain.

"Sit, sit," said the governor. "Now. I am out of a lot of mercenaries and a leader for them. These boerin have become too bold in their defiance. However, I don't want to start killing them. With the uncertain times, they may revolt and then we'll have to kill all of them and that would be unpleasant. We'd be out a workforce and the monarchy would want an explanation and I'm sure you and your men won't come across so well, having lost the prisoners. So," he smiled at the captain, "We need a strategy to get rid of these troublemakers without rousing the entire boerin population. And perhaps even some of the jotlin, who will no doubt protest the loss of their workers."

"Well," said the captain, "if you want to go that way, it's best to hope they tear apart from the inside, give themselves up. You can threaten to kill all the boerin. Seeing that they rescued them, it's obvious that they care for their people as well as the kalinag. Or..." the captain trailed off for a moment.

"What?" asked the governor.

The captain looked at the governor. "The mercenary, Lawrence Kit, he had captured one of the perpetrators, an old man. He has been trying to get him to talk but the old man resisted. He's one of the jotlin actually, probably funded them."

"He's been torturing one of my jotlin?" asked the governor sharply.

"He was boerin first," said the captain, "Not saikan."

"Still," said the governor. "I dislike not being informed of this."

"My apologies," said the captain, "I was only recently made aware of it following the... demise of Mr. Kit."

"Fine," said the governor.

"Well, if this prisoner is a part of their movement, why not threaten him instead? As he is already a criminal the rest of the boerin might not be inclined to revolt and the rest of the criminals might either give themselves up or attempt to rescue him."

"And how do we know that their rescue attempt won't be successful this time?"

"We'll spare the theatrics this time," said the captain. "We'll keep him in the jail and we'll have a man with a revolver standing right by him. The first sign of trouble, we'll shoot the prisoner. We let them know that, they most likely won't try."

"And if that doesn't work?" asked the governor.

"Then we move on to much more drastic measures," said the captain. "There are other ways to obtain a workforce after all."

"Yes," said the governor. He fell silent and then nodded. "Alright. Pass the word once the prisoner is secure in the gaol."

CHAPTER 39

Jamal, returning home from work at Ainsley's estate, heard the proclamation first.

"By order of the governor of Port of Gold, protector of Ierie under the monarchs of the Motherland, all boerin class members who are involved in the heinous crimes against saikan class lives are ordered to come forward and face justice. The governor of Port of Gold has offered this mercy: the life of the perpetrator in our hands shall be spared as will the lives of any of those who come forward. The perpetrators have three days to give themselves up. If they fail to do so, then the governor shall not extend any mercy to them and they will be condemned to be hanged by the neck until dead. If anyone attempts to release the prisoner, let it be known that he will be shot dead at any disturbance at the gaol. The perpetrators are hereby warned and commanded: accept mercy while it is offered to you and face justice for your crimes."

With that the speaker stiffly rolled up his paper and marched away.

Jamal blinked, and when the soldiers and speaker had passed by, he quickly went into the boerin section and headed home.

"Hey!" he said as he entered. "Allyuh hear dat?"

"Yes," said Jessica.

"Wha you doing home?" he asked in surprise. "Ah thought you was helping de people we rescued?"

"I was," she said, "We need some more bandages, so I came home to get some. I'm returning soon. Did they say they had a prisoner?"

"Yeah," said Jamal. "I think is the Child of Anansi that dey did capture dat night."

"Oho," said his father. "Well somebody best tell he daughter and de rest of de dark things that meeting today."

"De Dame Lorraines go do it," said Jamal, "Dem does know how to pass news. How de people?"

"Most of them are okay," said Jessica, "But they took some really bad beatings. It will take them sometime to recover. But they are doing well."

"Well dais good," said Jamal. He quickly spooned out some food in a plate. "Wait fuh meh, ah go come with allyuh, when allyuh going back."

"Well hurry up," said Jessica, "We are going back there soon."

The Bat almost crash-landed in the middle of the yard in his haste to give them the news. Sadika blinked at the staggering figure and then hurried forward to help him to his feet. A couple of Stickfighters beat her to him, hauling him up and setting him firmly on the ground.

"What happen?" asked the Midnight Robber, Kirish, Sadika recalled his name was.

"New proclamation," the Bat gasped out, "Have a prisoner. We have three days to turn we self in. If we do, they nuh going an hang we. If we don't dey go kill de prisoner and we go geh kill if we geh ketch."

"What prisoner?" asked a Moko Jumbie, a young woman by the name of Shamika. "One ah de boerin?

The Bat shook his head and turned to look at Sadika. "Is yuh father," he said.

Sadika clenched her jaw and nodded stiffly. "Of course," she managed to say.

"So, three days?" asked a Dame Lorraine.

"Dais about as much time as we have anyway," said the smooth voice of the Jab Jab, "Unless someone wants to risk more time for ah nex, how shall we say? Eruption."

"No," said Sadika as her mind whirled. Her voice was far away and distant as she spoke next. "Dais enough time." She turned and smiled at them. It was a trickster's smile, Anansi's smile when he outsmarted his enemies, and it held beneath it the fierceness of Ierie.

"Enough time for what?" asked the Jab Jab.

"To play a trick ah we own," she said, "to get a hostage of our own. The governor does have ah daughter, doesn't he?"

Protect the children of my womb!

"Hey," said Sadika later that night to Reshma. "I have to go for ah few days but ah want you to stay here. Eliza will take care of you. But I will be back."

Reshma stubbornly turned her face away. She hadn't been pleased that Sadika had left for the day and was even less pleased to hear she wasn't going to be around for a few days.

"Reshma," said Sadika.

"No!" snapped the little girl. "Doh go! Granpa done gone! Wha if dey ketch you too? Wha go happen to me?!"

"Reshma," Sadika tried again but the child stomped her foot and burst into tears.

"Dey going an kill granpa!" she wailed. "Ah hear dem! Dey say if allyuh doh give up allyuh self dey go kill 'im!"

"Oh Reshma," said Sadika. She pulled the young girl against her.

Reshma fought her. "Yuh said dey was going an let him go but dey not going to! Yuh just saying yuh going an come back! Yuh not coming back!" she blubbered. She finally stopped fighting and let Sadika hug her tightly.

"Hey, hey," said Sadika, "Watch meh now. Ay chile, watch meh." She carefully blotted the tears of the child's face and said, "I am coming back for you. Me and granpa, we both coming back. Okay? I not going to leave yuh. But ah have to do something so dat we could go home and so dat we could save granpa okay? I know you've been really, really brave for this whole time and I'm so proud of you, but I need you to be brave for just a little while more. We going an end this soon okay? And then we going home."

"Yuh sure?" Reshma asked in a small voice.

"Very sure," said Sadika. She hugged the little girl again and kissed her forehead. "Very sure."

It took four Midnight Robbers, one Child of Anansi and three Bats to successfully steal the governor's daughter without anyone knowing. The governor's mansion had been heavily guarded as a matter of course and the governor had added spyglasses to look for Bats. It had taken a cleverer illusion-making than Sadika had done before and the damping miasma of four Robbers to get in undetected. Once there, one of the Robbers knocked out the governor's daughter, a beautiful, young woman named Kristabella, with a practiced hand. Sadika winced at the growing lump the young woman would undoubtedly wake up with the next day, and quickly helped them bundle her up in her covers.

Getting out was a different story altogether and required a distraction. A brave Bat, Keston, had volunteered for the task. When one of the Midnight Robbers signalled, Keston shot into the air from just outside the governor's grounds and screamed. Instantly shouts went up; men quickly aimed at the Bat who was twisting and turning in the air, flying wide loops and diving on occasion. A few men shot at him before the order to hold their fire came.

While Keston was distracting the men, the Robbers climbed out of Kristabella's window and slithered down to the ground. Sadika helped to lower Kristabella down to them and watched as they picked her up like a log and waited on Sadika's signal. Once Sadika ensured that the guards' attention was on the sky, she nodded to the Midnight Robbers who took off on a slow creep across the yard to freedom.

Sadika watched them through the window and concentrated on maintaining the shifting illusion over them. She had wrapped all four Midnight Robbers in spiderweb as well as Kristabella's unconscious form. Any guard who looked at them would only see empty lawn and the Robbers' dampening miasma would help to hide any inconsistencies in her illusions.

It was a tense ten minutes. To Sadika it felt more like ten hours and she was sweating when they were finally over the fence and safely away. She signalled to Keston to fly away, and then slumped down inside Kristabella's room with relief. A few minutes later she struggled to her feet again and peered out the window. Far in the distance, a blob rose into the sky and Sadika breathed another sigh of relief. The Bats were on their way with their precious package.

Tamara and Vishal were chosen to be the last leg of the journey to transport Kristabella to a place where her father would never find her. While they sat waiting for the Bats to bring her to them Vishal said,

"Do you really think they go kill she?"

"Kristabella?" asked Tamara.

"Yeah," said her brother.

"I doh know," said Tamara. "We kinda hoping it doh go like dat."

"Yeah buh if he doh agree, you think dey go really kill she?"

"I... I hope not," Tamara admitted. "But…"

"But?" prompted her brother.

"But the whole part of this plan revolves on making the governor believe that they will, if he doesn't do what they want."

"So dey might," said Vishal.

"Yes," said Tamara in a little voice. "I think they might."

Her brother wrapped an arm around her and she leaned into him.

"Why does that thought hurt more?" she asked him.

"Cause she innocent, I guess," Vishal answered after a moment's thought.

"I really hope de governor have some love left in his heart for he daughter," Tamara said. "I, I don't want innocent blood on any of our hands."

"Me too," said her brother. "Me too gyul."

Just then the sound of wings flapping came to their ears. The twins looked upwards and soon enough two Bats came into view, carrying an unwieldy bundle between them.

The Bats landed and laid the bundle down very gently and then bent over and placed their hand on their knees and breathed deeply.

"Allyuh have water?" one asked.

"Yeah," said Tamara. She quickly found a canteen and handed it to him. The Bat drank deeply and handed it to his companion.

"She real heavy," said the second Bat when he had finished drunk.

"Really?" asked Vishal. "I thought she was kinda thin."

"She is," said the first Bat, "But after a while she does get real heavy. Be careful not to drop she."

"She still unconscious?" asked Tamara.

"Yeah," answered the second Bat. "Dat Midnight Robber hit she good."

"She alive right?" asked Vishal worriedly.

"Was last time we check," said the first Bat.

Tamara sighed and knelt next to the bundle. She pulled back the sheets which wrapped the girl, snugly but not tightly enough to cut off her air and placed a finger underneath her nose. A puff of air reassured her that Kristabella was still alive.

"She alive," she announced. "A little cold though," she said poking the woman's face which was stiff.

"Nothing we can do about that," said one of the Bats. "Allyuh just have to warm she up when yuh reach where yuh going."

With that bit of advice, the two Bats took to the air and began the long journey home. Tamara and Vishal looked at each other and then bent to try and figure out what was the most comfortable way to carry their unconscious passenger.

Jamal was patrolling the small encampment where they were keeping the boerin that the saikan had beaten, when a small figure came out from the mass of people and walked towards him. On closer inspection, he realized that it was his adopted sister.

When she came closer, he folded his legs and sat on the ground. Jessica blinked and then said, "That is very strange."

Jamal grinned but didn't reply. After a moment of hesitation, Jessica sat cross-legged on the ground next to him facing the camp.

"You think all of this will be over soon?" she asked.

Jamal shrugged.

"I hope it is," she said. "The men in there miss their families. A lot of them have children and their wives are all alone in the village, caring for them. They can't keep staying here. Their families need them."

"One way or another," Jamal said, "This go end. And probably soon."

Jessica sighed and wrapped her arms around herself. "Well I am hoping for a happy ending," she told him.

Jamal, looking out at the men who were all healing well but separated from their families for an unforeseeable amount of time, hoped for a happy ending too.

CHAPTER 40

Impersonating the governor's daughter for three days wasn't particularly difficult, but it wasn't particularly easy either. Sadika spent the first day in bed, claiming to have a headache from the heat. Maids catered to her every whim and dropped cool cloths over her forehead and Sadika didn't have to talk much, and risk giving herself away by some oddity in her speech. Sadika was also lucky in that the governor's wife was no longer alive. She didn't think she would have been able to fool Kristabella's mother if she were here.

Luckily the governor and his daughter did not have a deep relationship. The most Sadika saw him was for breakfast and occasionally at dinner. He appeared to be deeply in thought most of the times and barely answered her chattered questions as she rambled about the social goings-on of saikan life. She was very glad that she had caught up with all the news in the time she had spent at Eliza's house.

Sadika heartily wished that the three days would soon be over. Her only real grace was that the governor had not noticed that his daughter was missing at all. Hopefully he wouldn't notice for the next few days.

The saikan girl awoke with a groan. Amrika, sitting at the mouth of the tent, eyed her. After a few minutes of continuous stirring, Kristabella's eyes finally fluttered open. She blinked confusedly at the top of the tent and probably would have dismissed it as a dream if the pain hadn't hit her a moment later. She grimaced and reached up to touch the back of her head. Her gentle probing of the bump caused her to hiss and pull her hand away.

The jolt of pain seemed to wake her up more and she attempted to sit up. She sat up halfway, grabbed her head and sank back down into the thin mattress.

"Uh!" she moaned, screwing up her eyes.

"Yuh might wanta lie down some more," Amrika advised.

After a moment, Kristabella bent her head and slitted open her eyes to look at Amrika.

"Who are you?'" the young woman asked. "Where am I?"

"Who I is," said Amrika, "is no concern of yours. As fuh where you dey. Yuh quite far away from where yuh expected to be."

"My father," Kristabella began. She stopped, licked her lips and started again. "My father will kill you for this."

"Yuh father have no idea where yuh dey and probably never will," Amrika told her calmly. "Water?" she held out a canteen.

Kristabella eyed her speculatively for a moment and then reached out and took the canteen. She uncorked it and dropped the water into her mouth daintily, managing not to spill any. She swallowed and then said,

"If you release me now, I will ask my father to grant you amnesty, that is, not punish you for this."

"Nuh really an option," Amrika to her. "You're being held for ransom."

Kristabella let out a high-pitched laugh which evidently made her own head hurt, as she screwed up her eyes again right after.

"Money," she said when she could talk again. "All the money you would gain from this wouldn't save your life."

"We not asking fuh money," Amrika told her.

"And how long am I to be held here in these deplorable conditions?" the governor's daughter demanded.

"Three days," Amrika told her.

"And then you will return me to my father?" she demanded.

"Depends on what yuh father do," Amrika told her.

"And if he doesn't accede to your demands?" asked Kristabella sharply.

"Well," said Amrika, "Leh we jus say yuh wouldn't have to worry about anything anymore."

Kristabella paled at the implications.

"You would kill me," she said, voice wobbling, though she tried to keep it steady.

"That's de threat," Amrika agreed. "Leh we hope yuh father love yuh eh?"

"If you kill me," Kristabella began, "he will kill all of you. He will not grant you mercy. He will not grant your families mercy."

Amrika just smiled at her, knowing that even with the mask on her face, that the saikan girl would know.

"Leh we worry 'bout dat eh?" Amrika said to her.

"You will regret this," Kristabella warned her. Amrika didn't deign to reply.

Khion settled on a log next to Jiang. The other Stickfighter had finally gotten on her feet some days after Markus and him, but she was still moving stiffly.

"How yuh dey gyul?" he asked her.

"Better dan everybody seem to think ah is," Jiang retorted.

Khion laughed. "Hey, yuh was looking real bad off."

Jiang snorted but some of her ire left her form. She looked around at the kalinag encampment.

"Calm before de storm," she commented.

"Yeah," Khion agreed. Beneath their feet Ierie's beat was steady but waiting.

"Yuh think dis plan ah de spider's go work?" Jiang asked him.

Khion sighed. "I think we doh really have much choice. But she is ah trickster, she know better than we how dese things go."

"Will he stick to his agreement?" Jiang asked. "If de governor does agree?"

"Maybe," said Khion, "If he smart, he will."

"Leh we hope he smart enough den," said Jiang.

"I think," said Khion, "ah lot of people hoping he is."

"Hoping who is what?" asked Markus, coming over.

"Hoping de governor smart, "Jiang answered. Markus collapsed on the log next to them.

"Yeah," he agreed, "Cause if he play chupid, we all dead."

"Except de kalinag," Khion reminded him.

"Except for the kalinag," Markus agreed, "Buh ah doh think even dey go be happy with dat."

"Ierie doesn't care," Jiang said. "The land just want them alive."

"Yes," said a nearby kalinag woman, who had been listening in on the conversation, "Buh we care. It go be real lonely with just us here."

"Well," said Jiang smiling, "Leh we hope de dark things who negotiating know what dey doing."

It took a few hours before Kristabella summoned enough strength to sit up for long periods of time. She still had a terrible headache which she complained about but had refused to drink the herbal concoction Amrika had procured for her. Clearly the idea of being killed by poison had crossed her mind. Amrika telling her flatly that if they were going to kill her, they would just do it and not waste time with poison hadn't seemed to reassure her in the slightest.

When Kristabella felt recovered enough, she demanded to leave the tent for fresh air. Amrika gracefully stood away from the tent opening and allowed Kristabella to crawl out. The saikan girl stood up, winced and looked a little green. When the nausea had subsided, she looked around her and froze.

Amrika figured that she hadn't really believed that she was as far away from the town as Amrika had told her. The landscape certainly put that idea in the grave.

"Where am I?" Kristabella shrieked, looking at the field, no lake of black substance, pockmarked with green growth and turbid pools.

Amrika smiled grimly. "Not in Port of Gold," she told her.

"I demand to know where I am!" Kristabella shouted at her. She even stamped her feet a little.

"I thought yuh might have figured it out by now," Amrika told her dryly. When the saikan woman looked at her in question, Amrika said, "Black lake, south end of the island, pitch."

"The lake of pitch," said Kristabella, "I have only heard tell of it."

"Well even in description it's rather unique," Amrika responded.

Kristabella swallowed, looked around her again and then said, "For how long was I unconscious?"

"Only the night," said Amrika. "It's de next day."

"Only the night!" repeated Kristabella astonished. "But that's impossible. We can't have reached the southern part of the island so quickly. How long have I really been unconscious? Answer me boerin!"

"Only de night," Amrika replied again. "Relly. We have we ways ah getting yuh here so fas."

Kristabella pursed her lips and looked like she definitely didn't believe Amrika. Amrika didn't particularly care.

After looking sulky for a long time, Kristabella asked if they had food. Amrika handed her a sack of food from inside the tent and watched as the saikan girl opened the sack, inspected the food and peeled back her teeth in disgust at the fare. Still her stomach rumbled so she munched on the food, still twisting her face at it every now and then.

When she was finished eating, she said, "Is there some place I can have a bath?" She paused. "For that matter, are there any other clothes for me?"

"It have clothes," Amrika said, "And it have place to bathe. De clothes in a bundle in the tent."

When it became clear that Amrika was not going to fetch the bundle of clothes for her, Kristabella got up in a huff and stormed back to the tiny tent.

She emerged from the tent and stalked over to Amrika, "Where can I go to bathe?" she asked haughtily. Amrika pointed to one of the pools of warm water. Kristabella blinked at the pool and turned to look at her.

"Absolutely not! You jest!"

"I don't," said Amrika. "It's safe an clean. And I hear it good for yuh medically too."

"I will not!" snapped the governor's daughter.

"Den stay dirty," said Amrika. Kristabella stared at her in mounting fury for a few moments and then tossed the bundle of clothes at her face and took off across the uneven land, making a bolt for freedom.

Amrika tossed the clothes away, watched her running figure and wanted to laugh. She debated having one of the others catch the saikan but it was her job to guard her, so she set off after Kristabella, Stickfighter speed letting her catch up with the escapee quite easily. She snatched at the back of Kristabella's night dress and tugged her to the ground.

Kristabella fell with a yelp, tried to kick Amrika's feet out from under her and wound up holding her foot instead.

"Okay," said Amrika stooping down next to the prone saikan. "First off, yuh cah hurt meh. Secondly, I is not de only person guarding yuh." She pointed off in the distance where a female Moko Jumbie was leaning out from behind a tree, looking at them. Kristabella's face paled at the sight of the Moko Jumbie who was moving far too fluidly to just be someone on stilts. She blinked at Amrika and then reared back and punched her in the face. Amrika didn't move and winced on behalf of the young saikan woman.

"Ow! Ow! Ow!" yelled Kristabella as she now held her hand.

"Wha I just tell yuh?" said Amrika in exasperation. "Yuh cah hurt meh. Now get up and go bathe." She hauled Kristabella to her feet and pointed to the pool. Kristabella glared at her but slowly limped over to the pool. Amrika snorted. If this kept up she would soon find herself wishing to fight mercenaries again.

"What are you?" Kristabella asked when she was lying in a pool of pleasantly warm water.

"What?" asked Amrika.

"I've hit a man before," said Kristabella, "A strong man too. He was being too forward," she explained, "And still he moved when I hit him. Just a little, but he did move. You didn't. It was like hitting a wall." She inspected her knuckles. "My hands are bruised. So," she looked at Amrika, "What are you? You can't be normal." Her eyes flicked to where the Moko Jumbie stood guard.

"I'm a dark thing," said Amrika.

"A dark thing?"

"A dark thing of Ierie," Amrika elaborated.

"An evil thing," said Kristabella.

"No," laughed Amrika.

"Then why 'dark'? Why call yourself a dark thing?"

"Dark like the earth of de mangrove and de mountains" said Amrika, "Rich, fertile, teeming with life. Dark like the pitch here which bubbles up without end and is strong and binding and has unexpected benefits. Dark like de reservoirs of black energy which lie untapped off de shores of de island, in de waters dat belong to Ierie. Dark like that. That darkness runs in we blood and make it black."

Kristabella was silent for a moment and then said slowly, "This is because of that proclamation isn't it? The ones about the boerin who stole saikan property and killed some men. I think I vaguely heard something about a proclamation about that."

Amrika wondered what it was like to live so detached from the rest of the world that the proclamations that threatened the lives of an entire class of society was only a thing heard in passing, that hundreds of your own people dying was just a footnote.

"Yes," she said shortly. Then she cocked her head. "Do you know what yuh father trying to do?"

Kristabella shook her head. "Why should I? It is his business."

"Your father trying to kill out all the kalinag to take their land," Amrika said flatly.

Kristabella absorbed the news and then shrugged. "The island belongs to the Motherland," she said, "It is ours to do as we will."

"And killing innocent people is okay?!" Amrika demanded.

"They should move away and stay away," Kristabella said coolly. "They are not citizens of the Motherland. They don't deserve our protection. In fact, they probably just take up resources that belong to us."

Amrika felt somewhat speechless. "They lived here first."

"And they failed to keep their land," said Kristabella, "That's what conquest is, boerin. Besides, why do you care? The kalinag are not your people. You are not being threatened. Why are you putting yourself and your families at risk for people that are not your own?"

"Maybe," said Amrika, "Maybe because we doh need a reason to be decent people?"

Kristabella laughed. "I could, perhaps, believe that. But rare are the people who think that way. You'd never get so many of you who think the same. And I see no kalinag here. Surely, they'd care about their fate as well? Yet I see only you, the dark things here. So why do you care?"

"De kalinag are our brothers and sisters in spirit," Amrika said after a moment. "We doh take that connection lightly." She paused struggling to find a way to explain how she was rooted to the land of her birth, how she automatically classed the kalinag as to be protected because the land loved them dearly. She didn't know how to explain that she was expendable because the birthing of the dark things was a far easier birth than that of the kalinag. But most of all, she didn't know how to tell someone that the land of her birth had threatened her life and her black blood if she did not save the kalinag and she was okay with that, that she understood why; while simultaneously not knowing how to survive the loss of her status of a dark thing. Black blood had always run in her veins. To have it ripped out of her…she wasn't sure she'd survive the grief of its loss.

"I can't explain," she said after a long pause. "But duty and love and fear binds me to this."

Kristabella huffed. "It doesn't sound like a good reason to die for anyone. You should obey my father's proclamation and the laws of the Motherland which govern this island."

Amrika felt like slapping her but refrained by dint of much self-control.

"There is one thing you should never get confused about saikan, "she said after a long moment.

"What?" asked Kristabella.

"The land is not yours. De land belongs to nobody except itself."

The saikan woman gave her a confused but amused look.

"The land isn't alive," said Kristabella.

Amrika laughed in her face. "If the land isn't alive, Kristabella," she said, "where did de dark things come from?"

Protect the firstborn!

CHAPTER 41

Sadika was glad she was a good actor and had enough command over her facial expressions so that she didn't give herself away. It was little things that nearly tripped her up in her secret residence of the governor's house, tiny habits of the saikan that none of the jotlin or boerin had adopted, odd points of view that led her into awkward conversations that took some linguistic dexterity to extract herself from. But the three days passed, peaceably enough.

The morning of the fourth day, she managed to convince her maids that she wanted to visit her father at his office.

She spotted the captain of the soldiers leaving the governor's office but he didn't go far so it was obvious that he was still waiting for orders. Good.

Sadika made her way over to the governor's office and knocked, opening the door as she did so.

"Who" began the governor angrily, looking like he'd been startled out of thought. "Kristabella!" he said in surprise, brows creasing. "What are you doing here my dear?"

"I find myself terribly bored," Sadika said, mimicking Kristabella's voice, "I thought I would visit, cheer up your day a little."

"That's sweet my dear," said the governor, "But I'm busy. I will see you another time. Please. Entertain yourself in the stores today my dear. Your father is very busy."

With that he lowered his head and returned to thought. Sadika stepped into the room properly, closed the door behind her and said in her normal voice, "No really governor, I think you ought to listen to what I have to say."

At that the governor's head shot up and he stared at her, frowning. "Kristabella?" he asked confused.

"No," said Sadika smiling. She allowed the illusion on her face to flicker and change to another female's face. She wasn't stupid enough to let him see her true face. The governor blinked in shock and then scrambled for his gun. A hand chopped sharply down on his wrist, sending the gun flying. Sadika kicked it calmly into a corner while the governor stared at the Midnight Robber and Stickfighter who had come into the governor's office via his window, a feat only managed by the illusions Sadika had held on the spider webs they wore. Sadika spared a moment to be proud of Reshma. The child had wound the spiderweb perfectly around the two.

"Be quiet, governor," she cautioned.

"Who are you?" he snapped. "Where is my daughter?"

"Not safe at home," Sadika told him calmly.

His face grew red as he took in the news. "I will kill all of you!" he began, but his tirade was cut short by the Midnight Robber who said casually,

"Why don't you leave de threats for dem who know how to make dem eh governor? Shut up now an listen, yuh might learn something. We here to bargain. Play it right, yuh daughter comes back safe and sound. Play it wrong and then is just she body coming back."

The governor froze. "Are you threatening me?" he asked, slowly.

"Threatening your daughter actually," said Sadika. "We have some demands. We would like you to meet them for the safe return of your daughter."

The governor clenched his teeth but nodded. "Very well, "he said, "I would hear your demands. That doesn't mean I will accede to them."

"Our demands are simple," Sadika said, "First, leave the kalinag and their land alone, now and ever. Second, no harm shall be done to the boerin, they had no part in it anyway, thirdly, amnesty for the ones you call criminals and we call defenders and finally, you have a prisoner, one of ours, let him free, today. That's all. Four simple things."

"I, as you so graciously reminded me, have a prisoner too," said the governor, "I too can threaten the life of one of yours."

"We'll call your bluff," said Sadika flatly, "Will you dare to call ours?"

The governor sneered at her. "I have watched your people, read your movements. You'll kill mercenaries but you haven't killed any of my soldiers. You won't kill anyone who isn't threatening you. You won't kill her. You won't kill an innocent girl."

"That," said the Stickfighter very, very softly, "is where you are wrong, governor of Port of Gold."

"You see," said Sadika, "circumstances have occurred that find us all on the same side."

"And what side is that?" snarled the governor.

"The side where yuh island isn't destroyed," the Midnight Robber tells him, seeming almost bored.

"What?" the governor is confused again, but listening this time.

Sadika lets the illusions over all their faces switch into several faces rapidly. The governor jerks back and she smiles.

"Let's all agree that there are strange things afoot," she said calmly. "We can do things you wouldn't have believed a few weeks prior. Isn't that right? This is no drug, governor."

The governor pauses and then nods slowly.

"Then believe us when we say that there are worse out there than us," she continued. "The massacre on the river wasn't our plan. We tried to minimize the killing, but you are attempting to kill the kalinag and that has repercussions."

"Repercussions like the river," said the Stickfighter.

"And repercussion like the whole of Ierie being… nuh destroyed but uninhabitable for everybody but de kalinag," the Midnight Robber told him.

"There is another one of us," Sadika told him, "He is sleeping but because of what you are doing he is stirring awake. For your sake, and ours we need to keep him asleep."

The governor looked at them and then said, "Am I supposed to be threatened by this, this fairytale?"

"The dragon," said Sadika raising her voice slightly, "is awakening."

There was a heavy paused and then the governor started to laugh. He was cut off by a heavy hand slamming down on his desk.

The Midnight Robber let his dark miasma flood the room, let the governor shiver at the threat.

"The dragon,' he said harshly, "is awakening. And when he flies he will breathe fire over everything there is to burn in this land. He won't stop. He is not like we, to be bargained with. You cannot stop him. We cannot stop him. Once he awakes, all of Ierie goes down in flames save for where the kalinag lives. No saikan lives will be spared and we are very unsure if boerin and jotlin lives will spared as well."

"The dragon, governor," said Sadika, letting some of her fear creep into her voice, "can't fly. Even if most of the boerin lives are saved, undoubtedly there will be collateral damage. Someone will die. Destruction of that scale will never not claim innocents. Doh wake the dragon, governor. The dragon cannot be allowed to fly. If he flies through the sky, we are all dead."

"We are de dark things of Ierie governor," said the Stickfighter, "and you are de governor of Port of Gold. Would you choose to destroy thousands of lives for your pride? How would you explain that to the Motherland? You are charged with the care of the Motherland's property, aren't you? Make no mistake governor, you continue, and de dragon will come. Doh wake the dragon governor. The dragon cah fly."

The governor sputtered, unwilling to believe them but their utter seriousness was convincing him that, if nothing else, they believed in the threat. Fear crept over him and held fast, but he powered his way through for a final jab.

"I'm supposed to believe you about this? It could be a lie. You're, you're dressed as carnival characters, for goodness sake, ridiculous figures all of you, nothing more! And your threat is just as ridiculous."

Sadika laughed. "Oh, we're not dressed like carnival characters governor, they're dressed like us. The boerin like to imitate us, makes us less scary somehow. And in carnival there is a dragon mas and I know for a fact even the saikan do not think that mas is ridiculous. That's our only proof, that is how you know we are telling the truth, governor, because the boerin put it in their mas."

"And," added the Midnight Robber, "The dragon is one costume they do not ridicule."

The governor sneered again. "I have never seen anyone dressed like you, little girl."

"Oh no," said Sadika amiably. "No one masquerades as what I am. That's because no one knows what we really look like. Some people think it's considered bad luck to try, others don't, as an appreciation of our skill, a way to say 'you are too good to copy'."

But," the Stickfighter continued. "What dem two ah dem not telling you is dat even if we could stop de dragon we wouldn't, not for saikan lives anyway."

The governor blinked at him. "What?"

"Call our bluff when you like," said Sadika with a wry smile, "You have nothing over people who will not let anything stop them."

"Why?" snapped the governor. "Why would you do something so foolish? The Motherland will come down on you!"

"Because," said the Midnight Robber in a dark voice, "We have to save lives. Saikan lives we cannot spare, no matter how much we want to. So, we'll give them up for the rest of the people. You see, there are worse fates than all of Ierie being set aflame."

"So, what say you governor?" asked Sadika. "Will you risk your daughter's life and the life of everyone on this island and deny our demands or will you accede and save your daughter's life in the bargain?"

"You are mad!" said the governor, "All of you!" But there was fear in his eyes. Here before him stood impossible things. It should have been a far stretch to believe in a dragon. It wasn't. Not when hundreds of men were dead.

"No," said Sadika gently, "Sadly, we're not."

The governor was silent, weighing his choices but finally he said, "Give me a day to think of your proposal. No harm will come to any of your people in the interim."

"Very well," said Sadika. "We will meet back here then, the same time tomorrow."

The governor nodded and then the three of them walked out, Sadika walked out of the governor's office wearing Kristabella's face and the other two now looking like saikan soldiers. Once safely outside they disappeared into the crowd.

"An extra day?" said Khion.

"He's going to search for he daughter," said Kirish, "So he doh have to bargain."

"We have three days' head start on him," said Sadika. "He can't possibly find her."

"But we didn't tell him dat," Khion said. "He thinks she was taken today."

"Oh well," Sadika shrugged. "Let him search. Is not like he go find she."

"Yuh think he go keep he word if he agree?" asked Kirish.

Sadika sighed. "We can only hope. But I think we did really scare him."

"He will hate we," Khion observed.

"Dais fine," said Kirish, "So long as he doh try an kill the kalinag."

Protect the children of my womb!

CHAPTER 42

"It's been three days!" said Kristabella, angrily, "Release me!"

"Dat depends on wha yuh father do," Amrika reminded her. She was bored out of her mind and annoyed with the spoilt saikan girl by now.

"He will find me!" said Kristabella.

"I'm sure he'll try," Amrika said in a bored tone. "Buh dis island nuh small like others yuh know. It ha real place to hide somebody, living or dead." That statement shut Kristabella right up.

The first thing the governor did after his meeting with the dark things was, as predicted, to look for his daughter. Tamara and Vishal observed the search parties from where they hovered in the air, high enough to be mistaken for birds. Soldiers quietly ripped apart the saikan and jotlin sections of Port of Gold in search of Kristabella. Soldiers not-so-quietly ripped apart the boerin section but the governor apparently had kept his word about not hurting anyone.

Search parties spread out across the surrounding land, looking in every nook and cranny, searching distant estates and even the ruins of Chagna and Tarigua and as far up the road as they dared towards Aria, the sole kalinag village which hadn't been destroyed.

Riders were sent to all the civilized portion of Ierie at a speed which should surely kill their horses. Tamara felt sorry for the poor beasts. The search parties were kept going all night, but they turned up nothing. In fact, they didn't even come within miles of where Kristabella was stashed away.

"What now?" asked Vishal.

"Well," said Tamara, "I guess we go see if de governor will decide to kill he daughter."

As evening fell, Kristabella became more and more silent. Finally, she asked in a small voice, "Are you going to kill me now? No word has come from my father."

Amrika shook her head. "No." The Moko Jumbie had given her the news earlier from a visiting Bat. "Yuh father asked for an extra day while he thinks on we proposal."

Kristabella paled. "If he hasn't given an answer in three days, he won't save me for another."

"Relax," Amrika said, feeling sympathetic to the girl's fear. No one wants to think they're going to die. And no one wants to think it's because their father didn't care enough. "He didn't know you were gone until today."

Kristabella blinked. "But how can that be? How could he not know I was missing?"

Amrika smiled. "We have somebody who is very good at looking like somebody else."

Kristabella frowned and opened her mouth, then closed it. After a moment she said, "Is that person a dark thing?"

Amrika bobbed her head. "Yes."

"Oh," she said. She was silent for the rest of the night.

The governor sat late in his office as he contemplated his choices. He could hurt the boerin, could kill the conspirator he had captured but he knew, knew that these people would kill his daughter. He could not let that happen. He wasn't particularly fond of his daughter the way he would have been of a son, but she was very much her mother's child and he had loved her mother. He could not let her die at the hands of these, these things, for they were not human.

He needed some sort of leverage to hold over these people.

He struggled with his options, getting more frantic as the night drew on. But eventually his fear for his daughter morphed into something else. Anger.

He would not let these people dictate to him. He would not let their tales of an impossible thing sway him. Dragons were fairy tales. Whatever abilities these people had could be explained by some means or another. He would get his daughter back. These things were not so cold hearted as they tried to make him believe, they had after all saved those boerin who had been beaten. They would not let their own people die. He rang for a rider. When the rider came into the room the governor handed him a letter.

"Give this to Lord Ainsley," he said. "Go now!"

The rider nodded and quickly headed off into the night.

"Hmm," said Trevon, unfolding the note he had stolen from the rider. "I wonder what this is?" his eyes flickered over the writing and then he smiled.

"And wa is dat?" asked a Jab Jab from behind him.

Still smiling Trevon answered. "Ah good reason to geh rid of ah bad man." He sank back into the shadows and went off in search for a Bat.

Jamal heard the Bat's news, smiled, and went in search of his stilts. When he arrived at Ainsley's house, the rider was frantically patting himself down searching for the note that the Midnight Robber had stolen. Ainsley finally turned the man away in disgust and stalked back inside his house.

A few minutes later, the light in his study had drastically increased as a lamp was lit, just as Jamal suspected it would. Ainsley would know what the governor had sent for this late at night. He waited a few moments and then calmly walked up to the window of the study.

Inside Ainsley held up the bottle of whatever poison he intended to use on the boerin. Jamal took the opportunity to lean inside, reach forward and snatch the bottle from Ainsley's grasp.

The man gasped and made to move for a pistol, but Jamal pinned him with his stare. He struggled at first, this saikan who thought he should rule over everybody else, but he was unable to free himself. Jamal waited patiently until he stopped struggling and then said

"Lord Ainsley of the Motherland. You brought real evil to dis land. These grounds are steeped in yuh evil. The very air is rotted by yuh disgusting desires." Jamal took a deep breath and felt the evil in the air, felt the way the air was thick and slow with it.

"Yuh helped in trying to kill de kalinag and now yuh trying to kill de boerin too. Is time fuh you to done. Yuh hear meh. No more ah yuh games and yuh plans and yuh plots. No more ah yuh cruelty. Is time fuh yuh to pay now." And with that he reached out into Ainsley's mind and dragged out his fears to play. He feared a lot, Jamal mused, for a man who acted like little could hurt him. But men like him were always cowards anyway, their ambitions driven by their fear and hatred.

Ainsley trembled in his hold. His eyes widened, his pulse jumped, and he began to sweat. Soon enough he began to moan. Then he began to speak, softly at first and then louder as he spewed threats to all the people that he saw in his fears. He was practically foaming at the mouth after a while but luckily it was still not loud enough to attract the attention of others. His personal fears took a long time to pass. And when they were exhausted, Jamal started on the real stuff: all the fear his actions had caused to others, every evil thing he had done to the people around him for his entire life. Jamal did not spare him anything. Every person he had robbed, every life ruined, every reputation destroyed, every human being he had ever treated like filth, every time he blackmailed somebody, every person he had killed himself and every person he had ordered to be killed were all drawn back. Jamal let him feel the fear of his victims. It was a process that took longer to pass than the parade of Ainsley's own fears. This man had hurt a lot of people in his life.

Ainsley's heartbeat was hummingbird fast and he was gasping in breaths as hard he could. His eyes were wide, black pools, pupils dilated to the widest they could go. He had stopped speaking now, only letting out a continuous moan. Jamal ignored it, continuing without mercy until the very end.

When Jamal finally released him from his gaze Ainsley slumped onto the floor a blubbering, gibbering mess that moaned and rocked back and forth. The Moko Jumbie eyed him coolly and then stepped away from the window and disappeared into the night.

The incompetent rider who had lost his note to Ainsley the first time came back the second time looking thoroughly spooked.

"Have you lost it again!" the governor demanded irritated.

"No sir!" said the rider.

"What then?!" snapped the governor.

"Lord Ainsley sir," he said.

"What about him?" asked the governor.

"He's gone mad sir," said the rider.

"What?!" the governor sat up. "What do you mean?"

"When I went to deliver the note to him a second time, like you ordered, he was in his study. The butler said that he was not answering his knock. He asked if I could leave the note with him, but I said you told me to only give it to Lord Ainsley, so the butler tried again. When he didn't answer after ten minutes, they suspected something was wrong and broke in the door. That's when they found him on the floor, sir. Just, rocking back and forth and talking unintelligibly. He wouldn't respond to anyone."

"Were there any bottles in the room?" the governor demanded after a disturbed pause.

"No sir," said the rider, "Except for the inkwell."

"Very well," said the governor, "Leave!"

The rider left, and the governor sat back in his chair feeling very rattled. What had these people done to Ainsley, to drive him mad in so short a time? Could they do it to him? To his soldiers? And now, now they either had the poison or it was lost wherever Ainsley had secreted it away.

The governor poured himself a drink and shot it back, feeling the burn of it going down his throat. After a few moments, he suddenly realized that the first note hadn't been lost, it had been stolen from off the rider. Fear pooled in his gut, cooling the burn of the whiskey. Had he killed his daughter? Would they kill her for what he had been about to do? The governor collapsed heavily in his chair. Had he killed her?

CHAPTER 13

The morning dawned bright and clear. Blue skies soared above, and the sun was hot but not uncomfortable. If he listened hard enough the governor could hear the sound of the surf. The governor did not care for the day. He had not slept. Dark circles ringed his eyes but he splashed his face with water and dressed in fresh clothes as he waited for the people who had stolen his daughter to return.

They were prompt, entering his office to the minute that they had the day before. This time it looked like two of his own soldiers who walked in. When the door was closed, their images shimmered to reveal the same young woman, dressed in black, veiled this time, and the Stickfighter, the governor cautiously identified from whatever time he had spent looking at the carnival of the boerin.

A sudden click made him turn startled, only to see the Midnight Robber holding the governor's two pistols and his rifle from where he had hidden them. The governor blinked as he tried furiously to figure out where the Midnight Robber had even come from. The Robber simply smiled and said

"Ah go keep dem fuh now governor. In case yuh do something yuh go regret." He went to stand next to the other two.

The woman gestured at the chairs facing the governor. "May we?"

The governor nodded stiffly. The three settled themselves comfortably in the chairs and then focused on the governor.

"So," said the young woman who could apparently make illusions. "What have you decided governor?"

The governor clenched his jaw but then said, "I will accede to your demands. Now, release my daughter."

"Not until we have it in writing," said the Stickfighter causally. All three of them cocked their heads at the governor who trembled with rage, anger and fear but pulled out a piece of paper, sharpened a quill and began to write. He gave them all that they asked, wrote two copies at their demand, one for him to keep, and handed them the other.

"Now," he said when it was all done. "Where is my daughter?"

"She will be released today," said the young woman. "You'll probably get her back sometime this evening. We've hidden her quite a long way away you see. We apologize for the inconvenience. You may hold your prisoner until she is returned."

"She will be returned!" the governor threatened.

"Of course," said the veiled woman. "It wouldn't be smart to do otherwise." With that the three of them once more shimmered into looking like soldiers and they walked out of the governor's office.

The Bat landed next to the tent and grinned at Kristabella through her mask. "Good news!" she announced. "Yuh get to live saikan!"

Amrika watched as Kristabella's face lit up. "Really?!" she cried out.

"Really," Amrika told her. "Looks like yuh father really cares for yuh. Now. I am sorry."

"What for?" asked Kristabella frowning. Amrika hit her in the back of the head and she fell unconscious.

"Ouch," said the Bat.

"Yeah," sighed Amrika. She dragged the girl to the sheets she had come wrapped in and began wrapping her back up. The two Bats who had been stationed near them to return Kristabella came over and helped and then, holding her carefully between them, set off in the direction of Port of Gold.

CHAPTER 44

The governor kept his word. Once his daughter was released safely back to him, he released Sadika's father. The old man had been quicker than Sadika, putting masks of thick spiderweb over his face that the beatings hadn't been able to remove entirely. He had thus preserved his identity.

The mercenaries who had known which house he'd been captured from had all been killed on the river, leaving them surprisingly in the clear. Reshma had been overjoyed to get her grandfather back and thoroughly horrified when she saw the state of him, bursting into tears at the terrible mess that had been made of his face.

They stayed by Eliza while her father recuperated, not sure if their home was safe enough. But after a few weeks of peace they returned home.

The kalinag as well did not return to their villages, or what was left of them, very soon either. They didn't trust the governor not to go back on his word and try to kill them again. Instead they stayed in their encampments in the forest with a rotating guard of Stickfighters and other dark things. The boerin who had been beaten however, returned home as quickly as possible, eager to get home to their families.

"So," said Amrika to her brother one evening, as they both sat on a roof. "Yuh really think it over?"

"I doh know," said her brother. He wasn't currently the Robber, he was just keeping her company as they enjoyed the night air. "On one hand it looking so buh on de other, Ierie ain't settle down completely."

Amrika knew what he meant, there was still a tug on her bones, calling to the black blood in her veins.

"It's been almost two months though," she said.

"Time doh mean nothing to people who want revenge," Kirish advised her. "In fact, de longer it take de worse it might be."

"But people are watching him rite?" asked Amrika.

"Yeah," said her brother. "The Dame Lorraines, the Bats, de Jab Jab even and de Robbers too. All ah we watching buh yuh never know. Dem saikan can be real smart when dey ready."

"Well leh we hope he smart enough not to do anything, said Amrika, "And not so smart if he trying something."

Kirish laughed. "Leh we hope."

They were silent for a while and then Amrika elbowed her brother in the ribs lightly. "So yuh talk to Tamara lately?"

Her brother snorted. "Dais is none ah your business!"

Amrika laughed again and chose to change the subject. "Carnival soon," she said. "You think they'll have it?"

"Of course," said Kirish, "We nuh lehing the saikan frighten we so. Yuh playing?"

Amrika remembered the sailors' revelry and swallowed hard. "No. Ah doh think so. Ah go just watch dis year."

Her brother shrugged and turned to watch the streets of people below them.

CHAPTER 45

Kirish was right. Carnival continued as scheduled. Amrika woke up Carnival morning to the sounds of tamboo bamboo and drums. The vibrant beat made her smile and she danced her way into the kitchen. A note was scrawled on a grubby piece of paper in Kirish's handwriting.

'Gone J'ouvert,' it said simply. Amrika snorted and went about making herself breakfast. With breakfast in hand, she propped up in the doorway and watched as the J'ouvert mas players strutted down the street with their accompanying musicians: a mass of throbbing mud-covered people, moving in time with the beat. Amrika swayed to the music as she gobbled down her food, laughing at masqueraders who could not dance but were trying to anyway.

It was a perfect day for mas, she reflected as she returned inside to get dressed for the day. The sun was shining, there was hardly a cloud in the sky and the breeze was blowing in from off the ocean, bringing with it the scent of the sea. Amrika smiled, it was going to be a great day.

"Reshma hold still chile!" said Sadika in frustration as she attempted to affix the child's costume on her. The little girl was far too excited to keep still for very long, practically vibrating with excitement.

"If yuh don't stop moving yuh not going!" Sadika threatened. This got through and Reshma finally stopped moving long enough that Sadika could fix the Baby Doll costume onto her properly.

"Can we go now?" Reshma said excitedly. Sadika laughed.

"Yes but jus leh me geh meh mask chile." She grabbed her mask, put it on and held out her hand to the child. Reshma took it eagerly and pulled her down the stairs and to their carriage.

"Dad! We gone!" Sadika called.

Her father waved at them from the doorway, still moving stiffly, but he looked much better than he had been. Reshma and Sadika waved back and headed off to town.

Amrika sat on the roof of a store, not bothering to hide as she watched the parade that went on just below her feet. The sun was beating down on her head, the beat was thrumming through her bones and the boerin were wild and happy.

She danced in place to the music and admired the costumes of the people marching by. Some were of course dressed like the traditional figures. She could see several Midnight Robbers chipping along the road to the music. Just moments before one of them had finished their speech. As the Robbers passed her, Surish winked at her from under his hat, startling her into laughter.

Persons dressed as Jab Jabs prowled the streets, cracking whips and occasionally challenging other Jab Jabs. A solitary Bookman walked down the street, book in hand.

Sailors came next, a mas band that had Amrika shivering in the hot sun. But they were just ordinary people dressed as sailors.

Coy Dame Lorraines called to men on the sides of the streets. Amrika laughed as she noticed a few real Dame Lorraines among them, dressed in costume like the others.

A little band of persons dressed as cows came next, ringing their bells, followed by a few Pierrot Grenades. Following these, were persons dressed as Baby Dolls. Even as she watched, a Baby Doll ran up to a jotlin man and loudly accuse him of being the father of the child she was holding in her arms. The man reared back and tried to argue even knowing it wasn't real, simply because the Baby Doll was acting so well. His friends all laughed at him, softening the moment.

Some Bats came after doing their little Bat dance and flapping their homemade wings in time to the music. One of them was doing it very well and had managed to achieve the look of a true Bat.

Fancy Indians came next, screaming their loud cries and scaring half the people on the street. Then Moko Jumbies came dancing skillfully on their stilts. Amrika squinted up at them and yep, there were few real Moko Jumbies there too, but like the others they were simply on stilts and dressed the part. She laughed, almost kicked the head dress of a Fancy Indian who had stumbled far too close to her foot and waved to Jiang and her little sister who were among the Indians.

As she shifted on the roof, she caught a glimpse of something silver glinting from one of the windows along the parade. She cocked her head, curious, and noticed another glint from the window next to the previous one spotted. Another glint was in the window a house further down. Amrika frowned as she watched the parade spread out in the road before her. Then suddenly the glints wobbled, disappeared and did not return. She shrugged and turned her attention back to the tamboo bamboo bands that were passing.

"Fear," said the man.

The governor spun from where he was standing by the window, in a building overlooking the parade. He looked at the man who was standing inside the room, holding a book under his arm.

"Who are you?!" demanded the governor, "Where did you come from? How did you get in here?"

"Ah walked in," said the man. "Hello governor, doh go for the gun, leh we talk."

The governor looked longingly at the desk which held his gun, but was too far away from him to reach.

"What do you want to say?" asked the governor.

"Fear," the man repeated. "Is a strange thing, fear. It does make people do many things they wouldn't. Sometimes it makes them do commendable things. It can also make them do things that are very stupid. I'm afraid governor, that you fall in de latter category."

The governor's jaw clenched, and he said, "Did you come here to insult me boerin?"

"I did not," said the man clearly, switching into proper English for the governor's sake. "And I am not a boerin." He paused and then walked over to the governor's desk and leaned on it. "How long governor?" he asked.

"How long for what?" asked the governor through gritted teeth.

"How long did it take for the relief of having your daughter back safe and sound to drain away and be replaced by anger that your hand had been forced by people you considered inferior? And how long did it take for that anger to become fear? For you fear us, do you not? You got your darling Kristabella back and then stopped to take stock of your losses and realized that you'd lost a frightening amount of people. You realized what these people could do, how they could challenge you. Kristabella told you she'd been gone for three days and you realized they could have killed you any time they wanted. You began to fear dear governor. How long did it take?"

The governor lifted his chin and did answer the question. "You must all be destroyed. You are freaks and terrors that cannot be allowed to live on saikan land."

Outside, the tempo of the beat changed as the dragon mas came out. The governor's back stiffened and the man smiled at him from under his hat. The smile made the governor shiver.

"This is not saikan land," the man said very carefully. "Never, never make that mistake governor. This land belongs to itself. Ierie belongs to Ierie. It will never belong to the Motherland." The man tilted his head. "Do you know who I am?"

The governor, face red with anger, shook his head stiffly.

"I am de Bookman," said the man gently. "You would see a couple of the boerin dressed like me out there. I am the first of de dark things to ever have been made."

"Dark things?" the governor repeated in question, though he had a good idea what the dark things were.

"What you have called freaks and terrors," the Bookman explained. "You see, I was born first because I was born out of Ierie's hatred for injustice and the hatred of the slaves you brought over here. Their hatred was for the injustices they suffered also. I was made because Ierie is a free land and out of all the things in this world, Ierie hates slavery the most. I was made to dispense justice, to be the judge, jury and executioner of Ierie, not your paltry, biased court which does not understand anything of Ierie, of the people it has claimed as its children and the people it adopted as dear to its heart. That is why I was born. And you, dear governor, when you stepped foot on this land after I was made, you fell into my purview. Do you understand, governor?"

The governor shook his head dumbly even as a numbing terror was creeping over him. "Your greed would not have gotten you killed," said the Bookman. "If you had done as you agreed and left everyone alone, I wouldn't be here," the Bookman told him. "But your fear, your fear is what killed you." There was pity in the Bookman's eyes as he looked at the governor. "How were you going to explain the death of all the people in the parade to the Motherland? How deep is your fear that you would put snipers in the buildings to kill hundreds of innocent people, just to get rid of the dark things?"

"What did you do to my men?" the governor demanded, even as he fought down the kind of nausea that comes from utter fear.

"They are dead, governor," said the Bookman, "I killed them all before I came here because I knew they had orders to carry out your wishes even if you were dead." His eyes were sorrowful. "Some of them were good men governor; they were just following your orders."

The governor swallowed hard, and the Bookman spoke again.

"I am judge, jury and executioner, governor. I have judged you for your actions, the jury has found you guilty and now, now I must execute you. Goodbye, governor."

The governor moved then, diving at the Bookman, but the man simply flipped open the book and wrote in the last letter to the governor's name. The governor stumbled to a halt and fell to his knees, staring up at the Bookman. Then his eyes went blank and he fell over.

The Bookman closed his book, bent and closed the governor's eyes and then opened the door and stepped outside into the corridor. The Jab Jabs were waiting for him, next to the unconscious guards. He nodded and walked past them. They fell into the position after him as the honour guard they were, as he walked out the house and into the street.

Amrika, sitting on her roof, happened to look over the street and saw a figure coming out of a house with a book tucked under his arm and a Bookman's hat on his head. He was a small, innocuous figure in the sea of colours, but he was surrounded by real Jab Jabs. For a moment his eyes met hers, she saw the beginning of a smile and then masqueraders blocked her view of him. When the masqueraders had passed, he was gone and so were the Jab Jabs.

Amrika blinked, frowned and then frowned some more as Ierie finally settled, the tug on her veins easing and disappearing. Then she shrugged and decided for once to do as Kirish had said and keep her distance. She turned her attention back to the parade and continued to enjoy her day. It truly was glorious.

THE END

GLOSSARY

Bats: One of the dark things. Physical changes include gaining wings, claws, sharper teeth, slender ears, hollow bones. Abilities include sonic screams which can be used as a weapon or as sonar. They can also collect Ierie's song with their wings and release it as a shockwave of sound and force.

Boerin: Lowest class in Ierie. They are composed of persons who were brought over as slaves and indentured laborers by the saikan. As per the banishment of slavery and indentureship, the boerin have carved some semblance of independence and a culture of their own. They now live in an uneasy symbiosis with the saikan, though they consider themselves citizens of Ierie rather than citizens of the Motherland.

Bookman: The first dark thing ever made by Ierie. Has a book in which he scribes the names of persons meant to die. Once the names are written his victims die. He is the master of the jab jabs. The rest of the dark things generally consider that they will die at the hand of the bookman when their time comes if they are not killed by any other events.

Carnival: A festival instituted by the boerin after emancipation to mock the saikan and practice a culture they have been stifling for years. It consists of dressing in costume and parading down the street to music provided by tamboo bamboo or drums.

Child of Anansi: One of the dark things. They are the tricksters of the dark things and one of the rarest forms of dark thing in Ierie. They are capable of creating illusions with spiderwebs and of collecting spider venom in their bodies and expelling it as a form of defense or attack. They are also immune to spider venom though the first deadly spider venom they are exposed to takes a very heavy toll on their bodies.

Dame Lorraine: One of the dark things. Physical changes include an over-endowed bosom and butt, and a slender waist. The Dame Lorraine's are mesmerizingly seductive, both in looks and in voice. All Dame Lorraine's carry a knife and can be found haunting the dark alleys where they entice and then rob their prey. They may or may not kill their victims afterwards.

Dark Thing: These are persons who were granted abilities by Ierie itself. The abilities may be passed on hereditarily or they may be gained if Ierie considers them to be worthy. The dark things were first born out of the boerin and then later from some of the saikan-born jotlin. No dark things have ever been made from the saikan class.

Dragon: One of the dark things. Not much is known about the Dragon save that he or she can fly and breathe fire. The Dragon spends most of his/her time sleeping under a mud volcano.

Fancy Sailors: One of the dark things. These dark things operate rarely and usually along the coast of Ierie. They bring a fog or mist with them as well as music and can walk on water. Persons hearing the music are enticed to join the sailors' revelry. However, anyone who joins the revelry does not survive.

Ierie: Ierie is an island which belongs in the Caribbean Sea. The island itself is alive and sentient and anyone who lives on it does so by its suffrage. It is responsible for the formation of the Dark Things and for granting power to the kalinag.

Jab Jabs: One of the dark things. If the Bookman calls, they answer to him. Outside of his orders however the Jabs Jabs act as they wish. Their physical changes include gaining sharpened teeth, claws and blue skin. Jab Jabs carry a whip and can inhale and then burn the evil of persons. They are generally considered to be one of the scariest dark things.

Jotlin: This is the middle class of Ierie. They are composed of person who were born in the Motherland, but are too poor to mix with more affluent members of their society. The jotlin class also contains persons who were boerin born but managed to hit on financial success, though these persons are few in number.

Kalinag: They are the natives which had lived on Ierie before the Motherland conquered it. Of all the groups living on Ierie, they are the only ones not considered by the saikan to be citizens of the Motherland. As such the saikan do not consider it their role to ensure their safety in any way. The boerin generally consider them to be outside of the class system while the saikan consider them to be below the boerin.

Lake of Pitch: A large natural deposit of asphalt in the south of Ierie.

Midnight Robbers: One of the dark things. Like the name suggests, Midnight Robbers are thieves who terrorize anyone who they wish. They are recognized mostly by their dress which consists of a long coat, broad brimmed hat usually in some variation of black and white. The Robbers carry guns and knives with them as well as a whistle which they blow to strike fear in persons and to shatter their own dark miasma. They are known among the dark things for their eloquent but frightening speech.

Moko Jumbies: One of the dark things. Physical changes include fusing with their stilts and having their bodies slimming into a tall willowy figure. The Jumbies have the ability to bring forth somebody's fears and all the fears that they have inflicted on somebody.

Motherland: The country from which the saikans have come. The monarchy of the Motherland had been very interested in conquest, leading to the acquisition of islands such as Ierie.

Port of Gold: The capital of Ierie.

Saikan: The term saikan is used in two fashions among the people of Ierie. In its broadest sense, saikan refers to everyone who was born in the motherland or their direct descendants. In a narrower sense, the terms refers to those citizens of the motherland who enjoy wealth and power. Only persons born of the Motherland can enter this class of society.

Stickfighters: One of the dark things. Physical changes include enhanced healing, speed and strength. The Stickfighters can also change anything into an appropriate stick for fighting. Stickfighters generally feel Ierie's song through the earth and can use the song to tell which class of society is nearby.

Tamboo Bamboo: Lengths of hollowed bamboo rods which are beaten to provide a tune. A tamboo bamboo band is a band made up of players who beat different lengths of sticks to get various tunes.

www.ingramcontent.com/pod-product-compliance
Lightning Source LLC
LaVergne TN
LVHW041906070526
838199LV00051BA/2517